TREASURED BY THE HIMBO ZOMBIE

MAPLETOWN MONSTER MATES
BOOK TWO

IVY KNOX

To the women who've always felt like they're "too much." You are exactly as you should be, and the right people will see it.

CONTENT WARNING

If you don't have any concerns regarding content and how it may affect you, **feel free to skip ahead to avoid spoilers!**

This book contains scenes that reference or depict:

- Sexual harassment
- Physical assault
- Death of a parent to overdose (off-page)
- Death of a grandparent (briefly mentioned)
- Lost connection to Korean heritage
- Psychological and physical torture
- Racism
- FMC has trans preteen daughter
- Dermatillomania (FMC has it)
- Sexism
- Being drugged with the intention of sexual assault (to the MMC and only mentioned briefly)
- Divorce
- Murder

- C-sections (off page)
- Cannibalism (off page and only as it relates to his past as a newly turned zombie)
- Graphic violence

Please prioritize your mental health throughout this book.

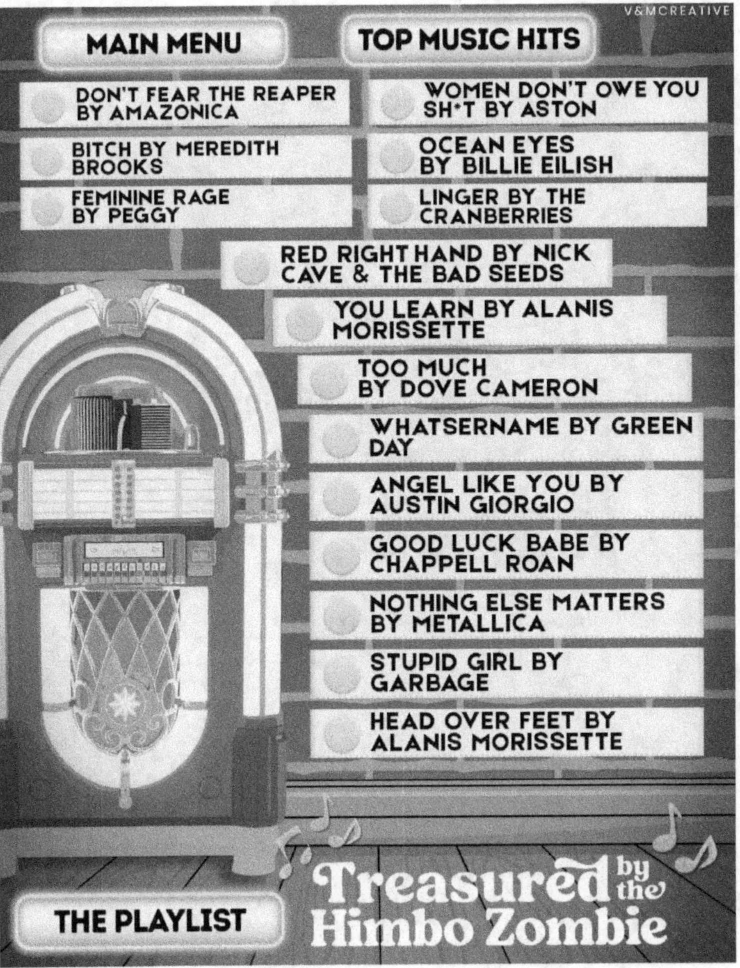
V&MCREATIVE
MAIN MENU
TOP MUSIC HITS
DON'T FEAR THE REAPER BY AMAZONICA
WOMEN DON'T OWE YOU SH*T BY ASTON
BITCH BY MEREDITH BROOKS
OCEAN EYES BY BILLIE EILISH
FEMININE RAGE BY PEGGY
LINGER BY THE CRANBERRIES
RED RIGHT HAND BY NICK CAVE & THE BAD SEEDS
YOU LEARN BY ALANIS MORISSETTE
TOO MUCH BY DOVE CAMERON
WHATSERNAME BY GREEN DAY
ANGEL LIKE YOU BY AUSTIN GIORGIO
GOOD LUCK BABE BY CHAPPELL ROAN
NOTHING ELSE MATTERS BY METALLICA
STUPID GIRL BY GARBAGE
HEAD OVER FEET BY ALANIS MORISSETTE
THE PLAYLIST
Treasured by the Himbo Zombie

Mapletown Forest
Caraway Manor
Mapletown Rock
Fast Glass
Tavern
Mapletown
Graveyard
House of Blooms
Flowers
Spellbound
Apothecary

COFFEE
blebrook Inn
Local Harvest
Hot & Steamy
Coffee Bar
Tome Time
Bookstore
Batter Spatter
Bakery
Crust Lust
Pizzeria
Mapletown
Post Office

CHAPTER 1
LINDSAY

Halloween Night

"Hit me again, Johnny," I shout, slamming my empty glass too forcefully on the bar top. I examine the bottom of it for any cracks and let out a relieved sigh when I find none. "Sorry."

"I'm only letting you get away with calling me Johnny because of your hot ass. You get that, right?" Vyla, the orc bartender with the jacked arms and purple face tattoo, asks with an amused and slightly annoyed smirk.

I nod. "Me and my hot ass thank you."

The flirty orc pours me another dirty martini, fluttering her long lashes. It's hard to tell if Vyla has a crush on me, or if she's like this with everyone. While I do find her attractive—that septum ring and long Viking braids would make anyone salivate—I've taken myself off the dating market. There will be no swiping, no matching, no messaging, no flirting, no first or second dating, no casual sexing, and absolutely no relation-ship-ing for me for the foreseeable future.

After many failed attempts, I've come to the conclusion that I'm simply not built for it. *It* being sharing my life with another person.

"How could you possibly look so glum on the best night of the year?" Vyla asks, leaning her elbows on the bar. Her eyes are bloodshot, and she sways on her feet. A strong earthy scent wafts in my direction, making me wonder if she's high, if she has any more weed on her, and most importantly, if I can have some.

I follow her gaze as it scans the room, packed to the gills with monsters of every species, surprisingly not wearing Halloween costumes. It's not like I expected the vampires of Mapletown to dress up as werewolves, but I assumed in terms of accuracy and creativity, monsters would crush the costume game on Halloween. Instead, most of them are wearing fancy dresses and suits more appropriate for New Year's Eve.

"I think this is the first time I've ever felt underdressed," I mutter, looking down at my ripped jeans and ratty sweatshirt. My hands instinctively wrap around my middle as embarrass-ment crashes over me. I'm *never* underdressed. I pride myself on being the one in a room making others question if *they're* underdressed. Holey jeans and hoodies are not my standard look.

"Oh, come on," Vyla says, interrupting my mental tallying of the dresses in my closet I should've worn instead. "I think you look cute. Relaxed."

"Depressed is the more accurate word."

"Depressed?" Vyla sounds aghast. "Baby girl, what for? Didn't you and Natalie just make up?"

Her confused expression has me reevaluating my word

choice. She's right, I did just reunite my best friend with the ghost man she's madly in love with, and right now, they're presumably in the middle of a bumping uglies marathon that will only cease when the sun comes up. I still feel like a fly-covered pile of turds for coming between them in the first place, though. Natalie seems like she'll forgive me, but will this always be a wedge between us? A layer of discomfort that keeps us from being as close as we once were? I sigh as I envision stilted conversations and forced laughs between us. "Mm, not depressed, exactly. More...emotionally exhausted."

In my defense, men are shit.

When Natalie told me, "So, there's this guy..." after years of heartbreak after heartbreak, I was thrilled for her. However, when she revealed that *this guy* was the ghost that had been secretly living in my late grandmother's house for over a century who's possessive and bossy and had been giving her the most incredible orgasms of her life, well, of course I was skeptical, because it sounds shady as hell.

The ghost thing was easy enough to get over, along with the idea that the monsters I once thought to be mythical are actually real. I'm not sure why that didn't bother me more than it did. Maybe because I've discovered more than a couple of people in my life whom I thought were decent human beings who somehow believe vaccines cause autism, as if autism is something to fear. We've reached a point in the downfall of society where I don't give a solitary fuck what you are, as long as you aren't stupid or evil.

The red flags waving frantically inside my head about Winston were due to my very vulnerable friend coming fresh off her mother's death and falling for a guy who never wanted her to leave the house. He never wanted other people around and was rude to anyone who interrupted their time together.

It sounded like a train wreck in the making, and I wasn't about to let her face another devastating loss just for some giant ghost dick. Of course I intervened. I was only trying to protect her chronically trusting heart. Thankfully, I was wrong, and they're madly in love with each other, and Winston's unpleasantness to everyone who isn't Natalie is something she finds adorable. My loving bestie has found the happy ending she deserved, so why do I still feel so heavy? It's like there's a boulder on my back that I can't shake.

I shrug, taking another deep pull of my martini. "It's been a long year."

"Christ, Lindsay," she says with wide eyes. "You need to slow down."

It isn't until the olives are in my mouth that I realize I've just emptied my fourth martini glass in under ninety minutes. Luckily, a pop cover of "Don't Fear the Reaper" blasts out of the jukebox, filling my ears and pulling my body off the barstool. My feet take me to the dance floor, and I shout over my shoulder, "Imma do the opposite of slow down," as I start to sway my hips to the beat. Soon, I'm in the middle of the crowd, bouncing and singing along, sweat coating my hairline as the booze settles in my blood.

The regret I felt about interfering in Natalie and Winston's relationship has receded in my mind, becoming a distant memory. The only thing that matters right now is this song and how my body feels as I move to it.

My sweatshirt and jeans are mildly prohibiting my dance moves, but that's probably for the best. Nobody wants to see a forty-one-year-old mom popping her booty. That's what my kid said the last time I chaperoned her school dance, anyway. However, given the way Mr. Hickson, her history teacher, was fucking me with his eyes for the rest of the night, I'd say there was at least one person who enjoyed the show.

By the time the song ends, my bladder is full and my bra is soaked through with sweat. I tug off my hoodie as I enter the bathroom, and take my time dabbing my chest, armpits, and the edges of my pink tank top with a paper towel before throwing my hair into a high pony. "Red Right Hand" is playing when I come out, and since it's not a song I can easily dance to, I make my way back to the bar.

Before I can get there, a blond blur of a man steps in front of me, blocking my path. I think he says his name is Finn, or Fergus, perhaps. It's too loud in here to know for sure, and I don't care enough about the answer to ask him to repeat himself. He's objectively cute, I guess, with straight teeth and a thick build, but I'm not the least bit interested in chatting him up. I wanted to drink enough to forget about everything I didn't get done this week and all the things I need to get done next week, and dance until my body demands sleep.

"Hi," I say, wary and irritated as I point to my chest. "Lindsay." I hope the vibe I'm giving off is Woman Who Desperately Wants to be Left Alone. Normally, I wear a plain gold band on my left hand to prevent this type of interaction, but I wasn't planning on hanging out at the Mapletown bar all night when I left my apartment in Boston, so I don't have it.

He leans into me, far closer than is needed, and I feel his hot breath on my neck as he says, "Lindsay, you're the hottest creature in this bar. Can I buy you a drink?"

It would be a decent line if he weren't slurring every single word, and if his breath wasn't acrid from what smells like a drink-a-thon of exclusively cheap beers.

"I'm good, thanks," I tell him, my tone courteous but firm. "Enjoy your night."

I successfully step around him, but he's hot on my tail as he corrals me to the only tall circular bar table that's empty.

"Come on," he pleads, his smile looking a little more predatory under the dim lights. "Just one drink. I'm buying."

If there's one thing I'm not, it's patient. Never have been. What little scrap of patience I do have tends to run out faster than lube at an orgy. Anger is the emotion that often takes its place, especially after a seventy-hour work week wherein I was interrupted in meetings by two different men named Jake. Two Jakes, same bullshit.

I could've told this guy I'm married or gay or scheduled to get hit by a train four days from now, but I prefer the power of truth. It's liberating to refuse to hide behind the illusion of a partner or some other excuse when someone's hitting on me. I don't need a shield to tell this dingus to fuck off. If he can't accept me at my polite decline, he deserves to get melted by the ball of fire growing in my throat.

"Yeah, I understand the offer," I reply stiffly, "because I speak English. I'm just not interested."

We stand there silently for a beat as I let the words sink in. I can tell that he's heard me based on the flash of hurt in his eyes. When it disappears, his smile widens menacingly, causing my stomach to tighten in a way that tells me to run in the opposite direction of his man. That this is some kind of game for him. But I don't move because fuck that and fuck this guy. I was having a great time before he showed up, and I'm not going to let him ruin my night.

If I didn't think I'd get arrested for it, I'd choose violence, but I have too much to do next week to get myself thrown behind bars.

"If you'll excuse me," I say, stepping to the left and trying to catch Vyla's eye from behind the bar. She's too busy pouring a row of shots, though, and doesn't look up. Can I successfully remove myself from this guy's path of destruction without putting myself in danger? I can't even tell what kind of monster he is. Truth be told, I forgot he was one until now. I assumed he was a human man, based on his disgusting behavior, because that's what I'm used to. Weren't the beasts who roam Mapletown supposed to be better than this?

I feel his thick fingers close around my forearm, and I wonder how much of a scene I'll have to make in the middle of this crowded bar just to get out of here alive. If the goal is to scare off a creep, I like to go big or go home.

"You don't want to be rude, do you?" he grits out, pulling me closer.

I look around for someone, *anyone,* to come to my aid, but no one is paying attention to me. They're all dancing and lost in their own worlds. I'm on my own in this.

Story of my fucking life.

The words come tumbling out, laced with venom. "Rude is actually my default setting, especially when dealing with shrimp-dick assholes who—"

"I really don't like what I'm seeing here." A low, rumbling voice from behind Finn or Fergus, or whatever his name is, interrupts my rage spiral, and I realize I've now been interrupted by three men this week. If this one's name is Jake, I'm pretty sure my brain will implode. "Care to explain, Finny?"

Ah, so the creeper's name *is* Finn.

I look around, unsure of where the hell this newcomer came from. One moment, I felt trapped and alone in the middle of the crowd with Finn, and the next, he's here, this giant man with a disapproving gaze narrowed on my harasser. He's wider and almost a foot taller than most others in the room, with striking light blue eyes and short inky black hair, a clump of it in the front already pure silver. The concentration of silver in that one spot makes it look intentional and effortlessly chic, but based on the small holes and stains on his t-shirt, and the thin scars covering his arms and neck, I'm guessing this is just how his hair looks naturally, and he's too busy to worry about the maintenance of a single chunky highlight on his head. His trim salt and pepper beard surrounds lips that look far too soft for someone who could have ties to the mob, and *why the hell am I staring at his lips?*

"I know you wouldn't be putting your hands on a lady in my bar without her consent now, would ya?" he asks the creep as he crosses his gigantic arms over his chest. The bulge of his biceps is almost comical, and I lean an inch toward him, waiting to hear the seams of his shirt snap under the pressure.

Finn lets go of me, and I rub the skin on my arm, trying to erase the memory of his hold.

"Nah, Dom. It's all good," Finn says, his eyes nervously flicking between me and Dom.

This must be the owner of the bar, I realize. Natalie's boss, Dominic. She went on and on about how he's too beautiful to look at, but in a rugged way, and I detect no lies. When his eyes land on me, a flutter in my belly catches me by surprise. He looks like he was carved from a block of marble.

When's the last time a single look made me feel this way? Not even one memory surfaces. Well, one does, but I was a teenager, so hormones likely deserve the credit there.

"I was trying to buy her a drink, is all," Finn adds.

I open my mouth to lay out how many times I said no, but Dominic steps forward, shaking his head. "See, I saw that happen when y'all were standing near the restroom. I also saw her say no." His Southern twang flows through me with a pleasant warmth, like a glass of barrel-aged whiskey. He clears his throat. "Help me understand why you continued talking to her beyond that point. Because we both know that's where it should've stopped. Don't we, Finny?"

"Well..." Finn replies, but Dominic grabs his shoulder, and I can tell by the slight narrowing of Finn's gaze that his grip is tight.

"You've been coming here, what, six years? Since the day I opened, yeah?"

Finn nods, his lips curving up on one side, making him look eager to impress the bar owner. There's a treasure trove of daddy issues in that expression that Finn will have to work out someday.

Whatever. Not my problem.

"Right, and"—Dominic puts a hand over his heart—"I appreciate that. I do. The thing is"—he tips his head toward the bar—"that sign has been here since the very beginning. And I know you know what it says, don't cha? Go on and recite it for me."

Finn shifts his body to read the sign, but Dominic's knuckles turn white as he keeps his top half immobile. The smile pulling at the bar owner's lips is friendly, but everything else about his body language and tone indicates that he's not fucking around, and based on the way Finn is trembling, I'd guess this level of seriousness is a rarity for Dominic. I also wouldn't be surprised if Finn was shitting his too-tight black jeans.

"Uh," Finn begins, voice shaky, "touch others without consent, be prepared to taste cement." Then his voice turns panicked as he pleads, "Look, man, I've had one too many, and I didn't mean any harm." He turns to face me. "I didn't mean it, okay?"

"It's fine," I say to Finn, my head starting to throb. I want this to be over. "Just leave me alone, okay?"

Things move quickly after that. Dominic calls a tentacled man wearing a finely tailored tuxedo over to us, and they discuss some kind of report.

"Dom, come on, man. You don't need to report this. Why

can't we just forget about it? She said it's fine. I-I thought we were friends."

"Report it? To whom?" I ask, eager to be filled in.

The tentacled man, whose name I learn is Otto, nods, patting his rounded belly. "All over it." He starts tapping on his phone, and I notice the Mapletown Sheriff's Department logo on the back of his phone case. An officer in uniform shows up a few minutes later, putting Finn in handcuffs and hauling him outside.

Dominic replays the events from his perspective once the officer returns inside, and when he's done, he nods in my direction. "Did I miss anything, um...?"

"Lindsay," I tell him. "Lindsay Abbadelli. My grandmother was Penelope Abbadelli. She lived in the Victorian house on the hill up the street. And no, you've covered everything."

I notice a twinkle in Dominic's light blue eyes, making them look almost silver, as his gaze roams over my face, down my neck, and lower, as he asks, "Natalie's friend?"

"Yeah." Why is he looking at me like that? What did Natalie say about me?

The officer thanks us as he leaves, and Dominic smiles at me, lopsided and boyish, distracting me entirely from the previous events of the night. "I've heard a lot about you."

Oh, god. "Whatever you've heard, just know it's my parents' fault, and my therapist agrees."

He lets out a deep belly laugh, throwing his head back and exposing his thick neck. My tongue darts out to wet my lips as I follow the veins and jagged white scars down into the neckline of his shirt, and I'm barely cognizant of it until his eyes land on my lips and he swallows. Do I suddenly have a neck fetish?

"Here," Dominic says, guiding me through the crowd with his hand a respectful inch from my lower back. Even without the contact, I can feel the heat of him through my clothes.

"Allow me to turn this night around for you." He has me take the empty stool closest to the kitchen. There's an opening on my right that allows the bartenders to go in and out, so there's no one else on that side of me. I feel protected here, on the outskirts of the crowd. "What can I make for you, Lindsay?"

I consider my options and shrug. "That whole thing killed my buzz, I'm afraid. I'll take an ice water."

When he places the water in front of me, he rests his forearms on the bar, lowering himself until he's at my eye level. "To each their own, but to make up for that earlier nonsense, drinks are on the house until you choose to leave."

"Seriously?" My mouth hangs open. I'm a sucker for freebies.

He seems amused by it. "Absolutely. This is the best night of the year. If I'm being honest"—he leans in—"I'll be more than a little heartbroken if you leave here with a bad taste in your mouth. That's unacceptable. So if you want to go back to drinking and dancing the night away, I'll make sure everyone else in this bar leaves you the hell alone. How does that sound?"

"What's going to happen to him?" I ask, pointing to the front door.

"Finn?"

I nod.

"He'll be required to enter a rehab facility for his behavior, since it's illegal. The facility is in Iceland, and the program takes a year to complete. If he passes the exam at the end, he can leave, but he won't be able to return to Mapletown. He'll be randomly assigned to one of the other towns populated by our kind."

"Wait," I mutter, trying to process this. "Grabbing someone without their consent is illegal here? And he'll never be able to set foot in Mapletown again?" That seems...harsh? Or maybe it's precisely the outcome he deserves, and I've grown too used to the lack of accountability for sexual predators in the human world.

"Correct." Dominic watches me for a moment, and his expression softens into a look that feels like a hug. "Mapletown is protected territory from most humans, but one wrong move could expose us. That would put everything and everyone in danger. You think we want a guy like that leaving here tonight, thinking he can behave that way with no consequences?" He lets out a sigh. "His next offense would be worse. Violent. You and I both know it."

"Wow," I reply in a stunned voice that sounded a little too breathy. Am I getting horny over Mapletown's laws? Maybe. Definitely.

No wonder Natalie wants to stay here forever. I never thought much of this place growing up. We'd come visit Nonna Penny, and it seemed like a boring, quiet little town without anything fun to do. Your average rural stretch of land where no one ever leaves and nothing ever happens. Well, *nothing* might be a stretch, but at least violence against women is minimal. That's something. A big-ass, meteor-sized something.

Out of the corner of my vision, and I spot a calico cat figurine sitting on the bar a few inches to my left. "What's that?"

He follows my gaze. "Oh, that's Polly."

"Polly?"

"Yeah, she was the original familiar of Mapletown. Martha Crane's familiar."

"Oh, the witch who founded the town and created the bubble around it?"

"Indeed," he replies. "Polly was known for wandering, stopping into the new businesses that would pop up, keeping her eye on things. We like to honor her this way." He presses the head of the figurine, and it bobbles adorably.

I feel my shoulders loosen, and as I watch the rest of the Mapletown residents continue to dance and drink with abandon, I decide to give this night another shot. "May I have a martini?"

Dominic chuckles proudly as he drums his fingers on the bar. "Coming right up, m'lady."

CHAPTER 2

DOMINIC

The pain in my neck is what rouses me. It takes a minute for me to realize where the hell I am, but when I look down at the old, paint-stained Fast Glass Tavern sweatshirt draped across my lap like a blanket, and the twisted shape of my body stuffed into the poorly cushioned chair, the previous night comes flooding back.

After the incident with Finn, I spent the rest of Halloween night serving Lindsay martinis. The bar was packed until last call, but Lindsay may as well have been the only customer in the building. That's how I operated once she took the stool in front of me. I served no one else. She had my full attention. Not only because I was determined to improve her mood, and not only because her striking different-colored eyes were so easy to get lost in, but also because this isn't the first time I've met Lindsay Abbadelli.

Long before I was bitten, and the virus turned me into a mindless, brain-slurping deviant, this radiant woman was my very first kiss.

Too bad she doesn't seem to have any memory of it.

I don't take it personally. We were kids. My skin was whiter than milk, nowhere close to the green shade it is now, and I had the awkward, gangly body of a boy stumbling through puberty. I've changed a lot since then.

A soft groan pulls my attention to the bed, and Lindsay turns on her side to face me, kicking her foot out from beneath the down comforter, her long toes flexing as the sunlight bounces off the white-painted tips. Her hands are fisted beneath her chin, and my lips tug at how adorable she looks.

I silently urge her to stay asleep, knowing how hard her hangover is going to hit once she's awake. She had three martinis before I encouraged her to switch to water, and noticing she had trouble walking, I got her a room at the Pebblebrook Inn to sleep it off.

She told me she didn't intend on interrupting Natalie and Winston's reunion by asking to crash in one of the spare bedrooms, and her plan was to sleep in her car. That was unacceptable to me. I would've offered her my bed if I thought she'd take me up on it, but after Finn put his hands on her like an entitled prick, I knew she wouldn't, and the last thing I wanted to do was to make her think I was anything like him.

I also don't think a woman like her would be eager to sleep in a trailer, on a queen mattress that's had multiple owners. Despite the jeans and hoodie, I can tell she's fancy. She smells like vanilla and bergamot, her hair is shiny like my truck after a fresh wax, and I'd bet my left nut she has more than one winter coat.

I'd been searching for her ever since that kiss, but without knowing her last name, my search never yielded any promising leads. I wouldn't say I've been *in love* with her since then—I'm not that much of a simp—but I couldn't forget her. Didn't matter how many times I tried. Now she's…here. In Mapletown. Mere feet from me. My dream girl with the different-colored eyes. A lock of her long black hair falls across her freckled cheek, and my fingers twitch with the urge to tuck it behind her ear. My need to care for her is overwhelming, and I'm not sure why.

It could be because she saved my life all those years ago, and part of me is eager to return that kindness, but it feels like more than that. In the memories I've kept of her, and the many ways I've imagined her, she never looked quite so dejected. Her fierceness hasn't faded, but the constant tension in her shoulders and narrowed gaze make me think the world has let her down, likely more than once.

I rub the back of my neck, trying to ease the soreness from the strain of sleeping upright in a wooden chair with cheap cushions. My gaze lands on the glass of water I placed on Lindsay's nightstand. She's going to need more than that when she wakes up. Something strong, with teeth, that'll fight off that hangover. Quietly, I shove my wallet and keys into the back pocket of my jeans and slip out into the hallway before putting on my boots.

I return twenty minutes later to a still-sleeping Lindsay with an assortment of bagels and pastries, and two steaming black coffees, one with cream and sugar, and one without.

Since recovering from the virus, my diet has been primarily raw meat. Most human food doesn't make me sick; it just doesn't taste as good as it did before I turned. There are a few exceptions, things I still enjoy eating since childhood, but I'm certainly not a member of the clean plate club. Though I do have a cup of black coffee each morning, out of necessity. The taste is rank, but it wakes my ass up, so I tend to drink it as quickly as possible without searing the taste buds off my tongue.

My phone buzzes on the table, and I grab it before the vibration wakes Lindsay. I'm in a group text with the rest of the bar staff, and Rizlan and Anton appear to be awake and chatty.

> Anton: Finn, man. The fuck is the matter with that boy? Was grabbing a woman truly worth blowing up his life here?

> Rizlan: He's a demon. What'd you expect? A strong moral compass? Dude has been on thin ice since he arrived. I never trusted him. Good fucking riddance.

Rizlan's reaction isn't surprising. I'm not sure what his beef is with demons, but as a dragon, it's in his nature to be fiercely protective of the women around him. It's why I hired him as a bouncer. He watches the crowd inside the bar as if every woman in attendance is his own sister.

Anton is a kraken and my cook at the bar. He's not big on confrontation, but he loves any fresh gossip he can sink his hundreds of teeth into.

> Anton: What an idiot. Did he think she'd enjoy being assaulted and beg him to take her home?

> Rizlan: You're applying rationality to irrational and disgusting behavior. It's never gonna compute. Besides, did you see the way Boss Man was looking at that soft little human after Finn was tossed?

> Anton: Didn't notice, but I'll throw a motherfucking parade in her honor if she pulls him away from Gemma.

I don't like the direction this conversation is taking. Gemma and I are not together. Not technically, anyway. She's reminded me of that more times than I have fingers. Not that it matters, since it's none of their business anyway. Even though their gossip is coming from a good place—these dingleberries are desperate for me to wife up and settle down—I don't want them getting the wrong idea about Lindsay. She's not my future anything.

> Boss Man has entered the chat and will put you on janitorial duties for the next two months if y'all don't shut your yaps.

> Vyla: Stop gossiping like little old ladies so I can go back to sleep, please.

I see the three dots indicating that the fellas are crafting their replies, but before those replies pop up, a sharp screech cuts through the room. I jerk to my feet, phone landing on the faded emerald carpet with a muffled thud. My hands are outstretched as I bounce on the balls of my feet, ready to strike and neutralize whatever threat has presented itself.

But just as quickly as my body readied for an attack, it deflates with relief. There's no threat. There's only Lindsay, her hair mussed and eyes wild as she stands on the bed, pointing her phone at me as if it were a sword she plans to shove through my chest.

"W-Who the fuck are you?" she shouts, her voice scratchy from sleep. "Where am I? Did you kidnap me?"

Shame is what I should be feeling, since this woman is clearly confused and terrified, and no part of me should find the sight amusing. But her tank stop is askew to the point that one bra-covered breast is popping out, and the sheet somehow got tucked into the waist of her jeans. She looks so fucking cute that I have to lower my arms to my sides to keep them from wrapping around her body and tucking her head beneath my chin.

"I'm Dominic. Owner of the bar," I offer in a soft voice. "Remember? Last night?"

She furrows her thick, dark eyebrows, her eyes darting back and forth as she searches her memory. "Oh. Right. What are you doing here?" Her gaze scans the room. "And where is here?"

"We're at the Pebblebrook Inn, Mapletown's B&B. You planned on sleeping in your car, but I offered to get you a room here instead. I–I…I slept in the chair the entire night. The only time I touched you was to remove your shoes," I explain, softening my tone even more to something calm and steady.

It's impressive how quickly she went from fast asleep to poised to attack, as if she's part lion or something, and memories from that summer, years and years ago, race back to me. She's always been a fighter, and even when she wasn't baring her teeth, you could feel her wildness simmering just below the surface, waiting to be unleashed.

When my focus shifts to the phone in her hand, I bite the inside of my cheek to keep from chuckling. "You can lower the, uh, the phone, by the way. I promise I'm not going to hurt you." I take a step back and gesture to the table. "I have breakfast, if you're hungry. And coffee."

It's then that she realizes she's not holding a weapon and lowers the phone as bursts of pink paint her cheeks. She steps off the mattress, still keeping her wary gaze trained on me. "You still haven't explained what you're doing here." Grabbing her sweatshirt from the foot of the bed, she pulls it against her chest, looking vulnerable and almost…afraid of me. I despise that look, but I understand it. "Why did you stay the night?"

With a shrug, I offer the truth. "Because you asked me to."

Her eyes widen, clearly not expecting that.

"I also didn't want you to wake up alone in a place you've never been. That's happened to me too many times, and I do *not* recommend it." I grab the coffee cups and hold both out to her. "Cream and sugar, or black?"

Lindsay hesitates, but when she licks her lips, I know she's about to cave. "Cream and sugar, please."

I pull out a chair for her at the table and take the one opposite her. We settle into a companionable silence as she nibbles on a pastry. I sip my black coffee and decline the bagel she offers me, encouraging her to eat that too.

It's incredibly difficult to pull my gaze from her mouth as she eats. Those lips create a flurry of filthy images in my mind. I can still remember the way they moved against mine all those years ago, and I envision the ways she could use them all over my body. A shiver rips through me at the thought.

"What are you thinking about?" she asks, pulling me from my indecent thoughts.

Shit. Be cool. Think of something that won't freak her out.

"Uh, I wanted to apologize for this morning. The way you woke up. If there'd been a better way to go about it, believe me, I would've done it. It must've been terrifying. For all intense purposes, I'm a stranger to you, and here I am sitting a foot away while you're passed out cold."

Her lips quirk as she studies me. "Do you mean, for all intents and purposes?"

I shake my head. It's a common mistake, so I understand why she needed to clarify. "Nah. I mean intense purposes. As in, this was an intense situation."

She opens her mouth to say something, then closes it. Eventually, I notice the barest hint of a smile as she takes a sip of coffee. "Right."

After she finishes eating, we head outside to my truck. When I reach the passenger side, she steps back, looking confused. I open her door, and the tension seems to leave her shoulders.

My forearm prickles with electricity when she brushes past me and her skin meets mine. It was brief, just the back of her hand, but I felt it down to my toes.

"Oh," she mutters through a sigh. "Thank you."

Her phone rings as soon as she buckles her seatbelt, and I make a weak attempt to avoid listening in.

"Hey, Isla. Is Jules okay?" Lindsay asks. She giggles at something, then says, "Yeah, I'm heading back now. I'll pick her up around lunchtime. That okay?"

The call ends, and I see her turn to me out of the corner of my eye.

"My daughter stayed at my sister's place last night."

"Right," I reply. "Jules. Thirteen. Loves Sabrina Carpenter."

She jerks back in her seat. "How did you—"

"You told me last night."

She presses her palm to her forehead. "Shit. Yeah, I remember very little after that second martini you made me."

"That's okay. You were mostly giggling, dancing in your seat, and telling me how incredible your daughter is."

Her smile is wide as she nods. "She's the best."

The rest of the drive back to the bar is quiet, so I turn up the radio when Alanis Morrisette's "You Learn" comes on and hum along with it. Normally, I'd sing, but I'm no Grammy winner, and I'm sure Lindsay's head hurts as it is. No reason to add to her pain.

"I love this song," she says quietly, her head leaning against the window.

"They don't make `em like Alanis anymore," I reply in agreement.

"Oh yeah? Is she one of your favorites?"

I scoff. "Of course. Along with many of her peers from the nineties."

She chuckles. "Yeah, same. That particular period of rock seems to get better with time."

"That's for damn sure."

I feel her eyes linger on me for several moments before returning to the passing trees, their remaining leaves desperately clinging to the branches. The chill in the air is getting sharper, indicating fall has one foot out the door and winter is moments from blasting onto the scene. My mind immediately ponders when the first snow will arrive, how many storms we'll get this season, and how that'll impact Lindsay's ability to come visit. If she even wants to.

She lives in Boston, a two-hour drive from Mapletown without traffic. Her best friend lives here, but how often would she want to escape her everyday life in the dead of winter to come see her? I swallow the hard lump forming in my throat.

Is this the last time I'll see her?

No.

It can't be.

There are too many things I still want to say. So much I don't know about her life from the day we kissed up to now. She doesn't know we've met before. Will I get the chance to tell her?

As I pull onto the gravel of Fast Glass Tavern's parking lot, I spot Lindsay's phone resting on the console between our knees. Before I stop myself, I swerve hard to the right before pulling into the spot closest to the door.

"Whoopsie daisy," I say with an innocent grin, as her phone slides off the console and lands next to my ankle.

Lindsay's eyes are wide as she brushes the long, silky strands of hair off her face.

"Keep forgetting to fill that pothole."

"It's fine." She grabs her purse and opens the passenger

door, giving me just enough time to do what I should've done while she was asleep.

I walk her to her car, nerves pumping through my blood as I figure out how the hell I'm supposed to let her drive away without knowing when I'll see her again, when the squeaky brakes of an old sedan fill the brisk morning air.

It's Camilla, and I can see her daughter's wild curls flying around her head in the passenger seat. Why would she be here more than two hours before we open? Camilla stops next to where we're standing and rolls down the passenger window.

"Hi, Dom, I'm so sorry to do this, but would you mind watching Rocío and Hugo for an hour?" Camilla asks with a panicked frown tugging at her lips. "I have a coven meeting and Morty got called into work at the hospital."

"Yeah, of course," I tell her, silently going through the tasks I need to finish before we open. I've watched the kids before, and they mostly keep to themselves as they sit at the bar, especially Hugo. I feed them as much soda and pretzels as they want, begging them to downplay the quantity to their mother. "I have a delivery coming in an hour, but otherwise, I'll just be doing prep."

"That's okay. Ro has homework to finish, and Hugo has his sensory bin, and I'll be back as soon as I can."

I wave dismissively. "Bah, take your time. Me and the kiddos will be just fine."

"You are an angel, Dominic!" She smiles widely and waves at Lindsay before pulling away to park a few spots down.

An *angel*. I almost want to laugh at the absurd comparison. If only she knew me...before.

When I turn to Lindsay, I find her staring at me, looking... the best way to describe it is baffled.

"What?"

"You babysit the children of Mapletown often while at work?"

I shrug, not understanding her level of shock. "Not that often, but when people ask, I usually say yes." Unless we're slammed, I couldn't imagine denying such a request. I love being around kids. They're brutally honest and curious in a way more adults should be.

Lindsay mutters something under her breath, and I only catch, "selfless *and* hot," before she opens her car door and tosses her purse onto the passenger seat. "Well, thank you for letting me drink for free and not using my inebriated state as a chance to chop me up in little pieces and scatter my remains on the side of the road."

"Jesus, is the bar really that low?" I chuckle.

Her lips form a stern line. "Statistically, yes."

I take her phone from my back pocket and hold it out for her. "It was my pleasure, Lindsay Abbadelli."

A twinkle in her eye makes my heart thump so hard inside my chest I place a hand over it to keep it from bursting through my skin. And the freckles that dot her nose and cheeks—damn, they're pretty.

"See you around, Dominic…"

"Jennings," I tell her. "Dominic Jennings."

She starts her car, and I loathe the sound of her soon exit. My lips part, but I swallow a desperate plea for her to stay before it escapes.

"Take care," she says, rolling up her window. I watch her pull out of the lot and turn onto Mountain View Road, my feet unable to move until I can no longer hear the soft rumble of the engine, knowing that this breathtaking woman from my past will occupy my every waking thought until I can get lost in her eyes again.

CHAPTER 3
DOMINIC

27 YEARS AGO...

BEAR HOLLOW PARK

OSSIPEE, NEW HAMPSHIRE

"Kenny, no!" I shout as his grip tightens around my forearm. He's dragging me toward the lake's edge, and his friend, Donald, is pushing me forward. No matter how deeply I dig my heels into the dirt, they bring me closer to the water. I can't swim. Kenny knows this. If he tosses me deep enough int0 that water, I don't know if I'll be able to get myself out. "Y'all don't have to do this!"

I scan the beach, panicked and looking for a grownup I can call out to for help, but there ain't any in sight. This is the rocky part of the beach, where the sign to my right says it's unsafe to swim. The pit in my stomach grows to the size of a boulder.

"This is what you get for eating my chips, shithead," Kenny sneers.

I feel his spittle dot my neck and want to tell him how rank his breath is, but he'd just punch me in the face, and if I have any hope of not drowning, I'll need to rely on all five senses.

Donald is laughing behind me, the sound brittle and sinister as he gives me a hard shove, and I jerk forward, but Kenny doesn't let me roll down the rocky hill. He lets me stumble and scrape both shins on the jagged rocks, but no, letting me go would give me a chance to escape, and he ain't about to let that happen.

Kenny continues hollering insults at me as he yanks me upright, and a sharp jolt of pain in my shoulder makes my vision blur.

There's a sound in the distance, I think. A shout from somewhere behind us. Hope fills my chest at the possibility of someone witnessing this and coming to my rescue, but that hope is dashed when the edge of my tennis shoe meets the water.

Time. I need time.

Time to fight back. Time to get away. No matter how pointless, no matter how much smaller I am than my older brother, I need time.

I throw myself backward, trying to create as much resistance and dead weight as possible. When my butt hits the dirt, I use my free arm to scramble backward like a crab on a stovetop. Two feet is the only distance I can put between my body and the lake before I feel Donald at my back, grabbing me by the hair and hauling me to my feet.

My eyes sting with tears as reality sets in. My brother might kill me today. If he throws me in the lake and walks away laughing, which I expect him to do, and I drown, there will be no one to take proper care of Mamaw.

I'm the one who checks to make sure she takes her diabetes pills every morning and night. I'm the one who buys her the tasteless brown bread from the grocery store for her grilled cheese sandwiches instead of the white bread with the higher sugar count. Mamaw relies on me to get the mail, mow the lawn, do the laundry, wash the dishes, clean the gutter, and all the other chores needed to keep her crappy old double-wide from falling apart.

Kenny doesn't do any of that. He's lazy and cruel, and it seems like he's in trouble with the law every other day. He's eighteen now, so I don't know what's stopping Mamaw from kicking him out. And I don't know why she invited him on this camping trip with us. She could've left him at home back in Tennessee. I really wish she had.

She and I could've had a nice week playing Gin Rummy and listening to her dusty Patsy Cline cassettes.

"Hey!" I hear the greeting roared moments before Kenny shoves me into the water with his hand pressing hard on the back of my head until I'm below the surface. My palms burn as I try to pull myself away, the skin tearing away on jagged rocks. Streaks of red chase my hands in the water, but I don't care how much I bleed. As long as I can avoid drowning, these rocks can cut my hands clean off for all I care.

My eyes squint as I struggle to hold my breath, and I start to panic. It's the last thing you're supposed to do when you're trapped underwater, but I can't help it. The clock is ticking.

I twist my body enough to get my feet under me and use that leverage to push against Kenny's grip. He's stronger, but I don't quit.

Suddenly, I shoot upward, Kenny's hand leaving my skull. When I land on my feet and rub the lake from my eyes, the sight before me has me sucking in a breath. It-it has to be a hallucination.

It's...a girl. A slender, very pretty girl with silky black hair whirling around her as she backhands my brother so hard across the face that he lands straight on his ass. Kenny cries out when his butt meets a sharp rock, and the girl whirls around to throw sand in Donald's eyes, causing him to stumble back and scream words I can't even understand.

With Donald no longer a threat, she faces Kenny once more and yells, "Suck on this, you little bitch!" as she brings her Converse-covered foot down hard on his crotch. He curls in on himself, clutching his frank and beans and wailing like she severed them from his body.

A strange rumble is coming from my chest, and it takes a minute to realize it's laughter. I shouldn't laugh at seeing my brother in pain, but well, shouldn't I? Most days, he terrorizes me. He's a prick who never leaves me alone. It's nice to see him get what he gives for once.

Kenny starts crawling toward Donald, and the girl kicks sand at both of them, some of it hitting Kenny in the eye this time. His crawl turns into a pitiful one-handed, keeled-over scramble to reach his still-blinded lackey and get out of her way.

"If I see you bullies again, I will scratch your eyes out!" Then she roars, actually roars a loud, menacing sound with her entire chest. The entire campground must've heard it.

I scan our surroundings, ready for someone to show up looking for an escaped jungle cat, but besides me and my fierce savior, it's just Kenny and Donald quietly whimpering as they huddle together and crawl back up the hill to the road that cuts through the camp.

My feet slosh through the water as I assess the damage to my body. There's a throbbing pain in my shoulder, but I don't think it's dislocated, so that's good. My knees are sore and I imagine there will be minor scrapes and bruises that I'll still be discovering tomorrow. The worst of it is my hands. Blood pools across the shiny, torn-up skin of my palms, and the sting is worse than a thousand paper cuts. I suck in a breath as my hands begin to tremble.

"You okay?" the girl asks, now only a foot away from me. She's shielding her eyes from the sun. I can't see her eyes, but the freckles that dust her nose and cheeks are awfully pretty. Her skin is a warm light brown, and her long limbs are lean and muscled.

She doesn't have an accent like mine, so she must be from around here. New England folks have a strange way of speaking. A rushed, halting sort of speech that doesn't have any R's. Hers isn't as thick as the others I've heard, but there are hints of it when she says certain words.

I reckon I look like a shrimp to her. She's at least four inches taller than I am. Hopefully, we're not the same age. That would be embarrassing.

"Yeah," I finally reply when I realize I'm staring. "Just some scrapes. I'll be fine."

Her fingers gently wrap around my wrist, and she lifts to inspect it. "Is this the worst of it? Your hands?"

I nod, trying to ignore the strange tingling sensation where she's touching me. My dick swells in my shorts, and I stick my butt out slightly to mask it. Clearing my throat, I repeat, "I'll be fine."

She rolls her eyes and mutters, "Come on," as she drags me up the beach. We find a break in the rocks, and she plops down on the sand, patting the spot next to her.

I ease my body down, wincing when I accidentally put too much weight on the arm connected to my sore shoulder. "Where did you learn to fight like that?"

Opening her neon-green fanny pack, she pulls out a pack of antibacterial wipes, gauze, and medical tape. "My dad. He told me to fight dirty when it comes to bullies."

I attempt a smile through gritted teeth as she wipes my wounds clean.

"Who were those guys?"

"My brother and his friend."

She nods knowingly. "The one I kicked in the pecker looks like you."

A laugh bursts out of me, and I'm not sure if it's because of her surprising choice of dick slang or the memory of her stomping so hard on Kenny's junk that his face turned as red as a tomato.

She's not laughing, though. Her expression is hard and probing as she asks, "Has he hurt you before?"

That's when I notice her eyes. They're not the same color; one is a rich brown and the other is green. I've never seen eyes like hers before. Her brown eye has flecks of gold and a ring of orange close to the pupil, and her green eye reminds me of dew-covered moss, with a tinge of turquoise near the outer edge of the iris. "Your eyes…" I trail off, mesmerized. I want to tell her how beautiful they are, how easily I could tumble into them and never want to climb out, but unfortunately, what comes out is, "…pretty cool."

She looks away, as if embarrassed. "Yeah, so I've been told. I fell into the edge of a table when I was little, and the injury changed the color of one eye." She shrugs and repeats her earlier question. "Your brother. Has he hurt you before?"

I nod. "He changed a lot after our ma died. He's angrier now. Distant."

"Oh, I'm sorry," she says in a quiet voice, gently placing gauze on my palm before securing it with tape. "How long ago was that?"

"Three years ago." The next part, I don't like to share with people, but this girl, whose name I don't even know, feels different. Safe. "She overdosed. Kenny found her."

She blows out a breath, the warmth of it tickling my wrist. "That's rough."

"Yeah."

We don't say anything for a while, and I feel like an idiot for bringing down the mood, not that it was particularly high to begin with. "Hey, um," I begin, attempting to change the subject, "thanks for helping me. You didn't have to do that."

She examines her work. My hands are cleaned and bandaged neatly, but still, her hard gaze makes it seem like her wound care is shoddy. "Bullies only stop bullying when you stop them"—her gaze lifts to meet mine, and I notice the corner of her mouth lifting slightly—"and I like stopping them."

"You're brave," I mutter, in awe. She really is like a jungle cat. "I wish I were as brave as you."

"How old are you?"

"Sixteen."

"I'm sure you'll get the opportunity to be brave someday. You've got plenty of time."

I nod in agreement. "How old are you?"

"Fourteen."

I scoff. She's taller *and* younger. What an embarrassing day this has turned out to be. "Seems like you've gotten a good head start."

She gets to her feet as she looks out at the water, brushing the sand off her hands. "Well, that's because I'm a national treasure, so..."

I laugh. Even though I can tell she's being self-deprecating, I want to shout, *You really are though!* I may be young, but I've certainly never met anyone like her. I doubt I ever will.

Her cheeks flush as she says, "Really?"

That's when I realize I said that last thought out loud. Before I can pray for a sinkhole to open beneath me and swallow me whole, she says, "You're sweet," and leans down to press her lips against mine.

I can't move. I can't think. This gorgeous girl not only saved my life but is now *kissing* me. Lip-on-lip kissing. The real deal. The kind you see in the movies. She tastes like lemonade and cherry Chapstick. I feel my heart thumping wildly, and my dick is like a steel rod in my shorts. I can't believe this is happening. My hands flex at my sides, and I wonder what I'm supposed to do with them. Should I put them on her back? Or her waist? Maybe her butt? It's a nice butt, and I'd very much like to know how it feels, but would she punch me after? *Likely*. And it's not worth it if it means she'll stop kissing me. I want this moment to last forever. I feel her hands land on my shoulders, and just as I reach out to touch her, to bring her closer, she pulls away.

A whimper escapes me at the loss of contact, and I can feel the blood rushing to my cheeks. "Wow," is all I can say, because aside from that word, my head is empty, or so filled with the soft feel of her lips that there's no room for anything else.

She giggles as she pushes a lock of hair behind her ear. "Yeah. Wow."

"Was that, um..." I stammer, "I mean, have you—"

"Kissed anyone before?" She finishes with a shy expression that looks out of place on her face. "No. You're my first."

"Lindsay!" I hear a soft, high-pitched voice call out from the road. A tiny girl with long black hair stands in the clearing with a Beanie Baby in one hand as she waves the other at us.

My savior turns toward the voice and shouts, "Coming!"

Lindsay. Her name is Lindsay. Beautiful. It suits her.

"I've gotta go. My dad is taking us to get ice cream."

"That your sister over there?" I ask.

She nods. "It was nice to meet you, um..." she trails off, waiting for me to offer my name.

"Nic."

"Nic," she repeats with a warm smile.

She doesn't leave, and it gives me the confidence to ask, "Can I see you tomorrow?"

"Lindsayyyy!" her sister shouts, sounding impatient.

"Yeah. Meet me here at noon?"

"Noon. I'll be here." There's nothing that could keep me from this spot of beach tomorrow at noon. Kenny could kill me, and I'd drag my corpse here.

"Okay," she says, shooting me another dazzling smile, giving me another chance to lose myself in her eyes. "Bye, Nic."

I wave as she jogs to meet her sister. "Bye, Lindsay." My eyes remain locked on her form even through the trees until she and her sister are completely gone from sight.

I spend the rest of the day replaying the kiss in my head. The memory keeps me up most of the night as I absently run my fingers along my lips. When I get up the following morning, my body aches and my head is groggy, but none of that matters, because I get to see Lindsay again.

At ten of, I go to our spot on the beach and wait. I've got a beach towel in hand and a pocket full of Airheads to share with her. Noon comes and goes, but I wait.

I wait.

And I wait.

I wait until the little hand on my watch passes the three before I grab my towel off the sand and head back to our campsite. My mind races at the possible reasons for Lindsay's absence, but I try to keep the self-doubt at bay. It's hard because she's *so pretty,* and I'm...me, shorter and weaker, and if I'm being straight with myself, dumber than her too. My grades are below average, and I often have trouble focusing. There's no way Lindsay's grades are worse than mine. I can just tell. So what do I have to offer her?

On the other hand, the memory of her smile after we kissed is burned into my brain. She didn't hate it. That much was clear, so the reason she didn't show up likely has little to do with me.

I don't see Lindsay again during our stay. Even as Mamaw pulls our minivan out of the campground lot four days later, my eyes search for her.

Lindsay.

I should've asked for her address so I could write to her, or even a last name. Something.

What I do have of her is so little, but has such a tight grip on me that I know I'll never be the same: her name, the feel of her lips, and the way she put herself in danger just to keep me from getting my ass beat on a humid, cloudy day on a rocky beach.

CHAPTER 4

LINDSAY

That fucking bartender. *Dominic.* With his perfectly heart-shaped lips, and his thick forearms, and that... that fucking Southern drawl that under normal circumstances I would find grating, but coming from him, felt like a warm cloak curling around my shoulders. He just *had* to lure me in with free drinks and then take care of me when I overindulged. Then he just *had* to buy me breakfast and practically leap at the chance to watch those random children at his bar.

Maybe it was an act. He can't really be that selfless, can he?

Anyone can maintain a mask of chivalry for a short time. I bet if I were to spend more time with him, that would fade. It always does. There are no greater actors in this world than men in a new relationship.

They all leave eventually.

My mom's words ring in my head. I was barely eleven when she told me that. She and my dad were in the middle of a massive fight, the one that would ultimately lead to their divorce—a divorce that her own parents vehemently opposed regardless of how unhappy she was because of how stigmatized divorce is in Korean culture—and she offered the four words that would stay with me even decades later. All when I tried to get her advice about a crush I had on a boy in my English class.

To be fair, my dating record has yet to prove her wrong. My most committed relationship was with Billy, the father of my child, and we were hardly a good match. Even at our happiest, he'd constantly let me down. In the best of times, it'd be little things, like ordering black olives on our Friday night pizza when I'd told him multiple times that I hate black olives, or forgetting plans we'd made and choosing to meet up with his friends instead. At our worst, he'd get mad at me for talking to another man in front of him and leave me stranded at the bar, or that time he showed up late *and high* to the birth of his child when I had been in labor for sixteen hours and had to get an emergency C-section.

Yeah, that one was the final straw. Even now, he's a sorry excuse for a co-parent. It's a miracle if he makes time to see Jules more than once a month.

So to witness a man joyfully offering to watch two kids while he's at work simply to help out a friend? It blew my mind.

It's been three days since I left Mapletown, and there's something about Dominic that I can't get out of my head. There's a familiarity about him that puts me at ease. Though, I'm pretty sure I'd remember meeting a zombie, so I must be imagining it.

I blame those lips of his for this weird fluttering in my stomach.

I'm in the middle of a video call with one of my clients when I realize I've been daydreaming about Dominic's lips for so long that I have no idea what my client just said. "I'm sorry, could you repeat that?"

His bushy gray eyebrows pinch together as he sighs. "I said, how does the data look for the Instagram ad?" He's the CEO of a local sandwich chain, and I know that having these calls with me is like torture for him. He underestimates the power of social media and is dying to prove to me that an online presence doesn't make a lick of a difference in their success. Most of the time, he looks one yawn away from dozing off while I'm talking.

I clear my throat as I quickly switch over to the Excel tab with months of analytics for each platform. "Promising. Engagement is up forty-six percent since the last ad with the new Bruins defenseman. Now, we know we aren't likely to beat that success, but if we can continue to ride that high into the seasonal menu change announcement in two weeks, I'm certain you'll see that reflected in your daily sales."

He chuffs with a roll of his eyes. "We'll see, sweetheart."

If only you could slap someone through a computer screen.

"The Revere location is still tanking us."

There's not much I can do about that, considering the surly former manager is the reason for the litany of one-star reviews. Instead of telling him that, I put on a determined smile and say, "Until the winter menu kick-off event, we have to be patient. The reviews have been steadily improving since the staffing change, but without a major catalyst like this event driving people through the doors, it's bound to be a slow climb."

I'm gifted with a skeptical scoff before I politely end the call, urging him to trust the process. The next few hours move at a snail's pace as I endure back-to-back meetings with the leadership team about budgets and acquisitions we're planning for Q1. When I make it back to my desk, I flop into my chair and gaze distantly out the window at the darkening sky. Pretty soon the sun will set long before I leave the office each day, and the commute home will become a deep dive into the question, *am I about to get fired or is this just perimenopause?*

There was a time when I enjoyed winter in the city. That first chill gave me an excuse to don my finest wool coat. The first flakes falling and dusting every surface, set against the scent of residential furnaces burning wood. But after the first year of icy, unshoveled sidewalks and dirty piles of snow that refused to melt, the magic began to wear off. I'm lucky that the building manager of my apartment shovels the sidewalks so I don't have to, but still, it's a hassle to go anywhere when you have to traverse tall mounds of muck covering the unshoveled areas.

A beat after starting the car in the parking garage, I feel my phone buzz in my coat pocket. I'm certain it's Jules begging for a veggie burger and fried mac and cheese bites from the place near the apartment, but a surprised squeak rushes out of me when I see Dominic's name. Actually, the name flashing across my screen is "Dominic the Beefcake," so I'm guessing he added his number at some point when I wasn't looking.

> Dominic the Beefcake: Has the hangover passed yet?

I feel my mouth pulling into a smile and actively work to undo it, silently cursing my body for its eager reaction to him. After typing and deleting a few replies, I decide fucking with him is the best way to proceed.

> Who is this?

His response is immediate.

> Dominic the Beefcake: Come now, Lindsay Abbadelli. I know you know. Have you changed my contact info yet, or am I still Dominic the Beefcake?

Why not Dominic the Buffoon? Or Dominic the Brutish Bonehead.

> Dominic the Beefcake: Say more big words.

None of those are big words, and I'm considering blocking you altogether.

> Dominic the Beefcake: That would be a damn shame.

Would it, though? Let's hear your pitch.

Instead of a text, I get a photo of him standing shirtless in an empty field as the sun rises in the background. Beams of orange and pink dapple his green skin in the sunlight, making the thin scars that cover his body glow in bright silver. I want to trace them with my tongue. His head is tilted down as one of his hands is pressed lightly between his naked pecs. With his other hand fisted at his side, the veins along his forearm pop from the surface.

"Jesus Mildred Christ," I mutter through heavy breaths, then quickly peek out the windows of my car to see if anyone is close enough to catch me salivating over this pretty monster. And that's precisely what he is: pretty. So pretty that I'm enraged when his next text appears and the notification blocks his face in the photo.

> Dominic the Beefcake: Annnnnd now a silly one.

The next photo is set in the same field, probably after the first one was taken, based on the slightly higher beam of sunlight coming off the horizon. Instead of a thirst-trap pose, he's hunched over with his palms pressed beneath his chin. Tiny rolls form beneath his ribs, and his eyes are crossed as he lets his tongue hang out the left side of his mouth.

I choke out a laugh as I stare at it. What a ridiculous man.

Dominic the Beefcake: Verdict? Still ogling?

I appreciate how aware he is of his beauty and how deeply unserious he is about it.

Okay, fine. Very persuasive argument.

Dominic the Beefcake: If I had a tail, it'd be wagging.

And the beefcake has me laughing again. Damn it. He's a relentless flirt, but I get the feeling he's like this with everyone, so I'm not going to think too much about it. It's also nice to talk to someone. I don't do much of that outside of work and Natalie.

Yes, the hangover has passed, but those were a rough few days. I might be too old to drink like that.

Suddenly, I'm self-conscious about him seeing me in that state. My fingertips graze along my chin, seeking the comfort only my worst habit can provide. What did my therapist call it? *Mapping,* aka the subconscious act of using one's fingertips to look for blemishes, scabs, or other irregularities on the skin's surface to pick at. Doesn't matter if picking said scab makes me bleed, and I don't know why. I'd still rather have the smoothness of a permanent scar than the rough exterior of a healing wound, and I hate myself for it.

> Apologies for being such a mess.

> Dominic the Beefcake: Nonsense. You were lovely. Uninhibited looks good on you.

I feel the blood rush to my cheeks.

> Steam was let off. I think the pain was worth it.

This is where the conversation peters out, right? We've addressed the reason that started the chat, had a few chuckles, and now we can move on. The text chain between us will move down the screen as others bump their way to the top with more urgency, and we'll eventually forget we ever met. I put my phone in my pocket and pull out of the parking garage, expecting silence from here on out. When I turn onto the main road, I feel my pocket buzz again, and my heart thumps against my chest. As I stop at a red light, I check the text.

> Dominic the Beefcake: Vyla told me to tell you to come back soon. She "misses your lush peach." Her words. What should I tell her?

Vyla has my number, so I find this game of telephone interesting. Did he make up this message just to keep the conversation going? I hate how adorable I find that. Granted, this particular description of my butt is very Vyla, so who knows.

I pick Jules up from school—science club, specifically—and she talks me into grabbing dinner from our favorite takeout spot on the way home.

"How was science club, baby girl?" I ask as she skips through the playlist I put on until she finds a song she likes.

"Ugh, fine."

"Doesn't sound like it was fine. Can you tell me one thing about it?"

A sigh rattles out of her chest. "We voted for our science fair project today."

"Oh yeah? What's it going to be?"

She crosses her arms over her chest. "A lava lamp."

My inner nineties child is jealous. "A homemade lava lamp? That's cool. Is that not what you voted for?"

"No, I wanted to build a water filter, but everyone else voted for the lava lamp." She shakes her head as she gazes out the window, as if the fate of humanity rests on her slim shoulders. "The water filter is useful. People need clean water."

My precious girl. She takes herself so seriously sometimes. Am I exposing her to too much news? I refuse to get her a phone until she's at least fourteen, but maybe I should check the search history on her computer. "Honey, at your age, there's no limit to how much fun you're allowed to have, okay? Especially at school. There's plenty of time to be exhausted and stressed and miserable in adulthood, but you're not there yet. Give yourself a break."

Her response is an affirmative grunt.

When I ask about the rest of her day, she tells me she learned "nothing" in her classes and that "nothing interesting" happened either, and I try to remind myself that this is the standard script of a budding teenager, and I'm not losing my precious baby forever. We get home and have dinner, and Jules goes into her room to finish her homework after she loads the dishes into the dishwasher. I change into sweats and a loose concert t-shirt that I cut into a crop top before making my way to the couch. Then I turn on old episodes of *Gilmore Girls* as background noise and pull out my phone.

I respond to Dominic's previous question about my next visit with a "Not sure."

Before I realize what I'm doing, I'm pulling up my work calendar, checking it against Jules's school calendar, and texting back, "Maybe next weekend? Not the upcoming one, but the next. Jules has a three-day weekend, and I'm taking an extra day off too."

Why the fuck did I do that?

I mean, I was planning to take that Monday off, but why did I offer to come visit? I don't even have a place to stay now that Nonna Penny's house belongs to Natalie and Winston. We could probably book a room at the Pebblebrook Inn, but...am I really considering dragging my daughter to a town filled with monsters?

It's not as if Jules doesn't know Mapletown exists. She knows I've been spending time there, trying to get things sorted with the house, but she hasn't come with me to visit since she was a baby. Certainly not since I discovered that the town is populated with mythical creatures and the town itself is protected by some kind of spell to keep it hidden from the rest of the world.

Will Jules be able to handle this? Will she run screaming from the first orc or werewolf she sees? I don't want to trauma-tize her. She came out as trans less than a month ago. She's got enough on her plate as it is.

"Hey, pumpkin?" I shout, loud enough to reach her room down the hall. "Can you come here for a sec?"

"Coming!" Jules shouts back. She slides into the kitchen on socked feet, twirling a finger in her loose black waves. "What's up?" She inherited my hair color, my hooded, angular eye shape, and freckles, and basically her dad's everything else, except for her spunk. That's all me.

Despite the genes of my Italian father, my very white ex,

Billy, and Isla's white husband, Jules, Isla, Kayla, and I are mostly Asian-presenting. I'm probably the outlier among us, with my heterochromia, height, and body shape. I tower over Mom, which she found amusing when I was a thin teenager spending most of my free time playing soccer and softball. But after I was in a car accident the summer before college and my knee injury put an end to my days as an athlete, the weight seemed to pile on, and her amusement turned into judgment. Her and Dad, and other members of the family—never Isla— have since learned how to censor their "concern for my health" after I told them to put a cork in it during a particularly tense holiday gathering.

"Do you have plans for next weekend? Want to drive up to Mapletown for the weekend with me?"

"Me and Kayla are staying at Gram's on Saturday, remember? She's making a cran-apple pie and showing us how to make something for cultural heritage day. Then Auntie Isla is taking us to the apple orchard on Sunday, and she said we could watch *Heated Rivalry*."

I spin on my ass like a top until I'm facing her. "You are absolutely not watching *Heated Rivalry*. You girls are too young."

"But Mom..." Her expression morphs into an anguished pout, and even though I feel a slight tug on my heartstrings, I stand firm.

"No way. You stopped believing in Santa last year. There needs to be more time between that milestone and when you watch a show with that much sex in it, okay, kid? Otherwise, someone is going to find out and have me thrown in jail." I also don't believe for a second my sister okayed this. I send her a text to confirm.

Jules says you agreed to let her and Kayla watch Heated Rivalry next weekend, but I smell bullshit.

She replies immediately with seven poop emojis.

Isla: But you and I are due for a rewatch at some point, yes?

I mean, I've watched the first season at least six times since the last time we watched it together, but it's not as if I'd ever get tired of Shane and Ilya's love story.

Obviously.

I should probably punish Jules for lying, but catching her in the lie itself feels like enough. She and Kayla play this game just as often as me and Isla played it when we were kids. Pitting the grownups against each other to see what they can get away with. Unfortunately for our daughters, me and Isla talk a lot more than our parents did, mostly because we don't hate each other, so our girls don't get away with much.

"Auntie Isla blew up your spot, kiddo. Nice try."

She throws her head back with a groan. "Sadie's mom let her watch, and she won't stop talking about it."

I fail to stifle a sardonic laugh. "Sadie's mom can make all the questionable decisions she wants. We won't be following her lead on anything, ever." Sadie and Jules have butted heads since sixth grade, mainly because, just like her mother, Sadie has the air of a typical empty-souled, spray-tanned mean girl, with her unnaturally white teeth, blemish-free skin, and acid tongue, and Jules has never conformed to beauty norms. I've let her choose her own clothes since she was old enough to speak, because who am I to tell another person what they'd feel their best in?

Even before she came out, her wardrobe consisted mostly of casual androgynous pieces. Now that she identifies as a girl, I've noticed more feminine accents have been added to her outfits, and part of me is terrified Sadie will use her gender identity as a way to bully her. To my knowledge, it hasn't happened yet, but is it just a matter of time before it does?

My fists have been clenched since the day she came out in preparation for it. Not just Sadie, but everyone. We live in a cruel and violent world, and for whatever reason, society seems to fear trans people more than domestic terrorism, and over my rotting fucking corpse will I let anyone insult my baby for living authentically. Ain't happening.

"Can I have an ice cream sandwich?" she asks, holding one up for me to see.

"Only if you bring me one." A calendar alert pops up on my phone a second later. "Don't forget, we have that appointment on Friday morning to get your shot."

Her lips tilt slightly downward. "Yeah, I know."

"Are you nervous?" I ask, folding my arms on the back of the couch. "The doctor said it's a quick pinch, and you only need one every three months. The medication is safe and everything it does is reversible."

She doesn't respond.

"You can also hold off on the shot if you're not ready. Isn't that what your therapist said?"

"Yeah." Her brown eyes drop to a spot on the tiled floor. "I know. It's not the needle."

I close the distance between us and lean against the kitchen counter, about an inch from her in case she needs me. "Do you want me to move the appointment back? We can get you in to see your therapist again first if you want."

"I just don't know what to tell people when I get to school." Her eyes grow wide. "Why I'm coming in late."

I pull her into my chest, and her arms tighten around me. When we first discussed her getting puberty blocker injections, she was thrilled and eager to begin her journey as the person she's always felt like on the inside. It wasn't until she started worrying *what others would think* that doubts began to form. "You don't have to tell them anything, coconut. But if you want to say something, keep it vague. Just say you had a doctor's appointment. If anyone pushes for more details, remind them that it's none of their damn business, okay?"

"But what if my friends ask?"

"Haven't they been excited for you since you came out?"

She nods.

I understand her reluctance. Her friends are few, but they've been a safe place to land since long before she came out. Jules is old enough to understand how quickly that can change, though. When she came out to her dad, he wasn't outright transphobic, but he also wasn't as supportive as he could've been. There are still instances when he misgenders her, and it dulls the light inside of her every time. He's still her father, but he's no longer a safe place for her to be fully herself, and that realization is like a knife to the chest.

"You're good at reading people," I tell her. "Feel them out and only share what you're comfortable with, okay?"

She sighs and nuzzles her head a little deeper into my chest. "Okay."

My eyes sting at the memory of her doing this as a wrinkly baby when she was hungry, then as a toddler when she needed comfort. I know there will come a day when she no longer needs these kinds of hugs, and I'm desperate for that day to be decades from now. My sweet, perfect pumpkin.

She releases me and spins toward the freezer, grabbing two

ice cream sandwiches and dropping one in my palm before heading back to her room.

I take mine back to the couch and resume my scrolling. As the first bite settles on my tongue, my phone buzzes.

Dominic the Beefcake: I'll get to meet the famous Jules? What's her favorite kind of soda? Or does she drink juice? I'll make sure we have some.

Why is he so excited to meet a kid he's only heard maybe three sentences about? And eager to ensure she has her favorite drinks, as if we'd spend the majority of our time at the bar. It's as odd as it is endearing.

No need. She just reminded me she has a two-day sleepover planned with her cousin that weekend. I'll be flying solo this time.

Dominic the Beefcake: That's too bad. Some other time, maybe. I'll let Vyla know how soon you'll be back. She'll be thrilled.

And because I can't resist the urge to flirt a little...

Only Vyla will be thrilled? No one else? 😟

Dominic the Beefcake: Maybe others are thrilled, too. But maybe those others are trying to play it cool because they don't want their excitement to freak you out.

I chuckle as the blood rushes to my cheeks and moves down my neck. As much as I loathe dating, flirting is what makes it fun. I suppose I've missed that part of it.

Acting "cool" is not hotter than being openly smitten, just FYI.

The dots appear and disappear a few times, making me question not only my last text, but also every decision I've ever made. My anxiety doesn't ease as the minutes pass, so I put my phone beneath a pillow and turn up the volume on *Gilmore Girls*. Lorelei is just getting into a heated argument with Emily when I feel the buzz of his reply.

Dominic the Beefcake: Then consider me a smitten kitten.

Beneath the message is a selfie of him with his elbows on the bar and his large hands beneath his chin. He's added heart emojis over each of his light blue eyes and illustrated cat ears atop his head.

This man is officially a menace, and I fear I might not hate him as much as I wanted to.

CHAPTER 5
DOMINIC

"You lost, Riz. Fair and square." Vyla holds out her hand with her palm facing up toward Rizlan when I emerge from the stockroom with a fresh jar of olives. It's quiet for a Sunday night, though the forecast said we're supposed to get a few inches of snow before morning, so perhaps people of the town have chosen to hunker down in their homes. Seems unlikely, considering how many residents could simply shift and fly here.

Rizlan shakes his head at Vyla. "Bullshit. We only heard three slurps. There was never a fourth."

"What's this bet about?" I ask Natalie, who's smirking at her coworkers while mixing a Fuzzy Doug mocktail for Tilda, an elder werewolf and Mapletown's only cab driver.

"Dead Fang Debbie just left," she explains. "Vyla bet Riz they'd hear her slurp her pint of AB negative four times before the glass was empty. Riz bet on three. Now they're arguing about what counts as a slurp."

"Come on. That last sip." She turns toward Natalie. "You heard it too, right? That was the fourth."

Natalie holds up her hands in surrender, saying nothing.

"That was a gulp, not a slurp," Riz clarifies.

Vyla slaps her palm on the bar. "Are you kidding me right now? Why even make the bet when you're just going to weasel out of it? Her dead fang has a big-ass hole. That's why she's always slurping. It's audible. There's no mistaking that sound for anything else."

As with most of their spats, I let their voices fade into the background, knowing they'll either work it out or start throwing drink garnishes at each other until they get tired. That's usually how it goes. They always clean up after themselves, at least.

"Are you excited for Lindsay's visit?" I ask Natalie after she delivers Tilda's drink.

She scrunches her forehead. "What visit?"

Dammit. Maybe they haven't spoken since Halloween. They might not even be on speaking terms, despite Lindsay's grand gesture to bring Natalie and Winston back together. I should've checked with Lindsay first. But since the cat's out of the bag, I can't exactly backtrack. "She's coming up this weekend. Saturday, I think. She didn't tell you?"

Natalie pulls her phone from where she stashes it beneath the bar. "That long-haired jabroni," she says quietly, though the lack of malice in her tone eases the tension in my neck. "I can't believe I'm the last to hear about this." Her fingers fly across the phone in her hands, and when it buzzes a moment later, Natalie's smile grows until it reaches her eyes.

"Okay, she's been thoroughly scolded, and she says she'll swing by here once she's checked into the Pebblebrook Inn."

Why is she texting Natalie back, but leaving me hanging? It's an embarrassing, needy thought that occurs to me, but I can't tamp it down. I texted her hours ago. *Hours.* It was a selfie I took yesterday morning, standing out in the cold with no shirt and a fuzzy yellow beanie while taking a sip of coffee from my *Where do zombies go for a group dinner? HeadQuarters* mug—a gift from Vyla that I still smile at whenever I pull it from the cabinet. It has a little cartoon of three zombies dressed up in fancy clothes that are predictably tattered, carrying utensils and drooling.

How does someone not react to a selfie like that? Honestly. It was easily in my all-time top five.

"Have you and Linds been texting?" Natalie asks. The way her voice lilts at the end tells me she's intrigued, and I need to maintain a straight face or Natalie will be able to tell how hard I'm crushing on her best friend.

I keep my chin down and breathe slowly through my nose as I reply, "Uh, a little since Halloween. Not that much."

"Oh yeah, Riz told me you took care of her that night. Thank you for that, by the way. Means a lot."

It's sweet that she thinks I did that as a favor to her, and not an opportunity to spend time with girl I've been searching for since I was sixteen. If she wants to give me credit, though, I'll take it. "Yeah, my pleasure."

The bar stays quiet until I lock up at midnight. Snowflakes melt in my hair and on my jacket as soon as they land, making me long for Christmases from my childhood when Mamaw was still around. We never got much snow accumulation in my small Tennessee town, but you'd never know that from the way she decorated. It looked like the inside of Santa's workshop. She'd keep the windows open all night so it was cold enough to make hot cocoa. We'd snuggle up with blankets and listen to Christmas tapes and pretend we lived somewhere close to the North Pole. I miss her all the time, but so much more this time of year.

My phone dings as I settle into my couch, feet up on the coffee table.

Lindsay: Work sucked. You've gotta have a Mapletown story that'll cheer me up, right?

Then she replies to my selfie.

Lindsay: You're as ridiculous as those abs. Don't ever let me inside your house because I will steal this mug.

The ache in my cheeks tells me my smile is wider than usual, which is not surprising. Lindsay seems to have that effect on me.

I tell her about Vyla and Riz's bet, and poor Debbie with her dead fang.

The only dentist in town is her ex from over one hundred years ago, but she won't take the portal to another town's dentist either, so who knows. Maybe vampires are allergic to floss?

Lindsay: I hate going to the dentist. The grinding sound brings back horrible memories from when I had cavities as a kid. Why haven't they developed silent dental tools?

We have cars that can drive themselves, yet dental tools are still as loud as goddamn lawnmowers?

Lindsay: Seriously!

Why did work suck?

She might not want to discuss it, but I'm eager to know, and since she brought it up, it seems like a topic that's not off-limits.

Lindsay: One of my idiot coworkers asked me for a Thai food recommendation for a date he has this weekend. I asked him why he assumed I'd know. He gestures at my face and says, "Because of your whole thing, obviously. Aren't you Thai, or whatever?" with a dismissive gesture. That happened during my first meeting of the day, and I had trouble focusing afterward. I've worked with this guy for years. I know his kids' names. How old they are. I even went to his ex-wife's baby shower before his eldest was born. But to him, we all look the same and I'm just another face in the crowd.

That's awful.

My urge to comfort her is strong, but the need to make her smile is stronger.

Why did the chicken cross the road?

I'm not sure how dark her sense of humor is, but based on her many drunken justifications for a Purge Night run by women, I'm guessing it's somewhere between charcoal and onyx on the dark end of the spectrum.

Lindsay: Are you seriously parroting the world's oldest joke right now?

Just answer the question.

I can practically hear her impatient sigh from here.

Lindsay: To get to the other side?

Yes, because your coworker's lifeless body is twisted up on that side of the road, blood pooling beneath him, clearly a lost cause. But his eyes…well, those are intact, and the chicken notices they are currently unpecked. And the chicken simply can't resist.

Lindsay responds with a GIF of a women spitting out her coffee with laughter.

Lindsay: Who knew the chicken had such sadistic urges?

Oh I did. The original version of that joke is much darker than most people think it is.

Lindsay: What do you mean?

"To get to the other side." You could take that literally and assume the chicken is going for a nice midday stroll, waddle, whatever, but I'm thinking that poor chicken wanted to die.

Lindsay: JFC that's dark.

The life of a chicken often is.

Lindsay: There's no way the joke we all learned as children is about a suicidal chicken. There's just crazy.

Is it? Weren't we all kids when Disney twisted the story of Pocahontas into a romance?

Lindsay: Fuck. You've got me there.

My fat thumbs keep pressing the wrong letters in my reply, and I get fed up with it quickly.

> Can I call you?

> Lindsay: What are we, married? Do you need to discuss bills and childcare and groceries with me for some reason?

What in the hell? Lindsay is my age. How can she be this averse to phone calls?

> Isn't your arthritis making it hard to type?

> Lindsay: RUDE. I'm in my early forties, which is basically late thirties, which means I still get carded when I buy booze.

I won't deny she's a smokeshow, but I ain't buying this.

> Liar.

> What are you afraid of? I'm just a Brutish Bonehead, remember?

The three dots taunt me for several minutes, but then I'm rewarded with not only a call but a FaceTime request.

"Evenin', beautiful," I say as I answer. She appears to be leaning against a modern, cushioned headboard and wearing a white V-neck shirt. The screen cuts off just beneath her collarbone, and I wonder if she's braless. If her nipples are peaked and poking through the thin fabric. Based on the lack of makeup and gold patches beneath her eyes, I'd guess there's nothing separating her shirt from her skin.

My mouth waters at the image in my head.

"Happy now?" she asks with playful exasperation.

"Very." I look at the clock on my nightstand. "Why are you up so late? Isn't it a school night?"

She nods. "I had to finish the deck I'm working on for our

upcoming board meeting. It's still not done, but my eyes have stopped working for the night."

I know she's an important marketing person for a restaurant group, but beyond that, I'm clueless as to how she spends her time. "On a day when your coworkers aren't acting like fools, do you enjoy what you do?"

Her lips purse as she looks off into the middle distance. "Yeah, I mean, I'm good at my job, so that makes it easy to like."

That's not what I asked, but I don't point that out. "What about it makes you happy?"

"When a campaign I created delivers and the restaurant sees a boost in customers. They make more money, they have proof they can trust us with their vision, and I get a pat on the back. Everyone wins."

She shifts the conversation from work to lighter topics: our favorite TV shows, books, which Green Day album is the best—it's *American Idiot*, no matter how much *Dookie* defined their sound, I don't care what she says—and before I know it, it's three-thirty in the morning.

Once she yawns thrice in the span of as many minutes, I let her go. There's a pinch in my chest the moment her face disappears from the screen, but that's okay. I got to gaze into her different-colored eyes for almost three hours tonight. At the end of the call, she thanked me for cheering her up, and that alone made me feel like I had won *two* prizes in my cereal box instead of just one.

I go to sleep thinking of her freckles, and the many shapes hidden inside them. She'll be in Mapletown next weekend, and if all goes according to plan, I'll get to be beside her for most of her trip.

I stopped believing in God once my heart stopped and my hunger for flesh became insatiable, but I'm thanking Him now for not timing her visit during my monthly rut. Luckily, that will come the following week. There's no way to know where this thing with Lindsay will go, but being a human, I doubt she'd understand or accept the change in me that occurs every thirty days. I plan on keeping that part of myself hidden for as long as I can.

CHAPTER 6

LINDSAY

"Baby, I need you to fold the laundry on your bed, okay? Then I need you to get dressed. We have a lot to do before I take you to Gram's. She wants to take you and Kayla to the diner for brunch so we can't be late."

"Yup yup yup," she mumbles as she tosses a stress ball in the air and catches it as she walks.

There's no sense of urgency in Jules this morning, and it's driving me up the wall. It's been that way all week while I've felt like a headless chicken, zooming from one room to the next trying to remember everything I planned to get done. I also can't stop thinking about that damn chicken joke and how deeply disturbing Dominic's take on it is.

He and I have been texting most nights, but on Tuesday, we had another phone conversation that went on for hours. I woke up exhausted but smiling. There are so many questions I have about his, *ahem*, condition, but it still feels too personal to broach. I can't recall what we talked about, really, but we didn't get off the phone until four in the morning. For about an hour, I was baking gingerbread cookies for Jules to bring to school, and he was doing laundry, so we weren't really talking at all, just listening to each other exist. It was nice. Comforting.

This morning is the opposite of calm. I still have to finish packing, make sure Jules is packed, take out the trash, and load the dishwasher, and that doesn't include getting myself ready to hit the road. The only step in my beauty routine that's been completed is the vitamin C serum. I still have all the other steps and only an hour before we need to leave.

"Mom, what do you think of this lip stain?" Jules asks as she strolls into my room and puckers her lips. The shade is a deep purple, almost eggplant-colored.

"The drama! I love it," I tell her. "How's the folding going?"

"Ugh, I'm doing it." She rolls her eyes as she stomps out.

"Watch that sass, cupcake. It's bad enough you landed yourself in detention next week." She earned that punishment by getting into a screaming match with Sadie, her nemesis, during math class, which I'm not thrilled about, but it sounds like Sadie started it when she whispered to her lemmings about Jules's eyeliner being "mid" and "a cry for an involuntary psych hold" and Jules overheard. What I won't tolerate, however, is her getting an attitude with *me*.

My hair is air-drying, and I'm doing that awkward hop one with a sturdy frame often does as I yank on the waist of my olive slim-fit pants to get them over my thick thighs.

"Hey, Mom, when you get back, can we do some more clothes shopping?" she asks, shouting from her room.

"I will not be taking requests at that volume, young lady," I shout back.

Okay, clothes are on. Jewelry has been selected. Shoes are next to my vanity. Time for makeup, then chores. My fingers trace along my jawline as I lean close to the mirror and examine the few pimples I'm sporting, but I'm quick to shake off the desire to pick and apply a thin layer of primer—after sunscreen, of course. Then I add a subtle cat-eye with dark brown shadow using my fine-edged brush.

"Can we go shopping when you get back from Mapletown? I found some stuff at Pac Sun that I really—"

"We went shopping a couple weeks ago, didn't we?" She's still wearing her pajamas, and I'm wondering if she's folded a single thing from that giant pile of clothes on her bed. "No, honey. Not until next month. We can't be blowing money on new clothes all the time."

"Didn't you just make a ton of money from the sale of Nonna Penny's house?"

The death stare my mother would give me for asking about her and Dad's finances would probably make Jules pee herself. She has no idea how easy I am on her.

"That money is not for new clothes. It's for your future, okay? Now go get changed. Scoot."

When we finally make it out the door, Jules is giving me the silent treatment. She doesn't even touch the playlist I put on in the car, or react when I crank the volume on "Nothing Else Matters" by Metallica—a song I know she despises.

I pull into Mom's driveway, relieved that the snow we got on Thursday seems to have been cleared from the pavement and the stone walkway to her front door. My sister talked her and my dad—who lives right across the street—into hiring someone to shovel all the walkable areas around their houses that the city plow doesn't reach. My dad was stubborn at first, convinced he could still handle it, but eventually caved.

It's nice having my parents live so close to each other. Dad kept our childhood home when they divorced, but bought Mom the two-bedroom house directly across the street when it went up for sale. Now that they're no longer married, they're basically best friends. Mom even gets along with Ruth, Dad's second wife, whom he married several years ago.

"Hey," I call when I enter the house. Jules has already run off somewhere, probably to find Kayla. "Sorry we're late."

"Heyo," my sister, Isla, calls back from the kitchen. "We're in here."

I round the corner and find my mom with Kayla at the dining room table as Jules sits in the chair next to her, while Isla and my dad are standing in the kitchen eating donuts from a big Dunks box while observing the scene.

"I thought you were taking the girls to the diner."

Dad shrugs. "We wanted donuts."

Guess I didn't need to rush after all. Thanks for letting me know, guys.

There are dozens of bundled nylon cords in a variety of colors covering the table. My mom is holding up a recently completed *maedeup* as she explains to the girls how she tied it. "I've been teaching myself how to make these, and I thought it would be fun to teach you."

She gets to her feet when she sees me and offers me a half hug, which isn't so much a hug as it is a shoulder squeeze, then a pat. We aren't overly affectionate with each other, not like she and Isla are. I've stopped taking that personally. Well, I've been trying to stop. It's an ongoing process.

My sister and I got two completely different moms in the same woman, and that's just how it is. I got the terrified mom who got pregnant younger than expected, whose professional dreams were dashed upon seeing the results of her pregnancy test, who had no support system once I was born, and wasn't encouraged to seek help when she was clearly suffering with postpartum depression. Isla got the mom nine years later, who was halfway through getting her law degree, who was regularly seeing a therapist, and eager to get the whole mom thing right the second time around.

Setting that aside, Mom and I have always clashed. She's

quick to tell me I need to "calm down" and "not let my temper take over," while Isla is her eternally serene princess.

"*Maedeups, huh?*" I ask, surveying the table.

"Yes, they needed something for cultural heritage day, and I thought this would be perfect."

"Hm." I pick up the one she made, going over the intricate loops with my fingers. "Wish I knew how to make these at their age. What else is on the agenda? *Bibimbap* for lunch?"

I hear my dad let out a warning grunt from the kitchen, where Isla is shaking her head disapprovingly at me.

"Easy, Lindsay," Mom says quietly. "This is supposed to be a nice weekend."

Oh, and another pain point between me and Mom is the lack of Korean culture she exposed us to as kids. It's not entirely her fault, given that she was an army brat and only child to Korean immigrants, making assimilation priority one whenever they moved around the U.S., but she's very much the kind of person to obsess about a new hobby one week, and lose interest in it the next since she retired, and I don't like thinking of the preservation of our roots being treated like learning the harmonica, breadmaking, calligraphy, or that month she wanted to become a reiki healer.

Growing up in Boston, I was around other Korean kids, but with my Italian last name and inability to speak the language, to them, I was an outsider. Too white to be accepted by them, not white enough to avoid being the butt of racist jokes by the white kids.

Since Dad was the cook in the family, we were always eating American or Italian food. It wasn't until I went to college that I started going to Korean restaurants. Isla and I got really into K-pop a few years ago and couldn't stop watching *KPop Demon Hunters* when it came out, then we started bingeing K-dramas, but whenever we'd invite Mom to join us, there was an odd reluctance about her. Almost as if she felt offended to be introduced to her own culture by her daughters.

It's a loaded subject to broach, to say the least.

Dad clears his throat. "The traffic looks decent right now," he says jovially as he approaches. "What route are you taking?"

I always take 93 North to 89 North, and he knows this, but I appreciate his very dad-like attempt to change the subject.

"We're supposed to get a few inches on Monday afternoon, so make sure you leave in the morning, okay?"

"Okay, Dad," I tell him, giving him a hug.

"Jules," I say as I brush the loose pieces from her braid off her forehead. "Call or text me any hour, okay? If you need me to come home, say the word and I'll be on my way."

"Yeah," she mumbles, her focus entirely on the nylon cord in her hands.

I wave to the group over my shoulder. "Okay, have fun. See you on Monday."

I'm comforted to know that visits between Jules and her grandparents are completely free of tension and awkwardness, but it wasn't always this way. As soon as Jules started dressing herself, I knew she was different, and I encouraged her to explore that in whatever form it took.

My parents—Mom, in particular—weren't as open-minded. Leading up to the day Jules came out, I had already had many difficult discussions with Mom and Dad about supporting Jules on her journey with her identity. There were countless emails exchanged with links to medical resources on what gender affirming care actually entails, and news about bigoted anti-trans laws to help them understand the reality of what living authentically would look like for her.

Ultimately, they knew I wouldn't tolerate any lack of support, and if they wanted to remain in her life, they'd have to accept her just as she is. It helped that around the same time,

Kayla started talking about having crushes on a boy and a girl in her class, which led to my dad throwing up his hands and saying, "Kids today. I don't know. Whatever, as long as they're happy." Since then, we haven't had any issues.

My drive to Mapletown is long and peaceful, thanks to The Cranberries and Dolores's stellar pipes. The iced hazelnut latte the size of my forearm didn't hurt either, though it did make me stop twice along the way to pee. As soon as I pass the sign that says "Mapletown Welcomes You," my heart does this gleeful skip while my shoulders lower with ease. I know it's not a perfect utopia, and I'm sure it's got its problems, but this little town is becoming very sacred to me.

A bubbly minotaur named Quinn gets me checked into my room at Pebblebrook Inn, and I can't look away from her... everything. From her pink hair to her orange platform sneakers, she looks like she was styled by Lisa Frank herself. None of what she's wearing seems to match, yet it somehow makes sense together as an ensemble. She's very chatty, but in a way that makes you feel like she's your best friend. As she sets my bag in my room, she offers me a free turkey sandwich on rye bread with a bag of chips and a soda, and my stomach growls so loudly that I can't bring myself to refuse. I mindlessly eat my lunch as I putter around, putting clothes on hangers, setting up my beauty products in the right order, and once I'm done eating, I give my makeup a little touchup before I get back in the car.

Natalie greets me with a squeal as I walk into Fast Glass Tavern, and any lingering worries about whether she's still mad at me melt away. She pulls me into a hug, and I know she's asking me questions, probably about the drive and my plans, but I can't focus on her words as I search the room for Dominic, finding him absent.

Didn't he say he was working today?

We didn't make plans to meet here, but I figured he'd be here when I arrived. Was that too presumptuous?

I feel Vyla's muscular arms wrap around both of us, and her wide chest blocks my view.

"Welcome back, gorgeous," she chuffs in my ear.

I wave to the few other members of the staff as Natalie pulls me toward a particular stool at the bar. She starts mixing me a martini, and I hear the loud swing of the door separating the bar from the kitchen.

"Lindsay," a sultry voice says from my right, and I feel my toes curl inside my boots. He's prettier and taller than I remember from the last time I was here. Sure, we've Face-Timed since but seeing him in person is different. A treat. A borderline honor. His smile grows wide enough to create several lines in his cheeks that look like they were carved just for me. My stomach pools with warmth as he approaches, and my feet close the distance between us despite my brain feeling like mush.

"Hi again," I reply, my voice dreamy. The last time I felt this awestruck was when I was ten and got to meet Jonathan Taylor Thomas at a fan event in the mall. I reach my hand out to shake his—no idea why since we've met before—just as he opens his arms to hug me. I end up shoving my freshly done acrylics smack dab into the middle of his sculpted chest. "Sorry."

We chuckle as we stand there, not knowing where to go from here.

A few small groups filter in, and the staff starts getting busy. I sip on my martini, enjoying the soft `80s pop hits humming from the jukebox, and the monster watching available to me as the townspeople fill the space.

If Natalie noticed a vibe between us, she doesn't comment on it. In between customers, she returns for short bursts of chatter about how wonderful things between her and Winston are now. I keep offering to donate any of my nonna's junk that she doesn't want, but she declines.

"Winston found this journal, though, and thought you might want it." She drops a heavy leather-bound notebook in front of me that I've never seen before. A brown leather string is tied around the middle, holding the many loose pages stuffed inside. "Winston didn't read it, but he said there were a ton of recipes in there, and since you love to cook, I figured you'd want to hold on to those."

"Hm," I mutter, mostly to myself as Natalie shuffles away to refill someone's beer. The journal's owner scrawled their name on the inside cover, and to my surprise, it belongs to someone I've never had the pleasure of meeting—my great-grandmother on my father's side, Lucia Russo. She's someone I've thought a lot about recently, as she might be the reason me and my late grandmother were able to enter this town at all.

It's hidden from the average human, unless invited by a resident. Otherwise, the only way to cross the town line and into Mapletown territory is if you have the ancestral blood of a paranormal creature running through your veins.

The only thing I've heard about my ancestors that could indicate I'm "special" in this way is that my great-grand-mother, Lucia, would recite spells while cooking. My dad remembers her collection of cookbooks that were passed down from her mother and grandmother, with recipes that included spells and other rituals for good luck while preparing a meal. If there's any kind of monster in my blood, it's got to be a kitchen witch.

I continue skimming the journal for a while, noticing that the written passages between recipes are mostly written in Italian, which I can't read. The recipes do look good, though, and I definitely want to try them when I get back home. I miss cooking so much. I can throw together a quick meal for me and Jules on a weekday, but my life is currently too busy to engage in the fun kind of cooking that I used to do. The red sauce that would take all day to taste just right, beef Wellington, paella—the dishes that are hard to perfect. I loved the challenge of them.

I've even made my own kimchi, and *gamjatang*. It took me a few tries to get them right, but I was proud to learn how to make a couple of Korean foods on my own, even though I had to rely on YouTube. What I still need to work on, is my spice tolerance. Unfortunately, I have the taste buds of a Midwestern farm boy.

When I let out a wistful sigh, Dominic stops in his tracks in front of me. "You okay, gorgeous?"

Even though I know his flirting is part of his bartender schtick, I still preen at the compliment. "Yeah, I was just wishing I had more than twenty-four hours in a day. Or could afford an entire staff to handle the daily tasks that I don't want to do."

He scratches his salt and pepper stubble and nods. "I feel you."

A woman with familiar curly brown hair sits down next to me, tossing her large purse on the bar with a huff.

"Camilla, what's wrong, babe?" Vyla asks, grabbing a wineglass from a high shelf.

She groans, looking exhausted. "My caterer has Covid and can't make it to Hugo's birthday party tomorrow. We were going to have pizza pinwheels, fruit skewers, and a cupcake design station. He was so excited."

Vyla pushes a glass of chardonnay with one ice cube toward Camilla. "That sucks. You could order a stack of pizzas, though, right? A few tubs of ice cream?"

"That's all we had at my birthday parties growing up," Natalie adds. "No one complained."

Camilla lets out a sigh. "Yeah, I know it's not the end of the world. I just know Hugo will be bummed, and I hate the idea of him feeling that way on his birthday." She starts staring blankly at the home screen of her phone—specifically, the large digital clock. "I guess I could make the fruit skewers myself. I'd have to do it in the morning..." she trails off, likely subtracting an hour of sleep from what she planned on getting tonight.

I could recognize that look a mile away—the look of an already over-scheduled and sleep-deprived mom trying to squeeze in another chore.

It breaks my heart, and without thinking, I say, "I'll do it."

"You what?" she replies, her eyes filled with so much hope I want to backhand her husband for letting her put this much on her plate. I know she has one because when she asked Dominic to babysit, she said the reason was that her husband had to go into work. Where the fuck is this joker now?

"Camilla, have you met Lindsay? Natalie's friend?" Dominic offers. "She's visiting for the weekend from Boston." He turns to me. "Lindsay, Camilla is a high-ranking member of the Mapletown coven."

Coven? As in witches? The timing of this interaction feels serendipitous.

"Not officially," I say, sticking out my hand. "You asked Dominic to watch your kids in the parking lot after he drove me to my car. Nice to meet you."

"Um, yes, nice to meet you too," Camilla says. "Are you truly offering to take over for my caterer? Because I'd understand if that's not how you want to spend your weekend."

"How big is the party?" I've made this kind of food before. Depending on the guest list, it wouldn't be that hard to do it again. I didn't have any official plans for the weekend anyway other than hanging out here.

"Eleven kids and probably," she pauses, thinking, "seventeen parents are expected to come."

It's a lot of people, but these are relatively easy foods to make. There's only one snag. "Nat, can I use your oven? Is it working right now?"

"Yeah, that'd be totally fine."

Though, if it gives me trouble—which it always has—I might have to start over, which would waste a lot of time.

Natalie tilts her head to the side. "We made lasagna last week, and it was mostly, definitely cooked all the way through. But the stove is completely fine."

That inspires very little confidence. "I'm staying at the B&B, so I could probably just make everything there. I'd just need to ask the owner if I can use her kitchen, but—"

"You can make them here," Dominic interjects. "I've got a huge kitchen, and we have a limited menu. It's mostly fried food. You can make the stuff today or tomorrow morning and leave it in the big fridge until the party."

"Are you sure?" I ask Dominic at the same time Camilla asks me.

Dominic nods with a bright smile. "Yeah, no problem at all."

"And obviously, I'll pay you for your time," Camilla adds.

I have other ideas, though. "How about instead of payment, you teach me some witchcraft 101? I'm realizing that my great-grandmother might've been a kitchen witch, and I'm curious to see if I have any talent in that area."

"Wow, really?" she asks, intrigued. "I'd love to."

"At the very least, I want to have a better understanding of my roots, you know?"

"Absolutely. We could always use more members."

I show Camilla my great-grandmother's journal, and she quickly confirms that she was indeed a kitchen witch. She even opens her grimoire to show me some of the most basic kitchen spells she learned when she was trying to determine her discipline.

"I'm a green witch, which is close enough in practice to kitchen witchcraft that I kept trying in the kitchen and couldn't figure out why I was failing miserably. But just because you manipulate food that came from a plant doesn't mean you have any business trying to prepare a meal with it." She chuckles softly, and I admire her candidness.

It's clear that her past struggles to figure out what kind of witch she is aren't clouded with shame. She's fond of the journey that led her to plant witchery. Envy hits me so hard in the gut that I almost bend at the waist.

It feels like this is coming out of left field—this desire to suddenly dabble in the dark arts. But ever since Natalie helped me realize that the reason Nonna Penny was able to live here in the first place is because of the magic in her blood, there's been a flicker of curiosity about my ancestors that's growing into a wild flame.

I'm not about to quit my day job and join the coven full-time—if they'd even let me—but I do want to explore it. It'd be nice to have something that I'm naturally good at, that I'm meant to be good at, and eager to practice in order to get better.

"Here, I'm sending you some screenshots." Camilla says. They're all from her grimoire. "Consider it homework. When you're cooking, try them out. See how you feel, if you sense a pull to a deeper layer of your process in preparing food, and let me know what shows up for you."

"Wow, thank you so much." I don't know much about witches, but I know their grimoires are private, sacred journals they carry with them at all times, and the fact that Camilla is so open to sharing hers with me means a lot.

She texts me a list of food allergies and how many guests will need to be accommodated, and I work on putting a shopping list together based on the recipes I'll be using. The party is at one o'clock tomorrow afternoon, and will run until four, so I decide to prepare the food in the bar kitchen in the morning, and drop off the food around noon. Once I add up the proper quantities of each ingredient I'll need, I drive down to the main square and park in front of Local Harvest, Mapletown's only grocery store. I've been here many times in the past and have always been pleasantly surprised by the selection, despite the small size of the store.

Dominic is waiting outside without a coat when I return to the bar. He doesn't even look cold. I assume it's a zombie thing, since it's only twenty-two degrees out, but who knows. "Look at all these goodies." His grin is lopsided, and his eyes are sparkling amid the dreary gray sky. My heart squeezes just looking at him.

Somehow, he's able to get five bags in one hand, and six in the other, leaving me nothing to carry inside. I urge him to let me carry something, but he ignores me.

Natalie breezes into the kitchen while we're putting things in the walk-in fridge and lets Dominic know her shift is over. "Are you guys free tonight?"

Dominic and I exchange a confused look.

"Both of us?" I ask.

"Yeah, why don't you both come over for dinner tonight? Winston is making a giant charcuterie board, and we got banana cream pie from the bakery for dessert."

It's not like I had any other plans tonight, but if it's just the two of us with Natalie and Winston, wouldn't that make it a double date? Or would Dominic and I be more like the third and fourth wheels? Winston and I barely tolerate each other, but do he and Dominic get along? That's a whole lot of Winston for one night. "Is anyone else coming?"

"Nope, just you two."

"I'd be honored," Dominic replies. Then he gently nudges me with his elbow. "Come on, Linds. It's just four friends having dinner together."

My head snaps up at him. Could he tell I felt panicked? Am I that easy to read? Doubtful, since Natalie and I have been friends for decades, and she doesn't seem to notice anything off with my mood. If anyone could read me that easily, it's her.

They're both staring at me expectantly, and I realize I haven't said anything in a very long time. "Uh, sure. Sounds fun. I'll just go back to my room and change first. What time?"

"How about seven?" Natalie asks.

"Great."

Dominic takes the butter from my hand and says, "I'll pick you up at six-fifty then."

"Wait, why?"

"It's silly for both of us to drive. Let's carpool."

The bar is right next to Natalie and Winston's house. It makes no sense for him to drive all the way down to the B&B, only to turn around in the direction from which he came, but he's offering to do it, so he clearly wants to. What reason could I have to decline his offer that wouldn't give away my feelings...wait, these are *not* feelings. At best, they're inklings, little tendrils of objective attraction to a man who is both generous and insanely hot. Anyone in my position would be on edge about it.

"Uh, okay," I stammer, my mouth suddenly dry. "Sure."

It's just a ride and then dinner with friends. What could go wrong?

CHAPTER 7

DOMINIC

My heart is hammering hard inside my chest, and I'm worried it's about to burst through my bones and land on her lap, which would be a shame, mostly because it would make a mess of her lovely silk dress. It's the color of cream with little roses all over it, and the fabric hugs her curves like it was made exclusively for her body. She's wearing a leather jacket over it, which obscures my view of her magnificent tear-drop breasts, but because the jacket stops at her hips, I'm treated to a clear view of her dimpled thighs through the thin fabric.

My mouth waters at the sight as she settles into the passenger seat.

"Thirsty?" I ask as I climb in behind the wheel. "There's a bottle of water on the door for you."

"Oh," she says, looking down at it. "That's okay. It's a quick ride. Thank you, though."

Quick, indeed. Too quick. It'll take nine minutes to reach Natalie's house from Pebblebrook Inn, ten if I drive at a snail's pace. I wish we had more time alone.

"Excited to see Winston again?"

She scoffs. "I'm not even sure why Natalie invited us over, considering how much Winston hates company. I bet it was a battle to get him to agree to it."

"Nah, I doubt that. When Natalie wants something, Winston folds like a piece of paper to make her happy."

I see her nodding out of the corner of my eye. "I can't argue with that. The love between them is unlike anything I've ever seen."

I'm inclined to agree on the rarity of it, but I have seen it before. Here in Mapletown, there are many species of monsters that are lucky enough to have fated mates. Even without such an unbreakable bond, there are couples here who share the same unconditional love that might appear boring on the outside, but only because of the stability of it. The two become so synched in their partnership that they're able to regulate each other's nervous systems.

A stab of jealousy slices through my chest at the idea of being loved so deeply. The longest relationship I've had is with Gemma, and we've never been exclusive. At one point, I was convinced that I was in love with her, but it began to fade when I found out she was seeing other people. She's always been honest about her lack of interest in monogamy, but part of me hoped she'd change her mind one day. She hasn't, and it no longer bothers me.

If I were anyone else, I'd move on and try to find my person, but after the things I've done, whomever he or she might be is likely better off with someone else. Someone normal.

My gaze drifts to Lindsay as she anxiously smooths the fabric of her dress. Has she found her person yet? Is she still looking?

The thought distracts me enough that I don't realize we've

climbed the steep hill to Natalie's front door until my foot lands on the brakes. "Here we are."

Lindsay gasps as she opens her door. "Oh shit, I forgot to bring something."

I reach for the paper bag behind her seat. "Don't you worry your little noggin'. I brought two bottles of wine from the bar. One from each of us."

"My hero." Her smile is easy, and I want to bathe in it.

Snowflakes are starting to drift down around us, not enough to get my scraper out of the box in the bed of the truck, but enough to land fully formed in Lindsay's long black hair, making her look like an angel.

Natalie whips the door open with bright eyes and ushers us in. We settle in at the new dining room table that she's still gushing over. She got it for a great price, and she's thrilled it matches the new kitchen cabinets they had recently installed. Winston has been quietly listening, with his loving gaze locked on Natalie. He can't eat or drink, but Natalie set his place with the same plates, glasses, and cloth napkin the rest of us have, I'm sure in an effort to make him feel included.

The rest of us have our glasses filled with water and wine, and our plates covered in various cheeses, jams, and crackers from the charcuterie board in the middle of the table.

"This jam is terrific," I mumble with a mouth full of it. "Did you make it?"

"No, Ethel made it," Winston replies, speaking for the first time since we arrived. "She enjoys the tedium of making small batches with the fruit she grows. It's keeping her busy."

"Well done, Garden Ghost," Lindsay says, holding up her wine as if to toast the old-timey specter who haunts their garden by growing a wide array of fruits and vegetables and leaving the harvest on their doorstep.

Winston leans forward with scowl. "If Ethel is the garden ghost, what silly nickname do you use for me?"

Lindsay rolls her eyes. "You're my friend's grumpy-ass boyfriend." She never hesitates to fight back, and it's my favorite thing about her.

His lips curve, amused. "I have no qualms about that."

To break the lingering tension, I decide to change the subject. "Winston, how's the fence repair coming along? Ready for winter?"

"I wanted to replace our current fence with an electric one to deter bears, but my Natalie won't let me. She doesn't like the idea of bears getting shocked, because her heart is as soft as butter." His tone softens more with each word when he's talking about her.

"Plus, bears are adorable," Lindsay adds.

"Instead, I've been spraying the perimeter with diluted neem oil to keep them away, along with a few motion sensors I've installed, and strings of tin cans. The scent, the lights, and the sounds combined should keep them away from the garden."

Natalie smirks. "Though we don't really need the tin cans when we can rely on Ethel shrieking at the top of her lungs if she spots one."

We continue chatting about home repair, the bar staff schedule, and upcoming holiday events for the town as dinner fades into dessert. The later we get into the evening, the more comfortable Winston is becoming with our presence, and the more touchy-feely he becomes with Natalie. For some reason, I can't look away when their fingers entwine on the table, or when he idly twirls the curled ends of her hair. Natalie leans into his touch every time, like she's hungry for it, like it's a nutrient her body requires to function, like she doesn't constantly have access to it here at home. It makes my palms itch with want.

When I look to my left, Lindsay's small, soft hand is *right there*, resting on her thigh. What I wouldn't give to reach for it now.

After dessert, we play Scrabble, and I get my green ass whooped. Lindsay, on the other hand, is crushing it. She's won twice already. Natalie and Winston are holding their own, but Lindsay seems to know...all the words. Every single one. Meanwhile, I'm over here putting down "supposably" and "brang" and having to remove my tiles immediately after because I guess they aren't real words. Nobody told me that, and I've been using both since as far back as I can remember.

Lindsay never makes me feel stupid, though. She smiles warmly and tells me that both are commonly misused in place of the correct ones. She also rubs my shoulder each time, which makes it difficult to remember any feeling of shame, or what shame feels like at all.

I hear Natalie let out a surprised squeak from the other room, and she runs in to tell us the snow is coming down hard. I follow on Lindsay's heels as she races toward the nearest window and throws back the curtain.

"Shit," she mutters. "That's a foot, at least."

"I thought we were supposed to get hit overnight," I add with a sigh. "We should probably get on the road before it gets worse."

"No way," Natalie protests. "You should crash here. We have a guest room, and I can make up the couch."

"Oh, that's okay, really." Lindsay's tone makes it sound like she'd rather sleep in the garden shed with Ethel than stay here. Then I remember that her grandmother died in the bedroom upstairs, and her tone makes perfect sense.

"Thank you kindly for the offer," I say to Natalie, "but I've got chains and snow tires. We'll be peachy."

Lindsay beams at me with so much gratitude, my stupid heart is hoping for a kiss on the cheek. She doesn't give me that, but she does give my wrist a gentle squeeze, and the prickles that race across my skin at her touch make it just as rewarding.

We say our goodbyes and trudge through the snow toward the truck. I help Lindsay into her seat before grabbing the scraper from the box in the back of the truck. It's light, fluffy snow, so it's easy to clean off, but it's falling so quickly that the windshield will be covered again soon if we don't get a move on.

The hill down to the road is treacherous, and that's putting generously. Even though my foot is steady on the brake and I'm only going three miles an hour, we slide and skid off a few times. Even if it's not plowed, the road toward the B&B is mostly flat, so it should be easier to navigate.

"Are we going to die out here?" Lindsay asks when I turn onto the road. "Because I read somewhere that when you freeze to death, you get all numb and sleepy first, which honestly doesn't sound like the worst way to go." She's trying to sound cool, but her white-knuckled grip on the overhead handle gives her away. "I just want to start mentally preparing if that's what lies ahead."

"We ain't dying out here," I reply confidently. "I can promise you that." Though with the visibility being so poor, it might take hours to get back to the main square.

That's when I feel it, the loss of connection between the tires and the road. My jaw grinds with tension as the steering wheel loses resistance and doesn't respond at all when I try to turn into the swerve of the truck like you're supposed to when you hit ice or hydroplane. "Hold on," I command in a stern voice I don't even recognize as my own. The truck turns and our bodies are thrown to the right. I feel us descending as the front dips down into a ditch, slamming into the earth and jolting us forward.

It takes a moment for the chaos of the last sixty seconds to register, but when it does, my attention lands on Lindsay, and I'm whipping my seat belt off so I can get to her. Without thinking, I wrap my arms around her, gently cupping the back of her head as I look her over. "Are you okay?"

She's breathing heavily and looks slightly dazed, but when she mutters, "Yeah, I'm good," my heart rate drops from ten times its regular speed down to two. Her different-colored eyes are wild as she looks out the windshield. "Jesus, that could've been really bad."

I urge her to move slowly as she hops out of the truck, and I do the same. I'm relieved to see that there's very little damage to my truck, likely a few scrapes on the grille, a dent in the front bumper, and I might have to replace the headlights. All in all, a solid outcome.

"Is it worth calling that cab driver you told me about? The one who...isn't a good driver?" Then she lets out a resigned giggle that lights me up from within. "Nevermind. I just heard it."

"Tilda," I offer, then check my phone for the time. "She doesn't drive past eight at night anyway." Grabbing my keys from the ignition, I lock the truck and come around to face Lindsay. "I've got a better idea."

"Such as?"

"There's a studio apartment above the bar. It's where I lived when I first opened, but now it's a crash pad for anyone who has to work late and is too tired to drive home. I say we stay there for the night, and I'll get you back to the B&B first thing tomorrow."

She pulls her leather jacket tight around her and gives me a wary look. "One bed?"

"No," I assure her. "Two twin beds, a kitchenette, and a bathroom."

Lindsay kicks her boot through the snow and finally says, "Okay, let's do it." Then she points a finger at me. "But if you try to murder me, I'll murder you first. Got it?"

I hold up my hands in surrender. "I wouldn't dare. A zombie is no match for a lioness."

"Lioness?" There's an edge of amusement in her voice.

Shit. That's more of a private nickname I've kept in my head since she kicked my brother's ass and kissed the daylights out of me. I never intended to reveal it to her. "That's kind of how I see you—a fierce, mother lion stalking through tall grass, ready to slash the throats of her enemies."

Her eyes light up. "I like it. Nickname approved."

She's already walking ahead with her back turned, otherwise, she'd be able to see the dopey grin on my face at her approval. She doesn't get far, though, as the snow on the side of the road is deep, and getting deeper.

I'm tempted to see how long she'll push through without asking for help. If I were a betting man, I'd say she'd wait until her extremities grew too numb to move. To avoid any foolish stubbornness, I lightly grab her arm and pat my back. "Climb on."

She laughs. "What? Are you serious?"

"Yes. Your legs are bare under that flimsy dress, and I won't let you get frostbite. Let me carry you there."

Her arms are crossed over her chest, but I can tell she's considering it, especially when her teeth start to chatter. Then she spreads her feet wide, or as wide as she can. "It's just...I think my dress might be too tight for a piggyback."

"Oh. That's no problem." I grab her purse in one hand and

use the other to sweep her off her feet into a bridal carry. She squeals in surprise and wiggles to get free, but I tighten my grip until she stills.

"I don't want you to hurt yourself." Her voice is quieter than I've ever heard it, and it wavers with uncertainty. When she tugs the front of her dress away from her stomach, I understand her meaning.

Still holding her with one arm, I lift her body into a bicep curl, and have to resist the urge to press a kiss to her gloriously soft belly. "Most of the time, I'm too big for chairs and doorways. What other use for my body is there than carrying a goddess through the snow to keep her feet from getting cold?"

Even beneath the inky black sky, I can see her cheeks turning pink.

"Were you this big before the, um…" she trails off. "Before you were…"

"Turned into a zombie? It's okay, you can ask about it."

"Yeah."

I shake my head. "I was tall, but much leaner. One of the many changes my body went through during my recovery."

"Recovery?"

"You know that stereotypical look of a zombie? Like in movies, with the dead eyes, skin falling off, bones exposed, and that wonky limp/run as they hunt?"

When she nods, I continue.

"Turns out, that's an extremely accurate depiction of a zombie, but only during our first year. That's the period of time right after we're turned that we're not even mentally present. Our only purpose is to consume human brains. That's it. But if you're able to survive past a year, and most don't, you start to come back to yourself. You remember things. You can walk normally. The body starts to heal enough that your skin stops falling off in chunks, and eventually those become scars."

I don't mind sharing these parts of myself with Lindsay, mostly because it distracts me from how much farther I have to walk to reach the bar, but also because I want her to know me. Well, most of me, that is. The parts that I know she can handle.

"Why don't most survive?" she asks.

"Because most are on their own in the wild. The only reason I did is because Dr. Yates found me and brought me back to her lab. She kept me in a cage during that first year."

"What?" Lindsay sounds horrified at the idea. "A fucking cage?"

"It's okay, she needed to. I would've killed her otherwise. And I have no memory of it, so it's not something that sticks with me." I clear my throat. "She reduced my intake of brains little by little and replaced it with regular food; grains and proteins, mostly, until my system got used to it, and eventually she introduced fruits and vegetables. I was also given Zomonax, a medicine she created for our kind, which lessens our cravings and improves cognitive function. I still have to take it twice a month."

"Was it just you she was treating?"

"No, there were others. It was a limited outbreak in a remote area, so she was able to keep it contained, but there were enough that she had to set up shop right next to it in order to capture and rehabilitate anyone who got infected."

"Huh. I thought you answering questions about this would satisfy my curiosity, but now I have a million more questions."

I chuckle at that. "Fire away."

"How were you infected?"

"Contaminated berries in Alaska."

Her eyes widen. "Tell me everything."

"Maybe later," I say, lowering her to her feet. "Because we're here."

"Thank fuck," she shouts, then trots excitedly toward the entrance of the bar.

The apartment entrance is next to the front door, but it's somewhat hidden by the awning that covers the outdoor seating area. I've always appreciated the separation of the two. Having to go back outside to access the apartment was an efficient way to mentally let go of the day and put my body into rest mode.

I turn off the alarm and follow her up the stairs, to a second locked door. Once inside, I turn on as many lights as I can reach and am pleased to find the place tidy. I'm not sure who stayed here last, but whoever it was cleaned up well after themselves, not leaving a stray cup or food wrapper in sight, and folding the towels and sheets neatly before putting them on the nearest bed.

The walls are a bland off-white, with nothing hanging on them, and the bedding was the cheapest I could find at the closest department store. There's an oak nightstand between the two beds with a teal lamp on it, and a cheap, black cabinet holding up the TV. It's not a cozy space, certainly not with how cold it is, but functional enough to use as a last resort.

"I'll get a fire going," I say as I gesture to the small fireplace in the corner. "There are some of my old t-shirts and sweats in the closet. Take whatever you want. I think there are spare toothbrushes in the bathroom too. The ones you get from the dentist."

It doesn't take long for a flame to grow among the logs and kindling, and once my hands are warm, I wash them in the sink next to the mini fridge. Then I make the beds, pull two bottles of water from the fridge, and turn on the TV. I need some form of noise to make me feel less like a teenager on their first date, which I'm well aware this isn't, but I can't seem to shake the knowledge that there's a very beautiful woman in *my* bathroom, putting on *my* clothes, who will soon be sleeping within two feet of me.

She emerges from the bathroom wearing a t-shirt that hits just above her knees, and a pair of knee socks that are big enough to pile around her slim ankles. Her hair is slightly wet from the snow, but it doesn't diminish how stunning she is. In fact, seeing her in my old, faded t-shirt makes my cock stiffen against my thigh, my pants growing uncomfortably tight.

"You're, um, out of toilet paper."

"Right," I mutter, unable to take my gaze off her muscular calves, the long white scar that runs through the middle of her left knee, and the way her juicy thighs disappear beneath the soft cotton. The expectant look she's giving me is what snaps me out of it. "Right. Toilet paper. That's out here."

She follows me out the front door of the apartment. There's a supply closet at the top of the stairs, which is where I keep the overflow of bar bathroom necessities and extra toiletries for the staff when they sleep here. I'm handing her three individually wrapped rolls when the closet light goes out, and I hear the signature *zzzip* of power being lost.

My palms immediately begin to sweat, and my breaths come out in shallow, uneven puffs. "It-It's okay. It's going to be okay." I'm not sure if I'm telling her or myself, but it does feel better hearing the words. "We'll be okay."

"Yeah, it's just the power. I'm sure it'll come back on soon." Lindsay sounds unbothered, which makes me feel like an idiot. Of course, she's not afraid of the dark. She's a lioness. I doubt she's afraid of anything.

My body trembles as I slowly close the closet door and guide her back into the apartment. If I hadn't started a fire, it'd be pitch black in here too. But even with the orange glow, it's still not enough light for me. "There's a l-l-lantern in here somewhere. I, uh, I think it's in the bathroom under the sink."

I'm starting to hyperventilate now, and Lindsay's brow furrowed with concern tells me she hears it too.

"Are you okay?"

"Yup," I reply, in a rush to get the word out. I don't want her thinking I'm a coward. "Totally fine." My body feels heavy, as if I shouldn't keep moving, and I lower myself to a seated position on the floor with my back against one of the beds.

She grabs the lantern and a flashlight from the bathroom and turns them on, placing the lantern at my side. When she sits down across from me, her gaze is assessing. Cautious. "So, how else did your body change after you became a zombie? If you don't mind me asking."

It's an attempt to distract me, and I'm grateful for it, because I automatically start going through the list in my head. "Um, in addition to the bulk, obviously the skin color. I was the whitest white boy before this."

At that, she chuckles, and the sound has my muscles unclenching all down my body.

"My eyes were a darker blue than they are now." I continue. "The scars…" I roll up my sleeve and point to the many jagged white marks along my forearm. "These are all from wounds after I was changed. I also don't need to eat as much anymore."

"Really?" she asks. "That surprises me. With your bigger frame, I would assume—"

"Fair," I interject, "but keep in mind, I was on an exclusive brain diet. One brain would be enough to sustain me for about four days. I didn't eat anything else in that first year. After Dr. Yates started introducing human foods, my stomach could only handle small bites. More than that, and I'd get violently ill."

"How much do you eat now? Like, on an average day."

"I can get by on one cup of black coffee, and one banana

and mayo sandwich a day, or a slab of raw top sirloin. I drink water, but I don't need as much of that either."

"Wait." She holds up a hand. "Did you say...banana and mayo?" Her face twists in disgust, and I can understand why.

It sounds like an odd pairing, but it was a staple in the South, especially if you were a family who struggled to afford food. For me, not only is it a comfort food, but I tend to eat three or four when I'm feeling particularly stressed. Like right now, for example. I'd trade a testicle for a banana and mayo sandwich to appear in my hand.

"Why would you do that to yourself?"

I chuckle. "It's not as bad as it sounds. In fact, it tastes kind of like a banana cream pie."

When I tell her it's my comfort food, her expression eases. "Ah. I have one of those too. Peanut butter and fluff. I always keep both in the house for bad days."

"See. You get it."

There's one physical change I haven't told her about, and I think I'll keep it to myself. She's already figured out I'm afraid of the dark. I don't need much else to scare her away, and the extra appendage that sits just above my dick would likely scare her away.

Lindsay shivers, and rubs her arms up and down. "It's still really cold in here."

"Let's get you to bed, then." If the night has to end here, at least she was able to talk me down from a panic attack.

She pulls the covers back on her bed, then pauses and turns to face me. "What if we pushed the beds together?"

Did she really just ask that?

"Together? As in..."

"As in two beds turns into one, yeah. For warmth."

Oh. For warmth. I do run warm, so practically, it makes

sense. I can still enjoy the benefits of her nearness, though. "Sure."

We move the nightstand back against the wall and pull the twin beds closer to the fire and pressed together. Once we're under our respective blankets, we face each other. The soft light of the lantern, paired with the orange glow of the fire, makes Lindsay look younger. Not that she looks old. But the shadows that dance along her cheeks make her look like she did when we first met. We were just kids. Part of me—hell, all of me—still can't believe we've been reunited.

"Afraid of the dark, huh?" Her mouth quirks up on the side, and I wonder if she's mocking me. "Have you always had that fear?"

"No," I answer honestly. "That changed after I was turned, along with everything else."

"Why the dark?"

I nestle deeper into the pillow, as if the tactile plushiness of it will keep me grounded here in the present. "I don't have any clear memories of that first year, like I said, but sometimes I'll get flashes. They're so fast, I'm not sure if it's a memory or a nightmare or what, but they feel real, as if a deeper part of me knows it too well. There's darkness, but it's not just that. There's palpable, suffocating fear, and then a scream. A scream that isn't mine. I don't know whose it is, but it's close enough to my ear that it hurts. I usually cover my ears, and then it ends, but not before reminding me of that time. The year I was something...else. Wrong. Evil."

Lindsay's hand brushes my cheek, wiping away tears I didn't know I shed. Her body is closer, too. Close enough that her nose is about an inch from mine, and I can feel her warm breath on my chin.

"I can't even imagine that version of you." Her eyes are

shining, and I'm baffled as to why she'd be on the verge of tears. "I'm so sorry you went through that."

Shouldn't she be moving away from me? Afraid to get too close after what I just revealed?

Suddenly, her hand moves to the back of my neck, and she's pulling me in. No, I have to stop this. She still doesn't know that we've met before. She doesn't know who I am, and more importantly, what I've done.

But my body disagrees. *Later*, it whispers, as my mouth closes the distance. Her lips look so soft, and the memory of the first time I felt them hits me like a sucker punch. Still, I can't stop. Don't want to stop, because this is Lindsay, my lioness.

The kiss is gentle at first. Achingly tender, as her lips press against mine. It's filled with empathy and adoration that I know I don't deserve. When I feel her tongue glide along my lower lip, I push away the part of me that wants to do the right thing, and allow myself to get lost in this moment, to keep it for as long as I can.

A moan from deep within my chest rattles out of me as I deepen the kiss, plundering her mouth with my tongue and learning each dip and corner. Her nails bite into my skull as she pulls me closer, and I feel her leg wrap around my hip. I swallow her desperate, needy whimper as my hand travels down her spine.

My cock is pulsing at this point, and I'm as sure as the sky is blue that the front of my pants are wet with precome.

Is it safe to grab her ass? *Fuck*, I want to. To have her soft cheeks spilling out of my palms would be heaven. But I can't just grab first and ask later. If this is going to happen, it has to happen the right way. The respectful way.

Then she whispers my name like a prayer, and it's like a bucket of ice water was dumped over my head. I pull back and instantly regret it. Her eyes are glazed, the pupils blown out, and her lips are swollen from my kiss. My hips protest this move by thrusting forward, and if I gave myself an ounce of leeway, I'd pin her lush body beneath mine and fuck her straight through the mattress.

I can't, though, because when she said my name, it brought me back to that rocky beach, to the tall girl who bandaged my wounds, and to the secret that will remain wedged between us until it's released.

"Lindsay," I say, chest heaving, "I need to tell you...we've kissed before."

CHAPTER 8

LINDSAY

I blink at him, wondering if I heard him correctly. "We what?"

He swallows and rubs a hand down his face. "We met...a long time ago, when we were kids. I was sixteen, you were fourteen, and we kissed."

The world starts to spin as I process his words. Scanning my memories, I know I kissed three boys when I was fourteen. One of them was Max Gebler, a kid in my math class who had braces and his breath always smelled like Mountain Dew. I also kissed Jared Dutton at the spring dance when he bought me a carnation and told me I had pretty eyes. The other kiss, my *first* kiss, was a boy who didn't go to my school. I met him during the summer when his brother was trying to push him into the lake. He was short and scrawny and kind. A Southern twang rings in my ears as I recall the details of that day. His name was... "Nic?"

He nods, his expression somber. "That was me."

Part of me can't believe this is true, despite the itchy sensation at the edge of my consciousness telling me he's not lying. I need to test him first. "If that was you, who else was on the beach with you?"

"My brother, Kenny, and his friend, Donald. Kenny was trying to drown me, and you stopped him."

"How did I stop him?"

He smiles, and the warmth of it envelops my body. "You threw sand in Donald's eyes, then you kicked Kenny in the crotch." The smile grows into steady, deep laughter. "At some point, you actually roared at them. They hobbled away like two dumb kittens who tried to pick a fight with..." he pauses, his eyes darting between mine, "well, a lioness."

When I say nothing, his smile dies, and he waits. And waits. And waits.

"What are you thinking?" he finally asks.

Truthfully, I don't know. I want to be mad at him for not telling me sooner, but when did he realize it was me? Was it yesterday? I'm not surprised I didn't recognize him, given how different he looks. Does it even matter when he recognized me? Does it actually change anything about this situation?

Granted, I crushed on "Nic" hard for the rest of the summer, and deep into the school year. Having learned only his first name, I had no way of looking for him, so the crush faded, and when he'd cross my mind over the years that followed, I hoped he was happy, wherever he was. Happy and brave enough to stand up for himself.

Knowing that the boy who kissed me with tenderness and didn't feel threatened by having a girl fight his battles is the man lying beside me isn't as shocking as perhaps it should be. In many ways, Dominic is the same now as he was then. He's just as thoughtful as I remember, and still a great listener. He aims to please without being a yes man. And with the way he reported Finn and had him arrested without a second thought to protect me, it's clear he gained the courage he was lacking back then.

There are a million things I could ask Dominic about why he's sharing this information with me now, but what comes out is, "Do you prefer being called Nic?"

Relief floods his expression as he lets out a sigh. He brushes some hair off my face and tucks it behind one ear. "Only by you."

"Did you change your name?"

He nods. "My birth name is Nicolas Jeffries, but Dr. Yates suggested I change it if I wanted to reenter the world. She made me a new license and all the accompanying identification documents with the name Dominic Jennings."

"Hm. Similar, but different enough to sell it."

"Exactly." He chews on the inside of his cheek, looking shy. "Why didn't you meet me that following day? At the beach. I waited. For as long as I could, I waited for you."

I let my memories take me back to that camping trip, to that sweet first kiss. I wish I could've met him that next day. It would've been a lot more fun than what actually happened. "My parents got into a big fight. They made us leave a few days earlier than expected."

I remember the hushed exchange of insults from their side of the camper so vividly. Before bed Isla and I were reading before bed on the kitchen table that morphed into a small bed inside our camper, while Mom and Dad were arguing on the other side of their thin bedroom door. Isla kept looking to me for assurance that everything would be okay, and that's what I gave her, because I had no idea what else to do.

The next morning, when they told us over breakfast we'd be leaving immediately, I completely lost my shit. As tears streaked down my face, I tried to explain that I'd made a friend and had plans to meet them at the beach that day. Both of them were too busy angrily packing to even acknowledge my emotional state. "Sorry, kiddo. We're leaving today," was all I got from Dad.

"I'm so sorry," I tell Nic now. "I wanted to meet you. I begged them to let us stay long enough so that I could at least meet you and tell you that we were leaving. They wouldn't even give me that."

"You know what?" he says, clapping his hands together. "That honestly makes me feel better, knowing that we were both miserable that day."

We share a laugh that lightens the tension significantly. When the laughter settles, I decide to take a chance. There's a question I've been trying not to ask, because it feels rude, but I think the time has come. "Do you still, um, need to eat brains? From humans?"

He seems to register the waver in my voice and gives my hand a reassuring squeeze in response. "The craving has waned significantly. I still need it as part of my diet, but less, and I probably always will."

I swallow the lump in my throat. "Are you craving it now?"

"No," he says softly. "Dr. Yates sends me the amount I need to hold me over for a few months. And it's not as bad as you're picturing. She grinds it into a powder and bakes it into a type of granola bar. I eat one a month."

Okay, that does seem a lot less frightening than what my imagination created, so that's a relief.

"Can you smell people's brains?" I laugh, embarrassed by the way I phrased it. "I mean, is that what triggers the craving? Is it akin to smelling brownies baking in the oven?" Before he can reply, I add, "Can you smell mine in my head right now?" I don't ask him what they smell like, but of course, now I'm wondering that too.

"No, I can't smell yours, or anyone else's." His smile fades. "Not while you're still alive, anyway."

"Oh." I don't need him to explain further. Once a person is dead and their skull is cracked open, the smell is there.

His eyebrows lift in a sweet, eager expression. "But your brain does tempt me in other ways."

I shoot him a smirk. "Oh yeah?"

He nods. "You might be the smartest person I know."

Other men would be intimidated by a smart woman. Not Dominic. There's nothing but wonder shining in his eyes.

We'll need to return to the powdered human brain food at some point, but I'm comfortable enough to move on for now.

"Whatever happened to your brother? Does he know you're like this now?"

Nic looks away, his jaw clenching. "Kenny and I were reported missing when we left Tennessee for Alaska. He was trying to get away from some people, and I followed along, liking the idea of starting a new life somewhere I'd never been. We went on a hike and found this discarded wooden crate filled with berries. At the time, we were out of money and starving, so I didn't hesitate to eat them. He was more reluctant." He rubs the stubble on his chin as he continues. "The next part is blurry, but I remember vomiting and feeling a crippling pain in my stomach. Kenny was shouting at me to get the berries out of my system because they were poisonous, and then everything went dark."

My eyelids are getting heavy, but this story is far too interesting to bail on. "Did Kenny turn into a zombie too?"

He shakes his head, still avoiding my gaze. "No."

A yawn escapes me as I ask, "Do you know where he is now?"

Nic pulls the blanket over my exposed shoulder and tucks it beneath my chin. "To be continued, lioness."

"But wait..." I protest, just as sleep pulls me away.

I wake up much warmer than I was when I fell asleep, and that's likely due to the large arm that's encircling my waist, and the solid wall of a chest pressed against my back. Not that I mind since I've never felt more protected. What does present a bit of a problem is the rock-hard dick that's poking me in the ass, and it's only a problem because based on the snore that's tickling my ear, Nic is still very much asleep, and I'm so turned on that it takes everything in me not to wiggle my backside against it.

Gray light streams through the narrow space between the curtains. It's that shade of gray that says it's way too early for my eyes to be open. I'd guess it was around four or four thirty.

There's a sticky pool between my legs, and though I can't remember my dreams from the previous night, I'm assuming they were exceptionally dirty. What am I supposed to do now? He's bound to wake up if I start masturbating beside him, and that would be utterly humiliating, but if I woke him up and made it clear that I'm horny as fuck and want to go for a ride, would he reject me? Would he pump the brakes and insist we take it slow? Does he have another secret that he needs to reveal before we go further?

I know I vowed to be done with men, but Dominic isn't technically a man. He's a zombie. A gentle giant of a zombie with veiny forearms and a very skilled tongue, and I have *needs*, okay?

"Mm," he groans as he inhales the skin of my neck, and I think maybe I woke him up because my ass is rubbing against his dick right now, much to my chagrin.

Clearly, the clappable material of my ass has a mind of its own. *Bitch.*

"You smell good," he says, his voice husky from sleep.

I notice that he's not pulling away, in fact, he's thrusting against my ass with equally slow, intentioned movements. He wants this too. Pushing all rational thoughts out of my head, I take his hand from where it rests on my ribs and place it on my breast. My hand guiding his, I cup and squeeze as my nipple becomes an aching, stiff point.

"Nic," I moan, turning my head sideways toward him. "Please touch me."

His eyes widen at that, and he stills. "Are you sure?"

"Yes." It comes out breathy and wanton.

Rolling me onto my back, his knees straddle my hips. "Lindsay, I..." He stops, looking so vulnerable my heart squeezes. "It will change things between us, don't you think?"

I shrug. "We were becoming friends, right? Now we'll be friends who have sex. That cool with you?"

Something flashes across his face that I can't decipher. That's when I start second-guessing every moment that led to this. Am I pressuring him? Did I misread the vibes? I thought he was into it.

"Friends who have sex," he repeats. Eventually, he nods before dropping his head and placing a kiss just beneath my ear. "Yes, I think I'd like that very much."

Once he gives the green light, we become a flurry of limbs and mouths and strewn clothes. His tongue swipes across my collarbone, making my bare chest arch into him, and he whispers, "You're so fucking beautiful."

His presses wet kisses down my chest and takes the time to flick each nipple with his tongue before sucking hard. He's leaving a trail down my belly when he adds, "If at any time you wish to stop, say the word."

I nod, but that's not enough for him. He grabs my wrists and holds them over my head with one hand. Then, with his free hand, he reaches down between my legs and traces a line along my inner thigh, so close to what I need, but not close enough. I lift my hips to get him closer, but I end up chasing his hand. "I need a verbal confirmation, gorgeous."

The authoritative tone brings me back to Halloween night when he was scolding Finn. As much as I hate the memory, I'm pretty sure I could survive on that calm, confident voice alone. Fuck food and water, just talk to me.

"Y-Yes," I whimper. "*Please*, Nic."

Five seconds into this, and I'm already fucking begging. Have I ever been on the verge of coming this quickly? No. Have I ever been attracted to anyone like Nic? Also no. I'm not about to get soft for this guy, but this does feel different, though I can't totally place how, or why.

When his hand dips beneath my underwear, his brow furrows. "You're bare."

A wave of early aughts shame washes over me. "Yeah, I had it lasered off in 2008." I scrub a hand down my face. "Thank goodness my eyebrows recovered from that time."

He responds by kissing me hungrily right out of the gate. "Bushy or bare," he says against my lips, "you're straight out of a dream."

It's really, *really* hard not to melt into a puddle at that.

"Tell me what you like," he groans. "What you need to come."

"I like..." I begin, and my stomach twists slightly with nerves. Will he be cool with my answer? Or will he judge me for it? He's asking, so clearly, he's eager to give me what I want, which is more than I can say for the majority of my previous partners. "I like being told what to do. Being bossed around." What can I say? Feminism leaves my body when the clothes come off. Or maybe it's because I have to make a million decisions from the time I open my eyes until the moment I pass out, and it'd just be nice to not have to think for a little while.

To know that whatever I do with my partner, it'll make us both feel good.

"Yeah?" he asks.

Nic's finger swipes between the lips of my pussy, and he moans like he's in pain. It does something to me, that moan. The sound makes me feel powerful. Like I could knock over a building with the back of my hand.

"I'd be honored to boss you around, lioness."

"W-What about you?" Speaking clearly is becoming a challenge with the way he's touching me, as is forming thoughts.

He nips at the shell of my ear before whispering, "I like it rough. Not all the time, but sometimes."

I very much like the sound of that.

"*Fuck*. You're gushing." He circles my clit a few times before inserting a finger, then a second.

They slide in easily, I'm so wet. It feels amazing, but not exactly what I need. Reaching down, I press the heel of his hand against my clit. "Ahh, like that," I tell him when he hits the right spot. "Pressure there." He finds a rhythm that has my thighs quivering as they wrap around his hips. I lift my hips to meet his hand, and we're moving faster and faster as my stomach tightens, and I feel like a bowstring about to snap.

Shit, this is happening so fast. Too fast. I wanted to explore him too. I wanted to study the details of the black grim reaper tattoo that covers his left pec, to trace every white scar with my tongue, and palm his dick through his sweatpants until he begged me to stop. I wasn't planning on this being all about me.

I reach down between us, beneath the hem of his boxer briefs, but he pushes my hand away. "No," he grunts against my neck through panting breaths. "Later."

As soon as the word leaves his mouth, he curls his fingers into a hook shape, and I'm barreling off the edge of a cliff, shaking and crying out into the early morning light as if someone is murdering me. He may as well have. As far as my pussy is concerned, it's dead, ruined for all other men.

When I come down, I'm still struggling to catch my breath and Dominic is smiling with his hand held up.

"What?" I ask. Then I see it. From the tips of his fingers down to his elbow, he's soaked. Dripping, in fact.

The fuck? How can all of *that* be from me?

"Have you ever squirted before?"

I lean up on my elbows to get a better look. "Is that what happened? Jesus Christ."

"I'll take that as a no." Then he glides his tongue up his forearm to the tips of his fingers, savoring every last drop of me with a gleam in his eye.

I shove his chest hard enough to roll us over until I'm on top of him. His hands settle on my hips, one of them very distinctly wet. Not gonna lie, I'm annoyed my body did something I didn't think it could and I didn't even get to witness it. On the other hand, it's hard to stay mad when I have a man the size of a tree beneath me just waiting to be played with.

His hands move up to my belly, and he proceeds to gently squeeze and cup my rolls with the purest adoration I've ever seen shining from his eyes. "I love your stomach," he says, continuing his tour of my body. His finger traces the horizontal scar just below my lower abs. "Is this a C-section scar?"

I nod. "I thought I'd be able to deliver her naturally, but they decided to cut me open instead."

He runs his fingers along the raised uneven skin once, twice more, and I feel the sting of tears forming behind my eyes. I'm not sure if it's the memory of how scared I was at the time, or because no one has ever touched that scar before, not even Billy, but I have to turn away to keep Nic from seeing.

I take a breath, and once I push the tears down, I return my attention to him. His body. His scars. This is about him now. "Is there a special meaning behind this tattoo?" I ask, drawing a bubble around the reaper's scythe with my finger.

"A reminder that I've met him before, and whenever he returns, I won't fear him." He looks down at it. "A little on the nose, I know, but I wanted to celebrate my recovery with a tattoo, so this is what I got."

"I love it." I reach up to touch the white scar beneath his left eye. It's bigger than a lot of his other scars, I've noticed. "How'd you get this one?"

He shrugs. "I don't know. Don't remember. When I started coming back to myself, it was an open wound that had just started healing. Took a long time."

"You never asked the doctor?"

"Nah. Didn't want to know."

I can understand. After surviving what he did, some things are better left unknown. To keep the sad memories from creeping in, I lean down until my chest is pressed against his and start inching backward. The moment he realizes what my plan is, his cheeks darken.

"You don't have to." He lets out a shuddered breath as I trace his abs with my finger, the muscles tightening all the way down to that delicious deep V shape directing me to the main event.

"But I want to."

He jolts to a seated position when I pull down his boxer briefs, the movement so lightning fast I almost fall off the bed. "Uh, I should explain."

When I look down, I don't understand what I'm seeing. "What, um..." How do I put this respectfully, without him feeling like a science experiment?

"This is another way my body has changed."

It explains a lot, but not enough. "You grew a second dick?"

I don't mean to sound so taken aback, but I can't help it. It's *that* jarring.

"No, not exactly."

"What do you call..." I begin, pointing at it, but my curiosity takes over. "Can I touch it?"

He nods nervously, holding his breath.

A second dick is the wrong way to describe this body part. His primary dick is long and thick, covered in veins and ending in a swollen mushroom head. Unlike the average human dick, however, this one is green, an even darker shade than the rest of him, and has the same little white scars that cover his body. The idea that he was injured here, and all over his heavy green balls, makes me wince on his behalf.

About an inch north of his primary dick, framed by neatly trimmed, dark hair, is a smaller appendage about the length and width of a thumb. It's not as hard as his dick, but not floppy and soft either. There's a slight stiffness to it, while still remaining flexible. "What's this part here?" I ask, pointing at the head of it. There's an opening that looks like a flower that's yet to bloom, with a dark green part in the center that resembles a tiny tongue.

"It's the suckler."

"This little thing in the center is the suckler?"

"No, the whole thing. The *second dick*, as you called it."

I have my theories on its function based on the name, and none of them make me want to call this off. Lining up our parts, it seems *the suckler* would fit perfectly against my clit. "Is it sensitive?" I ask as I circle it with my pointer finger and thumb, letting my breath fan over it.

"Not really." He scratches his head, looking boyish and cute. "I don't think it's for me at all."

"What do you mean?"

"When Dr. Yates discovered that this was a common thing

among newly recovered zombies and that it didn't seem to serve any biological purpose for us, she'd joke that it was God's apology for the virus. That he turned us into monsters, but if we survived, he'd ensure anyone who took a chance on us was well cared for."

A loud cackle escapes me. I'm not a religious person, but fuck, that's a great theory. Feeling bold, I press my finger against the head of the suckler, and holy shit, there's no better name for it. It sucks the tip of my finger into its hole, while its tiny internal tongue flicks against my finger at differing speeds. The feel of that against my clit or my asshole? I'll be done for. Possibly in a coma.

The longer my finger is connected to the suckler, the more my pussy drips with need. When I recall the reason my face is down here to begin with, I pull my finger from the suckler. I kiss along Nic's stomach, then the tops of his thighs, then move down as I pull his briefs all the way down. Now that I know the suckler isn't an erogenous zone for him, I ignore it and focus on his pretty green dick, throbbing and hot in my hand.

Just as I lower my lips to the head, Nic growls, "Spit on it."

Hearing the urgency in his voice, knowing how desperate he is to feel the wet friction of my mouth around him, so desperate that he actually wants my saliva covering his dick before it happens, I feel the blood rush to my cheeks. I'm eager to give him what he wants. My spit covers the head, and I use it to coat the rest of his length, stroking him down to the base.

"Fuck, Lindsay," he groans, his knuckles a pale green as he grips the sheets. I press soft kisses along his shaft as my free hand scrapes my nails down his thigh. He brushes the hair off my face and gathers it in his fist. "Fuck, you're so beautiful."

I only have him in my mouth for a second before I pull back with a sputter. "What the shit?"

"What?" he shouts, concerned.

"You taste like…" It couldn't be. "Like…" I must be having a stroke. "A peanut butter cup?"

Then he gives me a knowing look as his shoulders drop in relief. "Natalie never told you?"

I stare at him blankly.

"That the men of Mapletown are, um"—he's blushing so hard even the tips of his ears are dark now—"flavored?"

"Flavored?" That does ring a bell. I remember something about a spell one of the former mayors of Mapletown put on the men, something about…" When the image of a peanut butter cup pops into my head, I understand. "Ah, the favorite flavor of the person sucking the local dicks." I've never disliked blowjobs, more performing them on specific exes, but knowing I'm going to taste my favorite candy each time I put a dick in my mouth does make the process a lot more enjoyable.

"In that case…" I trail off, then give it everything I've got. I treat Nic's cock like a lollipop I need to get to the middle of, an ice cream cone that's melting, all while massaging his heavy balls. He thrashes and thrusts beneath me, but I don't let up. I relax my jaw and take him deep. Then I switch it up and suck on his balls for a little while before returning to the head and focus my lips and tongue right there while I stroke him.

It doesn't take long for Nic to whimper my name as he explodes in my mouth. I swallow as much as I can, but there's too much. It starts running down my neck and chest, but I don't care about the mess, because I'm too busy lapping up his special peanut butter cup sauce. It's fucking delicious, and I'm worried I'm already addicted to it.

His chest is damp with sweat when he gathers me in his arms and hauls me up his body. There he holds me tight and whispers "thank you" and "that was so fucking hot" over and over into my hair. At one point, I move to get up, knowing how sticky we both are, but his arms tighten. "Please," he begs, "not yet. Let me hold you for a little longer."

It's such a vulnerable request, and I can't resist giving in. "Okay." We fall back asleep a few minutes later, satisfied and a total mess.

The next time we wake up, the power is back on, and the overhead light is filling me with rage. Too bright. Too harsh. It makes me want to shove my fist through a wall. Why are all overhead lights so aggressive? I find the t-shirt I slept in next to my side of the bed and throw it on before stumbling toward the front door and turning the light off.

Nic rolls over and peers up at me with one eye open. "Morning, lioness. Sleep well?"

Nodding, I reply, "Both times. But I've got a children's birthday party to cater, and I don't feel right about preparing all that food while still covered in come."

He snickers and gives my ass a playful smack. "Reasonable. Towels are on the shelf above the toilet. You wash up. I'll make coffee."

"You never told me your biggest fear," he says, leaning over my shoulder to get a better view of the pizza rolls.

"Heights."

"Heights, huh? Is there an origin story?"

I think about it for a moment and come up empty. "I don't think so. As far back as I can remember, if there was a gorgeous view looking out over whatever, I got the hell out of there. No thanks."

I set my final wrapped pizza roll on the baking sheet and place it in the oven. There are vegetarian pizza rolls, pepperoni and gluten-free, so every guest should be covered. The cupcakes come next, and Nic helps me mix the batter while I whip up a large batch of buttercream frosting. I use chocolate and vanilla cake mixes, which hopefully, the kids like. For some reason, this man—who stress-eats banana and mayo sandwiches and doesn't like much else—is fascinated by each step of my cooking process. He wants to taste everything, then proceeds to make yummy noises with each bite.

After we had our morning coffee, Nic showed me around the kitchen and went out to shovel the parking lot. I made pancakes, and he was insistent on playing a `90s rom-com on the big TV in the bar when it was time to eat. Another thing I learned about Nic today is that he loves `90s rom-coms. We watched his favorite, *While You Were Sleeping*, and I watched his lips move along with the dialogue for the whole thing.

"It's the big family, I think," he told me when I asked why this was his favorite. "The banter between them, the loyalty, and the way they love each other. I've never had that."

To which my heart broke into a thousand pieces.

He went on to share his favorite lines from about ten other rom-coms from that era, and I made him promise to be on my team if the bar ever hosted a trivia night.

Once the cupcakes are in the oven, we have a bit of downtime before we need to make the fruit skewers. My hope is that they remain as fresh as possible for the length of the entire party, so I won't be making them until about a half-hour before we're supposed to drop the food off at Camilla's.

I find a menu on a shelf above the stove and look it over. It's the menu for the bar, and as Nic said, it's limited. There are fries with three kinds of dipping sauces, a signature Mapletown hot dog, jalapeño poppers, fried mac and cheese bites, fried calamari, and chips and guac.

He spots me staring at it and drops his chin onto my shoulder. "What's going on in that head of yours? Thinking about how terrible my food sounds?"

"It's not that," I say, not knowing how to end that sentence, because I have no doubt his customers love the food. "It's fried finger food. Of course it's delicious. But with such a humongous kitchen and a steady roster of regulars, have you ever thought about adding to it?"

There are only three or four restaurants in the entire town, so you run into repeats pretty quickly, and from what I've tasted, those options are mediocre at best. There's a pizza place, which Natalie said has recently introduced some pasta dishes, a Chinese food place by the gas station, and a diner in the strip mall by the highway. The coffee place serves a handful of sandwiches, but they close around five at night, so it's not exactly a dinner option.

"Not really," he says. "I'm not much of an expert on food, considering the state of my taste buds, so I figured I'd offer people the bar fare they're used to and leave it at that."

"Hm. Yeah, that makes sense." I put the menu down and look through the propped open door toward the bar. "This place is so much more than the local dive, though. It feels bigger. Like it has more to offer."

I expect him to be mildly interested, if not a tad defensive. In my experience, business owners don't appreciate an outsider's opinion on how to improve the day-to-day operations, even if they hire you to do just that. They're protective of their livelihood, and they often accept the status quo as the primary sign of success. This is a volatile industry, wherein restaurants often close within the first five years of opening their doors, so I get it. If you can afford to keep your doors open, why change anything?

What the restaurant owners I encounter often overlook— likely because they're spread too thin in order to cover the rising costs of rent, ingredients, and labor—are the little changes that can lead to major growth.

Dominic has a massive bar with unique architecture—the building is shaped like three massive wooden kegs, with the one in the center taller than the other two—a dozen beers on tap, an extensive wine and cocktail list, an outdoor seating area with room for lawn games, a dance floor, and a sprawling, immaculate kitchen. The only thing I haven't seen get much use is the kitchen, and since he owns the building and has a small staff, I bet he could afford to update his menu without breaking the bank.

He leans on the counter and gives me his full attention. "Such as?"

"Oh, I don't know." The question is unsurprising, but the pressure of it throws me off. I'm no chef—just a woman who spends her days staring at menus and looking for gimmicks to bring more people through the door. "Off the top, you could have an Italian grinder with a signature oil-based drizzle, glazed Brussels sprouts—everyone loves those—an antipasto salad with a unique twist to stand out, like, um, fried onions or diced roasted red potatoes. You could even offer a flatbread pizza with different types of cheese, caramelized onions and garlic, taleggio, and drizzled with local maple syrup. I know those ingredients sound odd together, but I promise they are"—I press my lips to my fingertips—"chef's kiss. Or you could focus on one food and perfect the condiments, like wings. Ooh, and you've heard of hot honey, right? Maybe Fast Glass Tavern could sell their own brand of spicy maple syrup."

"Plus, there's always merch. People love mugs. More themed nights. Private events." My brain gets flooded with Pinterest boards. "Weddings! That field behind the bar would be perfect."

His expression shifts from fascinated to wary because

clearly he hates my ideas and the fact that I've been rambling for a good three minutes straight.

"I don't know. That's just off the top of my head," I mutter, backtracking. "I can think of others, though."

Suddenly, my feet leave the floor, and I'm being whirled around in a very tight space filled with knives. Nic places me on my feet and cups my cheeks. His features are blurry, but I can tell he's smiling.

"You're fucking brilliant, you know that?" He rubs the tip of his nose against mine. "I could listen to you talk about food menus for the rest of time. I'm going to talk to Anton about all of these, and if you think of anything else, please tell me. Any hour of the day. It doesn't matter. Text me or call me. I want to know. Was that really off the top of your head? I think you just took Fast Glass to a new level. Man"—he stops, his light blue eyes scanning my face—"the way you light up when you talk about something you care about. *Fuck*, it's stunning, Lindsay. You're stunning."

The breath leaves my lungs entirely. My legs wobble, and I wonder if this is what it feels like to swoon. No one has ever been so happy to hear me talk about menu additions. Granted, I've never slept with any of the restaurant owners I made suggestions to, but still. Basking in the glow of this man's attention is like a full-body high. It's a new feeling.

A sad realization hits me.

It's a feeling I'll miss when I drive home tomorrow.

"Think you can extend your trip a few days?" he asks, as if reading my mind.

"I wish," I reply, and he has no idea how much I mean it.

CHAPTER 9

DOMINIC

Once the pizza rolls are done and the cupcakes are topped with Lindsay's homemade frosting, we work together to cut up the fruit and arrange it on silicone straws. There are grapes, strawberries, pineapples, watermelon, and cantaloupe. It's quite the bright, cheerful-looking snack.

My gaze drifts to Lindsay's profile between each assembled skewer, studying the slope of her nose and the shapes I can make out among the freckles on her cheeks. She's unlike anyone I've ever met. It's not just her body either—though that alone could inspire countless poems—it's the way her mind works. I wasn't lying when I told her I could listen to her talk about food for the rest of time.

Though, the more accurate statement would be that I could listen to her talk about anything for the rest of time. Anything that she cared about. The way her passion and knowledge about a certain subject transforms her features is captivating. Her body language is usually guarded and skeptical, with her eyes expressionless and her brows almost always pinched together, as if waiting for inevitable disappointment. But that melts away the moment she starts chattering like a hummingbird on speed. Her hands are open and constantly moving to express her opinions. Her eyes are bright. She doesn't stand still like a statue. Depending on the words coming out of her mouth, she might be shuffling her feet, tapping excitedly, or doing a little dance in place.

This is what was missing when I first saw her on Halloween night. She seemed bone-tired, but that's not the girl I kissed those many years ago. She was in there somewhere, though. I knew it. My lioness is fierce, always ready to extend her claws and go to war with the world to protect her people. I want to be the place where she can take a deep breath and unclench her fists.

Maybe there's no one else who can help her find that place. Maybe I was put back into her life for a reason. No, I'm certain I was.

I reckon I was brought back from the dead to show her the absurd beauty of being alive.

We cover the food in layers of plastic wrap and aluminum foil, and carefully stack the trays between our bodies in the truck. Camilla is thrilled to see us, especially after the snowstorm. The roads were clear on our way over, thankfully, but if the snow had continued into the morning, that likely wouldn't have been the case. We stay to help her set up the food along a foldable table in the living room, where the party is taking place. There are balloons and streamers along the walls and covering the ceiling.

Morty, Camilla's husband and the town's only jaguar shifter, is hard at work filling more balloons with helium at the kitchen counter. He gives me a friendly wave when I pass by. Rocío and Hugo are nowhere to be found.

Camilla is showering Lindsay with compliments about the

presentation and how she plans to sneak a cupcake before people start arriving, and I watch proudly from the sidelines, following Lindsay's instructions on where to put things.

She doesn't seem to enjoy the job she has, and she's already so good at this. It's not my place to tell her to quit her shitty job and be a caterer instead, but I want to. Especially if it meant she'd be here full-time doing something she likes to do.

While the two women continue chatting about witchcraft and some coven news, I head over to Morty and start tying ribbons on the ends of balloons that he's just closed and knotted. He's a man of few words, which I don't mind. This is a mindless task that allows me to observe Lindsay from a distance, and *fuck me,* one blowjob and I'm obsessed with this woman.

If I don't rein it in, I'm going to fuck this whole thing up before it even gets going. We haven't even had sex yet, and I'm picturing his and hers monogrammed hand towels in our bathroom. I shake my head, trying to knock the mushy shit loose, and Morty gives me a look like, *You good?*

I laugh, easing the tension from my stance and trying to be all nonchalant. Then, "Nope," falls out of my mouth, and I have no clue what to do next. There's really nowhere to go from here, so I hand him a stray ribbon and march away. "Linds, you ready to go?" Get me out of here before I ask Hugo to be our ring bearer.

More than one car is parking on the street in front of the house, and with guests arriving, my eager exit doesn't seem so strange.

Lindsay says goodbye to Camilla and promises to text her after she does her witch homework. I drive her back to Pebblebrook so she can take a "reset shower," whatever that is, and change clothes, and we agree to meet at the bar in a few hours. I wasn't planning on working today, but since I know she's coming in, I drive straight back to the bar and tackle the stack of bills in my office.

The silky caress of her voice meets my ears around three in the afternoon as she greets Vyla and Natalie. My body urges me to shoot to my feet and run toward her.

Close the distance. Do it. Do it.

But I remain in my seat. I just saw her a few hours ago. There's no reason to behave like it's been months.

I'm going to keep doing my job. I won't go out there until these bills are paid.

My knee bounces as I focus on clicking the "Submit Payment" button on my screen. It takes me much longer than it should to clear the stack. You'd think this was my first day ever using a computer with the way I slam one key at a time, but I'm relieved when the task is finally off my plate.

I'm leaning back in my chair, chomping on some breath mints and scanning the transactions tab of my QuickBooks account when Lindsay strolls in.

"Hi. You wanted to go over those menu additions I mentioned?" She's practically shouting each word.

"Uh, sure," I reply. Didn't we already do that?

She leans back against the door after closing it and locking the handle, and a mischievous grin appears. I don't understand what's happening until she's in my lap, and her lips are pressed against mine.

"Ah," I finally say with a laugh. It was a ruse to ravage me.

Her nose scrunches at first, and she tilts her head, like, *Really, dude?* But it's quickly replaced with warmth and amusement and a boop of my nose.

I wrap my arms around her and press her against my body, the softness of her stomach melting into the hardness of mine. "I missed you," I whisper against her lips.

She whimpers in response, our tongues gliding against each other in an erotic dance.

Her small hands travel from my hair to my neck, and soon she's lifting the hem of my t-shirt. As hot as it would be to watch her ride my dick in my office while my entire staff is busy working on the other side of the door, this chair barely fits my frame. If we take this further, I'm afraid it'll collapse beneath us in a sound so loud that everyone will run in with concern and catch us in the act.

I can't have that. I'm not even sure how comfortable I am doing anything sexual in here during business hours.

"Are you sure you locked the door?" I ask.

"Uh huh." Her tongue flicks my earlobe, and a jolt of electricity shoots straight to the head of my cock.

If we're going to do this, we need to do it right. "You want this? Here?"

"Mm," she moans.

I push the chair back as I grip her thighs and lift her into my arms. This seems to excite her. She starts grinding against me as soon as I straighten to my full height. Our bodies aren't even lined up properly like this, but *fuck*, I can feel the heat of her pussy through multiple layers, and I'm desperate to be inside her.

Once I decide how I want this to go, I lower her into the chair and get down on my knees. I yank the rolling chair closer, and she lets out an exhilarated squeak. Her pupils are fully dilated, and her lips are parted in a way that makes me think of how beautiful they looked wrapped around my dick, sucking me dry.

She's wearing a sleeveless sweater and tailored pants ensemble in a dark mauve color that brings out the pink in her cheeks. My fancy girl. I'm hesitant to remove her pretty clothes and toss them on the floor, but needs must. I unbuckle her belt, keeping my gaze locked on hers. She lifts her ass when I tug her pants down, carefully pulling her feet out and removing her socks before placing all of it behind me. Her lacy black underwear is still on, but that doesn't stop me from shoving my face against the scratchy fabric and filling my lungs with her scent. *"Fuck, Lindsay."*

How do I bottle this? How do I keep it on my sheets and clinging to my clothes like smoke after she goes back to Boston?

Those are thoughts for another day. Right now, I have a feast in front of me, and I'm not about to waste it.

Sliding her underwear down her thighs, I drop them in the growing pile and rest her calves on my shoulders.

"Oh shit," she keens as I spread the glistening brown lips of her pussy and lap at her center.

"Shh," I scold, looking up at her. "You have to be quiet. Can you do that for me?"

She sucks in a breath that reminds me she enjoys being ordered around. Not in her daily life, but during sex. And the way she pinches her nipples while glancing back toward the office door tells me another interesting thing about her. "You like this, don't you? The risk of getting caught. Of being seen."

"Uh huh," she replies, sinking her teeth into her plush bottom lip. "I'll be quiet. Promise."

I groan at her solemn vow. "Yes, baby. I know you can."

Her nectar covers my tongue once I descend on her pussy, and I transform into a desperate man in a desert, mindless with thirst as I drink her down. She tastes like honey and cream and something else tangy that makes my body tremble and my tongue push deeper inside her channel, seeking more, seeking *everything.* I feel her walls clench around my tongue, and if I had my way, she'd never release me. I could stay right here until she suffocates me to death.

"Yes, Nic," she chants quietly, tugging on my hair to the point of pain. "Just like that."

I suck and kiss her swollen lips as I hold her hips still, making sure every part of her pussy is worshiped before I move on to the main event—that adorable pink bud at the top.

As I wrap my lips around it, her feet buck next to my ears, and she shoves a fist into her mouth to keep from screaming. It's impossible not to smile as I continue to gorge myself on her. I'm only a man, and since we're historically bad at a lot of other things, being skilled at eating pussy feels like an honorable contribution to society.

"Oh fuck, oh fuck, Nic." Her words are garbled at this point as she says them around a mouthful of knuckles, but as I flatten my tongue against her and begin a quick flicking motion, the only sounds I hear out of Lindsay are soft, whimpering cries. It doesn't take much longer for her to unravel, and I will my mind to lock this away as a core memory before her thighs squeeze my head so hard it pops off my body.

Her lower half is shaking as I haul her into my arms and drop her down on the ledge of my office window. She wraps her arms around my neck and kisses me hard as she rubs herself against my body, driving me fucking crazy with need. I unbutton my pants and shove them and my boxers down my thighs in a rush. We break apart long enough for me to look between our bodies and feel oddly pleased that the ledge is the perfect height for fucking. That wasn't an intentional part of the design when the bar was built, but I'm inclined to send a thank-you note to the architect.

"Condoms?" she whispers.

Shit. Why didn't I think to get condoms? Although, even if I had, I couldn't have anticipated us having sex here. "I can't get you pregnant," I explain, panting. "Side effect of my medication."

"I'm on birth control anyway. Can you still pass diseases to me?"

"That I don't know, but I haven't been with anyone in months. Not since I last got tested."

"Okay, me too. I got tested last week, and I'm good." She guides me toward her entrance, her tongue tracing her top lip as I slowly push into her. "I can't stop thinking about the suckler."

I stifle a laugh, trying to remain quiet. "The wait is over."

Her heels cross at my lower back as I go deeper. It's a tight fit, and I don't want to hurt her, but based on the way she lifts herself to meet my thrust, it's clear that I'm not. "More," she begs, and a crack forms in my self-control.

"We need to go slow."

She rolls her eyes and presses her hands against my back, closing the distance between our bodies.

I should probably remind her who's in charge here, but her impatience is too fucking cute to address it.

"You feel so good," I say, pressing my forehead against hers. There's a tingling at the base of my spine, and I worry I won't last long. "So fucking good, Linds."

The moment I'm fully seated is also the moment the suckler attaches to her clit, and my worries fade in a flash.

She can't stay quiet anymore, so I swallow her quivering cries with a kiss that I refuse to break until she's come twice more. The first one unfolds like a boat climbing over a tall wave. There's an obvious tipping point, and the fall is a long, steady ripple. The second takes longer.

"I can't," she murmurs against my cheek. "It's too much."

"You can," I assure her. Part of me wants to ease off and let her body recover, but I have a strong hunch that she thinks she can't come again because her exes never took the time to get her there. That's about to change. "I know you can."

Her grip on my shoulders is tight as she holds onto me. I shift our bodies so the suckler can reach her clit from a slightly different angle, and within three thrusts, Lindsay's second orgasm has her silently screaming and body bucking wildly in my arms. That's what does me in. I come inside her wet heat, filling her up as I pepper her face with soft kisses.

By the time my heart rate returns to normal, I'm fucking spent, but I can't seem to let go of her, even to clean up. It isn't until I hear a knock on the door and Natalie's cheery voice ask, "Dominic, do you know when you'll have the schedule for next week ready?" that I extract myself from her warm embrace in a panic.

"Yup, it'll be done tonight. That okay?" I call back. I grab the box of tissues from my desk and hand Lindsay several before taking just as many for myself. Then I dispose of them in a small trash bag that I knot and tuck under my desk, where I'll keep it until I can personally drop it into the dumpster out back when no one's looking.

"Okay. Thank you," Natalie replies.

Lindsay and I struggle to right our clothes on unsteady legs, but we help each other, exchanging knowing looks and laughs when it seems like one of us is about tip over. When we look decent, I return to my desk and pretend to care about whatever is on my computer screen as Lindsay slips out the door.

Natalie invites Lindsay to Crust Lust for a slice when her shift ends, and I wonder if this is the last time I'll see her before she leaves tomorrow. I come around the bar and open my arms to give her a goodbye hug. She wraps herself around my middle and whispers, "Coffee tomorrow morning? Meet me at the B&B at eight."

I nod as I pull back, trying not to reveal how relieved I am, or our hushed plans. "Have fun," is all I say before she leaves.

I'm locking up the front entrance of the bar when I'm momentarily blinded by headlights. At first, I think it's Tilda looking for a late-night pint, or Vlad, in need of a tall glass of O negative, but it's neither.

"Hi," Lindsay says with a shy wave as she climbs out of her car. "In the mood for a rom-com?"

My smile is probably wide enough to show all my teeth. I don't care. It's her last night here until who knows when. This is not the time to play it cool. "Always." I gesture to the door of the apartment upstairs. "Shall we?"

She narrows her gaze. "Do you secretly live here? In the most boring apartment ever?"

"No. I live in a trailer out thatta way." I point toward the tree line, about a hundred feet away. "The interior is equally boring, I can assure you. Besides, this is closer." It's not that I'm ashamed of my trailer, it's more...that I'm deeply ashamed of it. It's not spacious at all, and beyond the appliances that were already installed when I bought it, I have a recliner, a TV, and queen-sized bed with a mattress that Vyla gave me when she upgraded hers. It's not clean, because I don't take the time to clean it. The apartment is clean, however, and that's where I want Lindsay to be. At least until I have the time to properly clean the trailer before her next visit.

We brush our teeth and put on *You've Got Mail,* but I can't seem to follow the dialogue. The woman of my dreams is here with me, wrapped in my arms, but the only thing on my mind is how long I'll have to wait before I get to feel this again.

CHAPTER 10

LINDSAY

Once I'm back in Boston, days fade into more days, which fade into weeks. It's a slog. Board meetings and pitch meetings and marketing meetings fill my time, and my patience wears thinner with each one. I knew it would be less thrilling, of course, because in Mapletown, there lives a zombie with a heart of gold and a dick tailor-made to give me the most mind-blowing sex of my life. I just didn't realize returning to my daily life would be this much of a bummer.

Since I got back, Nic and I still text throughout the day, and we FaceTime more nights than not. It's nice, but it's not the same. I miss his minty, woodsy scent, and the way he held me so tightly against him. I miss the way his body radiates warmth, even from a few feet away. We haven't discussed labels, and that's how I want to keep it.

I don't like missing him, let alone giving whatever it is between us a rigid designation that dictates every aspect of our lives when we don't even live in the same state. There's no chance of him leaving the safety of Mapletown to move to

Boston—a man walking around with green skin would not do well here—and it's not like I'm about to pull Jules out of school and away from her grandparents to move to a monster town.

He's a good friend and an excellent sex partner. We should all be so lucky to find both in the same person. When the physical part of this ends, which it will, I hope there's a chance for us to remain friends. I doubt it, though, since that hardly ever happens. He seems like the kind of guy who could be friends with his exes, which I've never understood. But when this thing falls apart, at least there won't be a huge mess to clean up. We have separate lives in separate cities and won't need to worry about awkward run-ins down the road.

It's on a snowy Wednesday night that I convince him to show me the inside of his trailer. "The anticipation is killing me," I tell him. "And if you're hiding decapitated heads in your freezer, I think I have a right to know."

"You sweet city girl," he says in that velvety rumble that I've grown addicted to. "They wouldn't be entire heads. Just the brains."

I let out a cackle that would make a swamp hag proud. "You're right. My mistake."

"Okay, this is the bedroom," he says when he turns his camera around. Maroon sheets and a navy comforter. Do all men limit themselves to these colors for bedding? Why is it always navy and maroon? There's one pillow in the middle of the bed, and one nightstand on the right side.

Then the camera turns one-hundred eighty degrees to the kitchen/living area/bathroom. I see a built-in dining nook that serves as a TV stand and mail collection area, and a black leather recliner facing it.

"Well, congrats," I say when the tour ends. "Despite becoming a zombie, your taste suggests that you're still a basic human dude."

He chuckles, his eyes twinkling. "Now you know why I prefer to take you to the apartment above the bar." Plopping down in the recliner, he slings an arm behind his head. "Are you still up for a rom-com, or are you too tired?"

I yawn but insist I can power through. "Do I get to pick this time?"

"Absolutely. What are we watching?"

"Hmm." I ponder my short list of favorites. "How about *The Wedding Singer?*"

"That's a classic. Let's do it."

We start it at the same time to ensure the dialogue is synched. Adam Sandler's character gets left at the altar by the woman who Ross cheated on Rachel with, Drew's boyfriend is a walking red flag right from the start, and my mind starts to wander down a familiar path. "I've always wanted to be more like her."

"Drew? Why's that?"

"She has this enviable softness to her. An easy smile. She has her own unique aura, of course, but no matter what she's doing, there are no hard edges. She's never too much, you know?"

"Mm," is his only reply.

I'm not sure why I'm following this thread in my mind, but I keep going. Maybe I'm just tired, or maybe it's because my period is in two days. I don't know. "In reality, my sister is way more like her than I could ever be. The angel of the family. The one who naturally fits into the shapes society deems correct." I sigh. "Meanwhile, I'm over here stomping around with my big feet and my large body, being too loud and too angry. A ball of sharp points. A middle-aged porcupine."

"I like your sharp points." His voice is soft. Reverent. "That's just the outermost layer anyway. You take that coat of knives off and the rest of you is butter. Anyone paying atten-tion could see that."

My heart swells, and I want more than anything to believe him.

"Hey, Linds?" he says, his brow furrowed as he stares at the phone. "Can I call you back?"

Clearly, he's getting another call. At this late at night, I'd assume any call I'm getting is an emergency. "Sure. Everything okay?"

"Yeah, just my friend, Gemma. I'll talk to you later."

The call ends as I'm saying goodbye.

Gemma. Who the hell is Gemma?

NIC

Gemma has either called me or shown up at the bar for three straight days. This is after not hearing a word from her for over a month. Vyla's theory is that she sensed I'm seeing someone and hates not being the center of attention.

"Toxic exes can always tell when you've moved on," she said. "Her favorite toy is being played with by somebody else, and because she's a fucking brat, she's trying to take it back."

Vyla's not a fan of Gemma. Her vitriol comes from a place of love, but it always makes me uncomfortable. Gemma and I have known each other for years. She's the reason I'm here in Mapletown. I owe her a lot, and that includes not letting others talk shit about her, even though my relationship with her has been, at best, rocky.

I'm trying to look at her reappearance in my life as a good thing. We've been on-and-off for as long as I've known her, and for the first time, I want to lock that off switch into place.

She needs to see me with someone else to fully understand that this dance we've been doing can no longer continue.

The only problem is that I'm not technically *with* anyone. Lindsay and I are in our forties, so it's silly for us to put stock in the label of boyfriend/girlfriend, and I know that for her, it's a way to protect herself from getting hurt. She doesn't know me well enough to trust me with her heart, or with Jules, and this is how she chooses to protect her bubble. That's fine with me, because I'm patient, and she's worth waiting for. Even though we haven't had a discussion about dating each other and no one else, I'm going to proceed as if we have.

There's no one else I'm interested in anyway. I'm not sure how, but I want to build a future with Lindsay. It'll likely take time, and there are logistics that need to be figured out, but I'm ready to have those discussions.

I'm not about to let Gemma or anyone else get in the way.

That night I ended our call to see if Gemma was okay—she was, and it was nothing more than a booty call—I immediately called Lindsay back. She asked about my connection to Gemma, and while I didn't lay my heart on the table and reveal my plan to build a future with her, I made it clear to Lindsay there was nothing for her to worry about. "I have no lingering feelings for Gemma. Not attracted to her at all," I told her. "We're friends. That's it."

Gemma doesn't seem to be getting the hint, unfortunately, with the way she keeps propping her heavy breasts onto the bar when I approach.

"Need a refill?" I ask, keeping my gaze on the wet pint glass I'm drying.

"Not a refill, but I would like a minute of your time," she purrs. Her red tipped nails trace the edge of her V-neck shirt in an attempt to draw my attention to her considerable cleavage. "Or wait, what was our record? Three minutes?"

"Can't recall," I reply. "You can have a minute, but you should probably refrain from the sexual innuendos. As I said the other night on the phone, I'm not playing this game anymore."

She rolls her eyes and props her elbows on the bar. "All for some boring human? You can't be serious."

The muscles in my jaw tighten at the slight to Lindsay. "She's not boring, and she's not a full human, either. She's part witch."

Gemma throws her head back with laughter. "Please. That's like saying she's the assistant regional manager, not assistant *to* the regional manager. Just because they have a few cute party tricks doesn't mean they're anything like us. They don't understand what it's like to be us, and they never will."

What a backward opinion about the majority of residents in all of our nation's monster towns. "Cute party tricks? The only reason we get to live in a town that's safe for monsters and protected from those who would persecute us is *because* of witches." I gesture at her tall black horns and shimmering purple skin. "Without the enchantments lining the borders, you'd never be able to walk down the street."

She waves a dismissive hand. "Witches aren't the only ones who cast spells, Dom. You know that. Anyone could do it."

"Huh. Are you saying you're a better wielder of magic than our current mayor?" Vyla pipes in with a menacing smile. "I bet she'd be *very* interested in hearing how unimpressive you find her and her entire ancestral line." She tosses her towel over her shoulder and puts her large hands on her hips. "Or would you like to tell her yourself? She usually comes in around this time."

Gemma drops two twenty-dollar bills next to her empty glass and gets to her feet. "I have better ways of passing the time." She keeps her gaze on me, never acknowledging Vyla's presence. Then she says over her shoulder, "Call me when you're ready to accept that a human couldn't handle you, Dom. Especially during your ruts."

Vyla growls. "If there's ever an appropriate person to call the c-word, it's her."

"Easy," I reply reflexively. Vyla continues her rant about Gemma, but I don't hear much of it. I'm too busy thinking about what Gemma said.

My ruts occur once a month and last for about forty-eight hours. During that time, there's no higher priority than sexual release. I have to leave notes for myself to remember to eat—that's how laser-focused I am on coming. Gemma hasn't been with me during my last two ruts, during which I relied on my hand, porn, and lots of lube. It's not the same, but it's manageable.

With Lindsay, though, it could be downright dangerous. I didn't have to hold back with Gemma, meaning I could be as rough as I wanted. Not only that, but Gemma preferred my roughness. There was even a time when I sunk my teeth into her thigh until she bled. The wound scarred over, and she got a tattoo of my teeth marks as a memento.

That's not something I could ever do with Lindsay. A zombie can't turn a demon, but a bite that breaks the skin even a little could easily turn Lindsay, no matter how much magic she has in her blood. Her biology is that of a human, which makes her susceptible to the virus that's currently dormant, but one I still carry.

Why haven't I considered this before? Am I putting a single mother in danger simply because I enjoy her company? If I'm this willing to put my own happiness over her safety, then I haven't changed at all. I'm still just as evil as I was back then.

CHAPTER 11

LINDSAY

My next trip to Mapletown takes place over Thanksgiving break. Jules has the week off from school, and as soon as the big family dinner ends on Thursday afternoon, we hop in the car and drive north. Jules spends the drive in a post-turkey snooze, while I listen to a podcast about modern witchcraft.

I'm hoping that listening to it informs my next steps on this journey because so far, my attempts at practicing magic have been...disappointing. It doesn't matter how many spells I recite while cooking, or when in the process I recite them, or if I have the correct supplies—the food always tastes the same and I feel nothing.

Camilla suggested trying green witchery, which is more focused on plants and the nurturing of surrounding nature. That, too, yielded very little in terms of results. The natural soaps I made smelled like feet. I tried crystal work, but it just felt like I was playing with pretty rocks, and when I attempted to honor the local land spirits with a ritual Camilla recommended, I felt like an absolute fraud, as if I'd used a baby witch kit purchased from Urban Outfitters.

I'm trying to ignore the discouragement I feel and follow Camilla's advice: "Check out astrology, dabble with the elements. Keep trying other disciplines until one fits like a crown, and that crown might be a grab bag of aspects from different disciplines. That would make you an eclectic witch. Very common."

But I'm starting to wonder if the magic in my blood has simply lost its power due to neglect. As far as I know, my dad never practiced, nor did Nonna Penny. What made me think I could open a grimoire, recite the spells, and I'd transform into one of the Sanderson sisters?

This might not be something I'm meant to do. That realization has led me to another—if not this, then what *am* I meant to do? And why am I having this crash out now? Until I inherited that house in Mapletown, I thought my life was fulfilling. I have a job that pays well, that I'm good at. I birthed the most fascinating and wonderful human being to ever exist. Most of my weekends are spent with family, whom I love and who loves me right back. My closet is full of beautiful clothes I enjoy wearing. These are most of the boxes teenage me dreamed of checking off by the time I reached my forties.

And yet.

I steal a glance at Jules, asleep in the passenger seat. She's wearing blue lip gloss today and has her hair in French braid pigtails. Ultimately, she's the most important box on the page. If she's healthy and thriving, I could take or leave the rest.

This weekend should be fun, though. After Camilla's son's birthday, I received emails from four other moms who wanted me to cater upcoming events. The one this Saturday will feature the same pizza rolls and cupcakes I made for Camilla, but with fewer people. Jules is eager to help out, and I'm eager for her to meet Nic when we make use of his giant kitchen.

Jules lets out a loud yawn as we pass the town sign, and I take this as an opportunity to offer a few reminders. "We're not going to gawk or stare at anyone we meet this weekend, right?"

She nods. "Right."

"What else are we not going to do?"

"We're not going to ask if we can ride them, or if they're temped to kill us and eat us."

"Right. Good," I tell her. "What about if we meet a vampire?"

She thinks for a moment, then says, "We aren't going to ask them if their skin glitters like in *Twilight*."

"Excellent. That's my girl."

By the time we get settled into our room at Pebblebrook, it's around seven, and Jules is still groggy from the holiday dinner. Quinn offers us some warm apple pie with vanilla ice cream, and we take those back to our room and watch *Elf*, because as Jules points out, "It's officially Christmas season now!" She falls asleep halfway through, and I text Nic that we aren't up for getting together tonight.

He understands, because of course he does, and sends three selfies with slightly different excited grins when I ask him to meet me and Jules for breakfast at Hot and Steamy the following morning.

We meet him outside the cafe at nine. The way he strides confidently toward us with that easy smile fills me with warmth. I didn't realize my teeth were grinding until the sight of him loosens my body. It's not just the way he makes me laugh and pays attention to the signals of my body when we're together intimately, there's a cellular reaction to his presence at this point.

Shouldn't I still be afraid of him, though? Maybe not pepper-spray-in-hand afraid, but like, keep-my-head-on-a-swivel afraid? I search deep inside the anxious part of my brain—which is almost all of it—and come up empty. My intuition is usually great at detecting danger, but whenever I'm with this goofy undead man, fear is never present. Instead, all I feel is peace.

I watch Jules's eyes widen the moment she sees him coming. I nudge her side, and she does her best to mask the shock, but she's a kid, so it's still pretty obvious. Nic ignores it and offers his hand.

"Delighted to finally meet you, Jules." His movements are slow, and his voice is soft. My heart squeezes the moment I notice. He doesn't want my baby to be afraid of him. Meanwhile, her jackass father won't even let her buy anything pink when he's around. "Your mom is really proud of you, you know. Will not shut up about how awesome you are."

Jules tentatively shakes his hand, her cheeks rosy, then leans against my side, suddenly shy. "Nice to meet you too."

"You hungry, muffin?" I ask, patting her back as if to say, *It's okay, he's one of the good ones.* "Want to get some food?"

We go inside and grab a table by the window after we order. She starts to open up as Nic asks questions about school, music, and her friends, while I try to keep my heart-eyes hidden behind a large mocha latte. When we're done eating, he pulls something out of his coat pocket. It's wrapped in gold tissue paper, and she's practically beaming when he hands it to her.

It's a makeup bag with illustrations of Sabrina Carpenter wearing her different performance costumes. She gasps and clutches it to her chest as she looks at me with a glimmering smile.

I cannot believe he remembered. I think I mentioned her liking Sabrina Carpenter once on Halloween night.

"Wow, that's a pretty great gift, huh?" I ask her.

She nods. "Thank you, Dominic."

He bows his head. "You're very welcome."

While she zips it open and examines it more closely, I lean toward him. "Where did you find that?"

"Didn't you hear? The internet delivers right to your door." Then he winks, and I want to smack him and kiss him at the same time.

After that, the three of us head to the grocery store so I can get the ingredients I need for the party, and we drive in separate cars to the bar. It won't open for another hour or so, which gives Nic the opportunity to show Jules around and play with the jukebox while I set everything up in the kitchen.

Jules mixes the cake batter while I prepare the pizza rolls, and we work together on making the buttercream frosting. She's a messy cook, but I can't get mad when she ends up with flour on her nose.

Anton, the kraken cook, arrives shortly after we make the gluten-free pizza rolls, and I'm impressed to see Jules confidently introduce herself despite his many tentacles and gigantic head. She doesn't even ask him what he is when one of his suction cups sticks to the inside of her palm, which is nothing short of a miracle. She just laughs it off and says it tickled.

Nic finds us near the fridge, and we go over the menu items I suggested during my last visit. Anton has been working on an antipasto salad with waffle fries, and a flatbread with shaved Brussels sprouts and their very own spicy maple syrup. Nic urges me to provide notes on each one that Anton made yesterday and kept in the fridge. Both are delicious, but I make suggestions on small changes he can make to see if that improves the overall taste. Anton is jovial and receptive to everything I say, and Nic has said that he's having a blast trying out new dishes.

His many tentacles also make it easy to do multiple steps of a recipe at the same time.

Taste is such a subjective thing, so I don't exactly feel qualified to tell a professional cook how to do his job, but if they get these dishes right, they could have a new wave of locals coming through the doors.

Since Nic is working until close tonight and Natalie has the day off, I take Jules over to Natalie's house once the pizza rolls and cupcakes are done, wrapped, and stored in the bar fridge.

"Jules!" Natalie shouts as she ushers us inside. "Look at you. Give me a spin."

Jules obliges, giving her a particularly sassy hair flip, and I beam with pride. Only thirteen and eating up every space she enters.

Natalie shakes her head in awe. "Shining brighter than a diamond, I swear to god. I can't believe how much taller you've gotten since the last time I saw you."

With my five-foot-nine frame and her father's six-foot-two, she was bound to be a beanpole; I just didn't expect her to almost reach my height this young.

"Ah, you're the child I've heard so much about," Winston says as he emerges from the living room. He offers his hand. "Pleased to meet you."

This is the friendliest I've ever seen him, despite wearing his signature scowl. When Jules lets go, he looks closely at his hand, as if concerned about cooties.

He points the book he's holding in her direction. "I understand children have a tendency to unknowingly cover themselves in sticky substances and proceed to touch every available surface."

"Winston, she's not a goddamn toddler," I snipe.

"I'm just saying," he's replying to me but still looking at her, "wash your hands, kid." And then he makes himself scarce for the afternoon. I make no objections.

Natalie gives us an in-depth tour, mostly showing me all the changes she's made since I was last here, which are primarily decor she's picked up from the nearby thrift store. We go outside and do a lap around the property, and Jules gets to meet Ethel, their garden ghost. She didn't make herself corporeal like Winston did, and Jules is entranced by Ethel's gray, translucent form while she points out various seeds she's planted outside the garden shed.

The hours pass with the three of us drinking mocktails and snacking on chips and guacamole. We play Uno while listening to pop hits, and I can tell by the volume of Jules's voice and the wild laughter bursting out of her that she's having a blast with her Aunt Natalie. We order pizza for dinner from Crust Lust, and drive back to Pebblebrook as the clock strikes eight. Jules has done a lot of peopling today, and I can tell she's hitting the wall.

I've been keeping my screen time limited today so I could be fully present with Jules, but once she falls asleep in the bed beside me, I grab my phone and smile as I read the texts from Dominic. They're mostly about the menu updates accompanied by pictures of the changes Anton made to the ones I tasted earlier. The last message, however, is unlike the rest.

Nic: Let me take you to dinner tomorrow. It's weird to have you so close but not being able to see you.

I've been thinking the same thing all day. There's one problem, though.

> I have Jules.

As desperate as I am to spend time with Nic and, let's be real, ride that glorious dick again, I can't exactly ditch my kid for the night.

> Nic: She's invited too, of course. We can show her the town. It'll be fun.

I have no doubt about that, and I'm touched he wants to get to know her better. Having the two of them spend time together was a worry of mine this week, because is it irresponsible of me to introduce my daughter to a guy I'm casually hooking up with? Yes, but that's not all Nic is to me. We're not in a serious relationship, but he's my friend, and a wonderful man.

There's also the fact that I truly enjoy being in Mapletown, and if I continue coming up here, I want Jules to love it too.

> Sounds great. Thank you for inviting her.

The next day, Jules and I drop off the pizza rolls and cupcakes, and run into Camilla and her daughter Rocío as we're leaving. Rocío is close to Jules's age, while Camilla and I are chatting about witchcraft, I notice the two of them start to talk. They exchange Instagram handles before we part.

Nic tells me to meet him by Mapletown Rock in the center of the square at five. It's a mild winter day, which is a huge relief. The sun is shining, it's forty-seven degrees, and the piles of snow on the edge of the sidewalks are rapidly melting. Since the town square is pretty small and the walk to it is quick, Jules and I decide to get dressed up. I wear a leopard print sweater, fitted black skirt, and knee boots, and Jules sports a knee-length maroon dress with black tights and platform oxfords.

We find Nic standing near a red and white blanket spread out on the grass next to the rock, with his hands behind his back.

"Uh oh, a picnic?" Jules says quietly at my side. "Mom, you hate picnics."

"Shh. We don't know it's a picnic, but if it is, we need to smile and be polite, okay?"

I give Nic a hug, and Jules gives him a fist bump. The day goes immediately downhill after that.

He hands me a beautiful bouquet of red roses and baby's breath, and in an instant, water runs from my eyes with the force of parallel waterfalls. The sneezing begins too, and the smoky cat-eye I took a long time to perfect is likely ruined. Jules has seen this movie before and knows to get rid of the flowers. I hear her say, "It's the little white flowers. I'm sorry. They're very pretty," as she takes them away, and I make a note to thank her later for complimenting Nic's efforts.

She digs out an allergy pill from my purse, and Nic hands me a bottle of water to suck it down. Once my symptoms pass, Jules does her best to clean up my face using a tissue. That's when I realize Nic has, unfortunately, set up a picnic. This is a problem for two reasons. First of all, I don't enjoy dining on grass, where bugs can easily get to me and whatever I'm eating. Secondly, there's no way I'll be able to go from standing to sitting on the blanket in the skirt I'm wearing. It hugs my body from hips to calves, so unless I'm trust-falling onto the stiff, still-frozen ground, it ain't happening.

But I try, oh do I try, because this was a sweet gesture, and I don't want Nic feeling like he biffed this entire day, especially after the flowers. I start by folding myself down to my knees, which isn't easy. Luckily, I have Jules to lean against on my descent. Then I shift sideways until I'm on my ass and my legs are bent to the side.

"Are you my mom's boyfriend?" Jules asks as Nic opens the picnic basket.

My stomach drops.

I suppose the roses did make this seem like a date. But... wait. That's not what this is, right? I thought the goal was to take me and Jules out to dinner. See the town. With Jules tagging along, I didn't anticipate there being even a hint of romance.

"No, pumpkin. Nic and I are just good friends."

Nic's hand pauses in mid-air at my words as he lifts a thermos out of the basket. His expression is unreadable, but the pause makes me think he didn't love my answer.

"That's right. Just friends," he adds, the corner of his mouth curving into a half-smile.

I guess that settles that.

There are a handful of people in the park, and I take a moment to watch them. There's a young couple making out in the gazebo, high school age, I'm guessing. I spot Vlad the vampire on a wooden bench in the far corner, ripping off pieces of bread and tossing them to a murder of crows hovering around his feet. Then there's the father holding his daughter's hands as she does that stiff toddler stomp across the grass while Mom snaps photos. They look human, so they must be witches or shifters of some kind.

"Mom," Jules says in warning, then knocks my hand away from my face.

Was I mapping? I hadn't even realized. That's the biggest issue, though, isn't it? I do it subconsciously.

"Everything okay?" Nic asks, his worried eyes scanning my face.

"Yeah, it's just..." How do I explain this? Do I want to? It's not exactly a turn on to hear the person you're fucking has a tendency to pick their face until it bleeds. "It's nothing."

"She was mapping," Jules offers. "That's what you call it, right?"

"Jules," I scold, then mouth, *Enough.*

I genuinely don't think she was blowing my cover to make me look bad. She's at that age where she's still discovering the variety of ways to feel embarrassed in front of the opposite sex, and I don't think she understands how much shame I carry with this disorder, despite dermatillomania being somewhat common, especially among women.

Thankfully, Nic was looking down into the picnic basket. "What's that?" he asks when his gaze lifts to mine.

"Nothing," I say, hoping he can sense the finality in my tone. "It's nothing."

He drops the subject by pouring steaming hot chocolate from a large thermos into paper cups. Then he sets out three paper plates. Wrapped in aluminum foil is a big, soft pretzel that he breaks into three big pieces, and pulls out small containers of what looks to be dipping sauces for us to share.

"Did you make this?" I ask after moaning around the first gooey bite.

"Can't take credit for the pretzel," he says, "but I did make the sauce."

There are three, which include a thick grainy mustard, a cream cheese with a brown-orange tint, and what I'm going to guess is honey.

Jules tries the cream cheese sauce, while I dip my pretzel piece into the honey. While we're chewing, she meets my gaze with panic and disgust. There's a sharp tingling at the tip of my nose, and my stomach churns the longer I chew. We don't spit out our food, but we chew quickly and throw back as much water as possible.

"Nic, what *is* that?"

He jerks back, shock and confusion twisting his sweet

green face. "It's our new spicy maple syrup. I put it in its own little cup and mixed it with cream cheese." His eyes dart between us. "No good?"

I shake my head while plastering on a sympathetic smile. "It was a good try, but I think there might be a bit too much spice and not enough syrup. What are the ingredients?"

"Um, maple syrup, red pepper flakes, sriracha, and this hot pepper sauce Anton bought last time he was in Cedar Grove, South Carolina."

Fuck. I know the answer before I even ask the question. "What kind of pepper sauce?"

"Something reaper, I think he said."

I take another swig of water. "Likely the Carolina Reaper, which is one of the spiciest peppers in the world."

"Oh, shit." Nic grimaces. "So he should leave that out next time, right?"

I place my hand on his and rub circles over his palm. "Nic, I don't know what the taste buds of the monsters in town are like, but if you serve this sauce to a human, one burp could set the whole bar on fire."

I watch his face fall, and it cuts through my chest like a rusty knife.

"Most hot honey is made with honey, chili pepper flakes, and an acid element, usually apple cider vinegar," I explain. "If Anton gives this another try, which I really think he should, I'd encourage him to make a batch that's safe for the human tongue. Cut out the sriracha and the Carolina Reaper sauce, okay?"

"Yeah," he says with a sad nod. "Will do."

Normally, I would enjoy the sight of a man in visible agony over the choices he's made, but seeing Nic in this state is unbearable. I want to wrap him up in a blanket and massage his scalp while promising him that everything's going to be okay. Instead, I grab his face in my hands and say, "Stop stressing, okay? We can easily turn this day around by packing up the picnic and going to that Chinese food place on the edge of town, yeah? There's no problem good food can't solve."

At that, he perks up a bit. "I guess it's good that I struck out so hard today. Now I know what never to do again." Under his breath, I hear, "And to never take advice from Riz."

"What was that?"

He rubs the back of his neck. "Riz said all women love roses. All women love picnics. All women love when you cook for them. Now I have proof that none of that is true."

"Every girl is different," Jules adds pragmatically. "We don't all like the same things."

"Agreed. Whenever someone generalizes like that, especially if they aren't a woman themselves, I'd just stop listening. Nine out of ten times they're dead wrong."

Jules raises an eyebrow at me. "Only nine?" My girl knows me well.

"Fine. Ten out of ten."

I'm relieved when Nic lets out a deep barrel of a laugh, making it feel like the awkward fog over our picnic has lifted. We hop in his truck and head over to the Chinese restaurant. Nic makes a point of ordering almost everything on the menu so we can try it, and the picnic debacle feels forgotten.

Later, when Jules is fast asleep, I get a text from Nic, asking, "Care to go for a moonlight stroll?"

Jules is conked out.

Nic: Just the two of us then?

I don't love the idea of leaving Jules alone in our room, but I have left her home alone in our apartment on occasion to run errands. We're on the second floor of the B&B, and Quinn has been at the front desk every time I've come or gone, no matter what time of day it is. Don't minotaurs require sleep like the rest of us? Maybe not.

I decide to leave Jules a note on my pillow in case she wakes up and notices that I'm gone. I promise to be back in under an hour, because how long could a moonlight stroll actually take?

Nic offers me his arm when I meet him outside. I push up onto my tiptoes to kiss his cheek and say, "Glad we get a little alone time."

He pulls me to the front of his body and lifts me off my feet. "Me too," he says, his voice like velvet as he presses a quick kiss to my lips. "I've wanted to do that all day."

I brush a finger across the stubble on his chin, and kiss him again, reveling in the minty taste of his lips. "You always taste so good."

A chuckle bursts out of him, and he gives me a bashful look. "I might be a tad paranoid about tasting or smelling like the powder in the granola bars Dr. Yates makes for me."

Oh Christ. I hadn't even considered that. "Did you just have one?"

"No, I had one about three days ago, but there's certainly an...aftertaste, and the last thing I want is to make it anyone else's problem."

"What, um," I shouldn't ask. I really shouldn't. "What does it taste like?"

His gaze darts between my eyes. "Do you really want to know?"

I nod.

"Well, even in powder form, it retains a lot of the original flavor, which is nutty, and a little sweet."

I'm not sure what I expected brains to taste like, but it wasn't that.

"The aftertaste is different, though. It's sharp. Sour."

Ick. Thank god for those mints he always carries.

He sets me on my feet, and we walk arm in arm, enjoying the quiet. We pass a few people on the sidewalk—those out for dinner or enjoying a walk like us—and I realize how incredibly safe I feel, given the time of day. I don't think it's simply Nic's presence, either. Mapletown might be the only place where I could walk around by myself at night without keys wedged between my fingers in one hand, gripping pepper spray in the other.

The pessimist in me whispers, *Give it time.*

The optimist in me, much quieter and always on vacation, doesn't disagree, but clarifies, *Give this place a chance. It has more to show you.*

The cemetery is next to the flower shop, which feels like top notch city planning, and is much bigger than I was expecting. I know monsters die too, but there are several species who live for hundreds of years, and some are even immortal. Beyond that, I assumed the rest had their own rituals for honoring the dead that didn't include having a standard burial.

We pass hundreds of gravestones, though, and I'm impressed by the tidy condition in which each one is kept.

"It's beautiful here," I say, taking in a deep breath of the crisp New England air. "So peaceful."

"The dead are a quiet bunch," Nic agrees with a smirk. He stops to lean against the waist-high stone fence that surrounds the dearly departed, and pulls me into his arms, my back pressed against his front. "Almost a full moon."

I look up and bask in the moonlight, warm in Nic's embrace, taking in the smattering of visible stars. *This trip was a great idea,* I think. *How soon can I come back?* I turn in Nic's arms and press my chin into his hard chest as I gaze up at him.

"I still can't believe you're the skinny boy I kissed twenty-seven years ago."

He chuckles softly. "Quite the glow-up, right?"

His tone is sarcastic, but I know he knows how pretty he is. Somehow, I don't think that's what he means, though. There have been times, few and far between, when he seems unsure of himself, or that he knows he's lacking and wishes he could disappear. It could be old wounds from when his brother bullied him, or maybe something else. The only thing I do know is that I hate the sight of it. I want to reach inside his mind, track down the memory that'll tell me who put those wounds there, and beat the hell out of that person.

For now, I offer him the truth as I see it. "You're remarkable, Nic. I've never known anyone like you. I felt that way when we met the first time, and it's still the case today."

His features soften, and his blue eyes swirl with gratitude. Rather than respond, he cups my jaw and kisses me. He drinks from my lips as his hands get lost in my hair. It's unhurried and sweet, but as soon as I feel his hardness pressed against my belly, my hunger for him steers my movements, and I change the tempo.

Our coats come off quickly, then his shirt. When I remove my sweater and my bra, he gives me a scandalized look and wraps his arms around me to cover me up. "It's too cold to do this here."

"No, it isn't," I reply, pulling him back in for a messy, passionate kiss. "I'll be fine." Then my skirt drops down to my ankles, my underwear with it, and I stand before him in nothing but my boots.

He scans our surroundings. "Someone might see." I raise an eyebrow, and he smiles wide. "That's the point, isn't it?"

I let my hands do the talking as I undo his belt and unbutton his pants.

For a second, he looks like he wants to protest this whole thing, but when his eyes drop to my nipples, hard and aching to be touched, I hear him mutter, "Fuck it," under his breath before he gets himself seated on the fence. He pulls me between his spread legs and wraps his lips around my nipple.

I grip the ends of his soft, fine hair as I moan at the contrast of his hot, wet mouth on my cold skin. It feels fucking spectacular. A gust of wind lifts the ends of my hair as he inserts a finger into my pussy, and I'm so wet the squelch of him fucking me with his hand echoes around us.

"Do you think the dead are offended?" he asks before running his tongue up the center of my chest.

"By us? Not a chance," I reply confidently. "If they still had the ability to fuck, they would be, doesn't matter where."

"Mm," he grunts with a laugh. "Good point. And it's not like we're on top of someone's grave."

I climb into his lap and straddle him, his hands gripping my hips tight enough to leave handprints. "Exactly." I'm panting now, desperate to mold myself to his body and feel the sweet friction of him rubbing against my clit. "They're getting a show." I reach between us and remove his hard cock from the slit in his boxers. It's hot and already pulsing beneath my gaze.

As I sink down on his length, he cups my cheek. "Hey," he whispers, demanding my full attention. It's not easy to provide, given the thick pole that's currently rearranging my insides. "You're incredible. Every part of you is incredible."

The words have me dropping the rest of the way down until I'm fully seated. I cry out, the stretch overwhelming, while feeling utterly filled by him balancing the discomfort.

"Hold on to me," he commands, and I obey. I love him like this, bossy and in charge of my body. It's a side of him no one else gets to see, and knowing the boundaries of my safety that he'd never dream of pushing allows me the freedom to let go.

It's the most vulnerable I've ever been in bed with someone, and the best sex I've ever had.

His fingers dig into my back as he slams me down until our hips meet. My arms are wrapped tightly around his neck, and I'm kissing his scalp between moans as his suckler teases the hell out of my clit.

"Oh g-god," I whimper.

He pulls back to look at me. "Okay?"

Something thrums in my belly at him checking in like this. Something warm and new. I nod, and he kisses me like he needs me to survive. It's messy and rough. Our teeth gnash, but I love it. There's no time to do it the right way, or the most aesthetically pleasing way. We need each other too badly for that.

"Nic," I beg as his tongue traces my jawline. "Bite me, please."

He stills and pulls back. "I can't."

"What? Why not?" I'm panting and losing the edge he was pushing me toward.

"If I bite you, I'll turn you." His expression is somber, like he knows he's disappointing me, and maybe surprised by the disappointment he feels too. "And if you bite me, same thing."

"Okay," I reply, gripping his scalp once more. "Whatever. It's no big deal." Because it truly isn't. I thought it'd be hot for him to leave his mark on my neck, but if it's too risky, that's fine. We'll just keep roughing each other up without using our teeth.

I pull him in for a deep kiss, long enough to make him forget we ever paused to talk about biting, and soon my pulse is racing as quickly as it was before.

My toes curl, and every muscle tightens as I race to meet the tidal wave quickly approaching. When it hits, my mouth falls open in a silent scream, and his quivering whimper meets my ears as his hot seed fills my core, my walls fluttering around him, sucking it into the deepest parts of my body.

It feels like hours pass while we come down, still clutching each other for dear life. He tucks himself into his boxers and helps me back into my clothes before putting on his own. Then he rubs my arms through my coat as if concerned I'm about to get frostbite.

Amazingly, I forgot it's winter. That was way too hot to drop my body temperate too low.

When we pass the town bookstore, Tome Time, a slender woman with black horns and sparkly purple skin comes toward us, smirking in a way that instantly annoys me.

"Well, well, well," she says, coming to a stop in front of us, her gray eyes locked on Nic. They land on me, then my arm looped through his, and I watch her smile slip into a sneer. "This must be the human I've heard so much about. Laura, was it?"

I don't need Nic to tell me who this is. I know who she is just by the way she intentionally gets my name wrong. Oldest trick in the book. I'm not about to let her get to me though. I don't give a fuck what kind of monster she is. "Lindsay, actually." I hold out my hand. "You're Gemma, right? The one he chooses to no longer spend time with?"

Nic lets out a nervous laugh, and I wonder which one of us he's nervous for. "Gemma, nice to see you," he says in a hurried tone. "This is Lindsay. Lindsay, Gemma."

All I know about this woman is that she's a demon, specifically a succubus, and they've been fuck buddies on and off since he first moved here. Nic told me that Gemma is the one who got him the placement interview with Mayor Crane to see if he was a good fit for the town. This was not long after his recovery, when he was at his most vulnerable and cloaked with self-loathing for what he'd become.

I'm not saying Gemma has been manipulating him this whole time, but it doesn't surprise me that he gives her so much grace and feels like he "owes" her for the life he's built. Back then, he was convinced he deserved nothing, and here was this person who gave him a chance anyway.

The rule I've decided to follow with her is that I'll be as polite to her as she is to me. I know she's important to Nic, but the game she's playing is as clear as day. She's had the luxury of popping in and out of his life, and for the first time, her ability to toy with him is gone because his attention is elsewhere.

If she truly values their friendship, I'll be able to see it, and I'll be nice. But if she's going to pull this petty bitch nonsense every time we run into each other, I'll shove it right back.

"I hope you're enjoying your stay in our enchanting little town," Gemma says to me. "You must have to head back to Boston soon, though, right?"

Nic replies before I can. "Yeah, she's heading back tomorrow, unfortunately." He squeezes my hand and looks at me adoringly.

I probably would've lied to make it seem like I'm a steady presence here, no matter what my mailing address is, but Nic must not have noticed the unspoken words in her question.

I clear my throat. "Yes, but I'll be back soon." I put my other hand on his bicep and lean my head against his shoulder. "Mapletown is becoming my favorite place." It's the truth, if not exaggerated a little in tone.

"It must be hard with your whole life so far away." She blows out a mock sympathetic breath.

"Not that far at all, actually," I reply, steeling my spine. "I'd draw you a map to help you understand, but sadly I left my crayons at home."

I watch the fury flicker in her gaze. It was there and then

gone, but I caught it. "Anyway, I should be going. Safe travels back home, Lindsay."

I want to scream when my mom's warning pushes itself to the forefront of my mind.

They all leave eventually.

Nic brushes off the interaction as soon as she's out of earshot, but I can't. That demon bitch knew exactly which buttons to push to send me into a mental spiral of doubt. I'm falling fast, thinking about the two-hour commute each way, the long hours I work, and the fact that Jules and my family are deeply rooted back there. Away from *him*.

"Sorry about that," he says when we reach the front gate of Pebblebrook. "She can be a lot sometimes."

He thinks *she's* a lot?

"A lot" is how I've been described my entire life by people who either didn't like me, or by those who once did and realized the error of their ways. Is that how he's going to see me one day?

Nic and I are in this delicate bubble of new feelings and long talks and amazing sex. How long before the distance, or Gemma, or just me being myself pops it?

CHAPTER 12

DOMINIC

Time passes slowly in December. It's like this every year. I shouldn't be surprised by it anymore. After Mamaw passed, the Christmas season stopped being fun. She was the one who went all out for the holidays, and without her, it became an annual reminder of everything I'd lost.

This year, December is annoying for a new reason: it keeps getting in the way of my time with Lindsay. The days are shorter, and it seems like her workdays are longer than ever.

"It's the end of the year, so I have a million different decks to prepare for the board," she told me. She went on to explain why this is the case, and I only understood half the words.

When she does have free time, she's distracted by the holiday shopping she has to do for her family, various holiday functions she's invited to by coworkers or Jules's school. She's exhausted at the end of each day, limiting our nightly Face-Times, and *fuck*, I miss her so much. The sweet vanilla scent of her hair. Those deliciously thick thighs.

We keep trying to nail down her next visit, but things pop

up left and right. I hate it. I feel like I finally have a person to celebrate this holiday with, someone I want to do all the stupid Hallmark Christmas movie things with, and I can't.

It's not just Lindsay, either. I want to spend time with Jules, too. She's such a fun, interesting kid. Lindsay's told me how much she loves Christmas, and I want to watch her eyes widen in that wholesome way while looking at Christmas lights.

Instead, I'm maintaining the Fast Glass Tavern tradition of boycotting the holiday altogether. It's not an anti-religious crusade or anything, and we don't diss the holiday or those who choose to celebrate.

Christmas is an overwhelming celebration that lasts over a month; for some people, it begins on the first of November, and is next to impossible to opt out of. Even if you don't listen to the music, watch the movies, or decorate your house, everywhere else you go will be shoving it in your face. Grief is heightened this time of year for a large percentage of people, and being surrounded by the happy faces of those who still have their loved ones to celebrate with is difficult to endure. It's a staunch reminder of the people and material things we lack, dressed in red and green.

From November first to the first of January, Fast Glass Tavern remains a Christmas-free zone. If there are any decorations at all, it's snowflakes in the windows, which is a nod to the season, not the holiday.

The first year I did this, I thought there would be backlash from the locals. I expected demands for holiday playlists on the jukebox, and gingerbread-flavored cocktails. Amazingly, the opposite happened. Those grieving flocked to the bar, and it didn't matter what stage they were in, either. People appreciated having a neutral space to escape to when the holiday cheer became too much, and it's grown over time.

The bar is packed tonight, a random Tuesday in the middle

of December, and the entire staff is here working their asses off.

Vlad is sucking down blood pints faster than we can pour them. Tilda is cackling with an empty wineglass in hand as she plays Connect Four with Dead Fang Debbie in a booth along the back wall. Camilla, Morty, and their kids are enjoying our new menu items, splitting two flatbreads with Brussels sprouts and the antipasto salad. Even Mayor Crane and her chief of staff, Ezra, are here, nibbling on jalapeño poppers while in deep discussion about some town council matter.

It feels like the entire town is here, and I can't even fully enjoy it. My mind is with Lindsay, wishing she could see this too.

LINDSAY

It's on the seventeenth of December that I get three back-to-back calls from Jules's school during a marketing meeting. I don't hear my phone buzz on the first call. When it rings a second time, I assume they'll leave me a voicemail, and I can deal with whatever it is once my meeting ends. The third call comes and goes faster than I can step out of the conference room without being disruptive.

When I call back, the vice principal tells me that Jules has been in a physical altercation with another student, and that I need to come down immediately. I race out of the office like a bat out of hell, my mind a blur of horrifying images of Jules with a bloody lip and a black eye. When I reach the front office of the school, I find Jules in a chair on one side, and Sadie and her mom seated on the other.

The only thing keeping me from pouncing on the two of them is the fact that Sadie's face is scratched up, covered in bandages, and Jules only has an ice pack pressed against her nose. It looks like Jules won the fight—as long as her nose isn't broken—and I'm flooded with as much pride as shame the moment the thought pops into my head.

"Jules, what happened?" I drop to my knees in front of her and slowly remove the ice pack.

"I'm okay," she says with a sniffle. Her eyes are bloodshot and puffy, like she's been crying. There's dried blood crusted in one of her nostrils, but her nose looks intact. The ice pack is covering a red bump on her cheek, just below her eye, which I'm guessing will turn into a nasty bruise in a few days.

"Come on in, everyone," Principal Torres says, waving us to follow him into his office.

Sadie and Jules take the two chairs in front of the principal's desk, and me and her mom stand behind them. Her mom, I think her name is Bianca, keeps trying to catch my eye. I ignore her.

"So how did this start, Manny?" I ask Principal Torres. He and I grew up on the same street. My sister introduced him to his husband, and if there ever was a time to milk my connections, it's right fucking now.

"Principal Torres," he corrects with a stern glance that I know is just for show. "It started just outside the cafeteria after lunch. Several teachers witnessed an argument between Sadie and Jules that turned physical with Jules shoving Sadie to the ground."

"She pushed me first!" Jules protests. "I was defending myself."

"That's *not* what happened," Sadie insists with a sour expression.

I sigh, growing impatient. "Then what did happen?"

Jules speaks up first. "Sadie was snapping my bra straps at lunch, and I followed her after to tell her never to do that again."

"What bra?" Sadie crosses her arms over her chest and gives Jules the stink eye. Or more like, the my-shit-don't-stink eye. "That's a tank top that you cut yourself."

Though I'm loathe to disagree with this tween menace, I know that Jules doesn't own any bras. None that I've purchased for her anyway. Not that it matters, since Sadie clearly can't keep her hands to herself. "This sounds like text-book sexual harassment, Principal Torres."

"Uh, well, let's not get carried away here," Bianca says. "To me, this sounds like typical teenage girl behavior." Then she has the audacity to turn to me. "You can't tell me this never happened in your day."

Slowly blinking, I give her the attention she's clearly so desperate for. "You're right. This was par for the course in my teen years. That still doesn't make it okay." I turn to face Manny once again. "I was under the impression that touching another student without their consent was cause for suspen-sion, which is precisely what Sadie did. Has that changed?"

Bianca is aghast. "Excuse me. This feels like a huge over-reaction."

I roll my eyes. "Oh, does it? Color me surprised."

Manny's trying to mediate, but it's not cutting through the tension on this side of the room.

Bianca starts talking again, and Jules looks back at her and shouts, "God, just shut up! The sound of your voice makes me want to sit on a knife!"

Silence fills the room, and my mind is in an extended state of buffering. I've never heard my daughter raise her voice like that before. Not ever, and that's not even the worst part. I'm remembering a fall weekend last year when Bianca and I chaperoned a school dance. We only spoke for a few minutes, but I knew she was Sadie's mom. I could tell. This was confirmed shortly thereafter by another mom. On the ride home from the dance, I told Jules that the sound of Bianca's voice was so irritating that it made me want to sit on a knife.

It was an offhand comment that was mostly intended as a joke, but with the gift of hindsight, I can see now how inappropriate it was for me to say. Sometimes I forget that Jules is my daughter, that she's constantly absorbing everything I do, even when I don't notice. Since it's just the two of us, and she's getting older, there are times when I treat her more as a confidante than a growing kid.

I can feel the blood rushing to my cheeks in embarrassment. When we get out of here, I need to have a long talk with her, because I've never felt like more of a failure than I do right now.

"Principal Torres," I begin, not even knowing what to say, but desperate to take the spotlight off of Jules. "I—"

"I've heard enough," he says, and I notice the tautness in his jaw, almost menacing. He scrubs a hand down his face, clearly over our bullshit. "Jules and Sadie will be suspended for two weeks, excluding the holiday break. They can access the student portal to stay on top of their schoolwork during this time, but they aren't allowed on school grounds. Understood?"

"Two weeks?" Jules asks, her voice shaky. "What about science club?"

He sighs. "Your group will have to complete the project without you."

Sadie leans forward, putting her hands on the desk. "But wait, I can still go to soccer practice, right?"

"Absolutely not. No extracurriculars."

"This is ridiculous," Bianca says haughtily, shaking her head.

I want to agree and vehemently protest the fact that Jules is getting the same punishment as Sadie for defending herself, but after she yelled at Bianca, I don't have much moral ground to stand on at the moment.

Jules will manage her schoolwork just fine; I'm not worried about that. She thrived during Covid. Her grades were the highest they've ever been. But I hate that she'll be missing out on science club. I know how much she loves it, even if she's not a fan of the project they chose.

I walk Jules to her locker so she can get the rest of her books, and we keep a safe distance behind Bianca and Sadie as we head toward the parking lot.

"Why did you cut your tank top into a bra?" I ask Jules. "I didn't even know you wanted to start wearing bras." It's not like she needs one yet. Then it hits me. "Is that what you wanted to go shopping for last month? After I got back from my weekend in Mapletown?"

"Yeah," she says softly. "There are so many different kinds. I wanted to see what it felt like to wear one."

I stop in my tracks, and my eyes sting with tears. Here I am priding myself on prioritizing Jules's needs when it comes to gender-affirming care, and I fucking blow it on one of the simplest ways to do that. Dressing like a girl is one of the easiest ways for Jules to embrace this new identity, and I stood directly in her way. Why, because we'd gone shopping the month before, and I didn't want to spend too much on her? The fuck is wrong with me? It's not like I don't have the money to spend. I was purposefully saving it for gender-affirming care, and when I get the chance to spend it on that, I become an ignorant tightwad.

She didn't specify she wanted to buy bras at the time, but I should've asked.

I'm also not about to drop a grand on bras for my daughter. For basics, we tend to go as cheap as possible, and when we shop the popular brands, I use the coupon code app on my phone to secure discounts. Shopping smart is something I've always been good at. I can do this without letting Jules turn into a spoiled brat.

I wrap my arm around Jules's shoulders and guide her to the car, walking quickly. Once we're safely inside, I crumble.

"Shit, honey. I'm so sorry. This is all my fault. All of it." I pull a tissue from my purse and wipe my eyes. "If I'd just gotten you the bras you wanted, today wouldn't have happened, and if I'd kept my wise ass to myself, you wouldn't have said what you did to Bianca. Which wasn't okay. You know that, right?"

She nods, her lip trembling. "Yeah, I know. I'm sorry."

Beneath the ice pack, I can tell she's crying too, now, and that makes me feel like an even bigger pile of shit. "I never should've said it to begin with, though. And my temper..." The list of ways I'm failing as a parent is piling up in my head now. I've opened the floodgates. "I'm sorry you inherited that part of me. It's always been my biggest flaw. The thing your grandparents are most ashamed of." My nose is running, and keeping up with the endless string of snot becomes a trying task. "I don't know, maybe I need to speak with someone. Get back into therapy."

I probably shouldn't even be sharing these thoughts with Jules, right? I'm sure there's a parenting group on Facebook that would tell me to lead by example, and stay strong for my kid, because kids need stability above all else. That I'm letting her down, and maybe even her dead-beat dad would do a better job than I have.

But aren't you allowed to be human in front of your kids? Aren't you allowed to screw up and feel lonely and break down in tears when you're convinced the world is falling apart and you're doing everything wrong?

Fuck if I know.

"Never mind," I eventually say. "I'll figure it out."

I start the car as I will my tears to stop falling. Jules turns on the radio to the all-Christmas station, but she doesn't sing along like she usually does.

"A two-week suspension, not including the holiday break, means you'll be out of school for a while," I say, setting up my attempt to lift the mood. "Anything you want to do?"

Her head jerks back. "I'm not in trouble?"

I shake my head. "I need you to promise me two things. First, that you won't speak that way to another adult unless they're making you feel unsafe. Second, that you won't repeat the things I say about anyone else to their face, okay? This needs to remain our little peapod of trust."

A faint smile tugs at her lips. "Promise. To both things."

I shrug. "Then we're good, peanut. If someone pushes you, you have the right to defend yourself. I don't care what Principal Torres said."

Her shoulders loosen, and I take it as a win. It doesn't cancel out the other missteps, but it's something.

"So...how should we spend this extended holiday break? Other than keeping up with homework, of course."

She bites her lip, thinking. "I've been talking to Rocío on Instagram. She's really cool. We like a lot of the same things." Her speech has sped up, a clear indication of her excitement. "She sends the funniest memes and the prettiest makeup tutorials. Could we go back to Mapletown? So I can see her?"

I nod. "Yeah, I think we can make that happen. I'll talk to her mom and see if they'll be around the next few weeks."

Jules bounces in her seat, and the next thing I know, she's screeching the words to "Jingle Bell Rock." When we pass the street I'd normally take to go home, her brow furrows as she asks, "Where are we going?"

"Shopping," I reply with a wink. "Let's get you some bras, baby girl."

CHAPTER 13

DOMINIC

This was a bad idea. Was it a bad idea? Will she be happy to see me? This was a mistake.

The same thoughts keep circling, making my palms sweat as I run my hand through my hair for the seventh time.

Just knock, idiot.

I take a deep breath and knock.

A gasp sounds from behind the door, and Lindsay opens it, but only a crack. She's looking at me like I'm something out of her nightmares, and my brain confirms that this was definitely a mistake.

"Nic?" she whispers before looking over her shoulder. "I'll be right back." Her comment is for whoever is inside her apartment. My mind provides many guesses, none of which calms my nerves. She slips out into the hall and closes the door behind her. With wide eyes, she asks, "What are you doing here? Is everything okay?"

"Yeah, I took the day off. Wanted to come surprise you and Jules." I lean down and press a kiss to her cheek, trying to pretend like this is fine. That Lindsay doesn't look terrified to be standing near me. That the tension coming off her body doesn't make me feel like I'm her dirty little secret in the enchanted town she occasionally visits.

I knew Lindsay would be at home today because Jules is two days into her suspension, and Lindsay is working from home until Jules goes back to school. I had hoped she'd be excited to see me, and I could talk both of them into playing hooky for a few hours to show me around their neighborhood.

"But..." She looks me up and down, like she's just now realizing I'm a zombie. "But *how* are you here? I assumed you couldn't leave Mapletown."

"Lindsay," I hear a female voice call seconds before the front door opens. "Oh, hello there." The woman is several inches shorter than Lindsay, with paler skin and fewer curves, but with the addition of soft creases in the corners of her eyes and silver streaks in her hair. Her mother, I'm guessing. The woman turns to her daughter. "I didn't realize you were having company today."

I notice that Lindsay is looking between me and her mother like we're both covered in blood. My heart sinks when I figure out why. She's ashamed of me. Her fear is in her parents meeting me.

"Well, come in," her mother says with a smile. "There's no need to hang out in the drafty hallway."

I step around Lindsay and offer my thanks to the person who doesn't mind hosting me. "My name is Dominic. Pleased to meet you, ma'am." I offer my winningest smile and most gentlemanly bow.

She giggles. Jackpot. "I'm Annabelle, Lindsay's mother."

"Who's here?" a man's voice calls out from another room. He's got gray hair, a tall, thick build, and the same olive skin as Lindsay, who's still hovering by the front door, unable to speak. "Hi there. Linds, you going to introduce us to your friend or what?"

After a long, awkward pause, Lindsay clears her throat and takes a step in our direction. "Right. Uh, sorry, I just..." her eyes dart between the three of us expectantly. "Never mind. Mom, Dad, this is Dominic Jennings."

I'm both eager and anxious to hear the way she introduces me. What I am to her.

"He owns a bar in Mapletown."

Factual, but without any attachment.

"Nic, this is my dad, Matteo, and my mom, Annabelle."

"Dominic!" Jules shouts as she rounds the corner and runs toward me, wrapping her arms around my middle.

"Hey, princess." I called her that once while she and Linds were making pizza rolls in the bar's kitchen, and she looked at me like I'd just given the keys to a Lamborghini.

"What are you doing here?" she looks up and asks.

"Took the day off to come see you."

"Really?" She's delighted. Grabbing my hand, she drags me toward the living room. "Come have a scone. I made them. They're peppermint!"

"I'll pour us all some coffee," Matteo offers.

"Actually, Nic," Lindsay begins, "can I talk to you in the bedroom really quickly? I have that book you asked about."

"Book?" I ask, before realizing this is a ruse. A performance. One that Linds is not selling. Not even a little. "Oh, sure."

We step into the bedroom, and she closes the door quietly behind her, then rounds on me like she's about to scream. "What the fuck is going on?" Her voice is barely louder than a whisper.

"What do you mean?" I reply quietly. I still have no idea why she's acting so strange. I'm hoping I get an explanation before we return to the living room, because I'm feeling extremely deflated right now. "Why are you so upset to see me? Did I do something wrong?"

Her eyebrows pinch in confusion. "No, of course not."

"Then what is it? Are you ashamed of me? You don't want your parents to meet me?"

She puts her hands on my forearms, offering reassurance. It works. Her touch releases the tension in my neck, as much, if not more than, a neck massage. "What? No," she scoffs. "They've been trying to set me up with their friends' sons and nephews ever since I turned forty. You could have a machete in your hand, and as long as you say please and thank you, they'd tell me to give you a chance."

"Then what?"

"Nic, you're the size of a tree and your skin is fucking green," she says, rubbing her temples. "Aren't you concerned about being here? Outside of Mapletown, outside the enchanted bubble and wandering around in your true form? How is this allowed? How is it safe?"

Oh. *Oh.* She's worried about me. About my safety. I'm so relieved she isn't ashamed of me that I pull her into my chest, my hand cupping the nape of her neck.

"Nic!" She pushes out of my embrace and looks at me with wild eyes.

"I got approval from the mayor to leave town for the day. For those like me, who can't shift into a form that naturally blends in with humans, her approval comes with a mask spell."

"Mask spell? What is that?"

"Everyone who's never seen me before can't see that my skin is green. To them, I look like a regular white guy, just with a lot of scars."

She chews on the inside of her lip. "So Jules and I can see

the real you, but when my parents look at you, your skin looks white."

"Yep." I'm realizing that her fear could've been avoided if I'd given her a heads-up that I was coming to visit, and now I feel like an asshole. "Sorry for the scare. I'm perfectly safe anywhere I go as long as I'm back in Mapletown by midnight. That's when the spell wears off."

"Oh god. Okay." She lets out a trembling breath and leans into me. "Fucking hell. I was standing there like, why are my parents so comfortable around this giant green stranger?"

I'm realizing now that Jules had the opposite reaction to Lindsay, despite her being able to see my green skin. "Why didn't Jules freak out?"

"She probably assumes I explained the existence of monsters to my parents the same way I did for her." She fans her face. "Shit. You just aged me, like, fifteen years."

"Maybe this will make up for it." I pull my gift for her out of my coat's inside pocket.

It's nothing special. I didn't even wrap it. But that doesn't seem to matter, based on the little excited hop she does.

"Peanut butter cups? You got me peanut butter cups?"

I nod. "For when you miss me."

She lets out a loud, unhinged cackle, ending in the most adorable snort I've ever heard. "This is perfect. Thank you."

I'm awarded with a heated kiss that makes my knees wobble.

She puts the candy on her nightstand and gestures toward the door. "Come on, let's go have scones."

We join Lindsay's parents and Jules in the living room and nibble on scones while her father flips the TV channels between two different hockey games.

"So, Dominic, how long have you owned your bar?" Matteo asks.

"About six years now."

"Have you always worked in the restaurant industry?" Annabelle asks.

"Not always." I tread carefully here. Not all of my work experience is technically legal. "I worked as a server on and off after high school. Then a bartender for a couple years in Memphis. I enjoyed it, especially once I got good at it."

"Oh yeah? Did you learn how to flip bottles in the air and pour cocktails behind your back?" Matteo asks.

I chuckle at the image. "No, sir. None of that, but I can mix a mean martini."

We go around sharing our signature drinks, and I tell them the hardest cocktails to make. They seem genuinely interested. Perhaps that's why I thoughtlessly utter, "After I was turned, I really wanted to be my own boss, you know? And since bartending was something I knew how to do, it felt like the perfect fit."

"After you were...turned?" Annabelle asks with raised eyebrows.

Fuck! I'm not used to interacting with normies. My filter came down way too easily.

"Uh, he meant—" Lindsay begins, looking panicked.

"After I, uh..." I'm urging my brain to come with something. *Anything.* "Turned against my community," is what spills out.

Lindsay and I exchange a *what the fuck* look before she adds, "Yeah, he was in a cult. A bad one. Very oppressive environment." She keeps nodding, almost manically. "He's lucky to be alive."

I suppose it works, if I were to think of that first dark year before my recovery as cult-like. There wasn't a leader, although I guess the leader here would be the virus? It's too late to walk it back anyway, so I play along. "Yes. Lucky."

Once we're past that minor hiccup, the conversation flows smoothly. Matteo and Annabelle are both kind and don't seem overly judgmental, but I find I'm unable to relax until I'm back in the truck and driving toward the highway.

A memory floats upward, of the time Gemma introduced me to her brother. We were having dinner at a fancy restaurant, and I struggled to follow their conversation. I couldn't tell if the references they were making were too inside, or I was too dumb to follow along. The way Gemma kept rolling her eyes and laughing whenever I spoke made me think it was the latter.

That was the only time I'd ever met a girlfriend's family, and she wasn't even my girlfriend at the time. Maybe she was testing me, seeing if I was worthy of the title, and I failed. Since then, I've had trouble gauging how people perceive me. Specifically, if I'm in on the joke or part of the punchline.

Recalling the details of the day, I think I made a decent impression on Lindsay's parents, but it's impossible to know for sure. Based on the way Linds has spoken of them, I get the feeling she wouldn't need their approval to date me, or anything more serious, but that doesn't mean I'm comfortable with them thinking I'm some uneducated loser who can't provide for and protect their daughter. I'm capable of both.

What I'm starting to realize, a realization so strong I can no longer push it aside—is that I *want* to provide both. I want to spend the rest of my days with Lindsay and Jules. If the only thing I'm good for is making their lives easier and putting smiles on their beautiful faces, I'd be honored to fill that role.

There's just one problem.

Would Lindsay let me?

CHAPTER 14

LINDSAY

I'm sitting at Isla's dining room table on Christmas Eve, eating roasted beef tenderloin and staring mindlessly out the window behind Dad's head. It won't be a white Christmas this year, as no snow is coming. Rain will take its place, but not until late tomorrow night. There's a steady hum of chatter around me, but I'm not taking part, because I'm not even really here.

Under normal circumstances, I'd be thoroughly enjoying this meal. The tenderloin is delicious and practically melts in my mouth, but no matter how hard I try to focus on the food and people in front of me, my mind wanders to Nic. That's where I'd like to be.

It's not because he's been spending time with Gemma, which he has. That's not it at all. I mean, it's not *not* it, but it's not the primary reason I wish I were in Mapletown. They're friends, and she keeps hanging out at the bar when he's working. It's not like he can refuse to serve her. Well, I guess he could, but unless she does something truly egregious, I know he won't.

The reason I'm spacing out is that not spending the holidays with the person you have the most fun with just feels wrong. Like there's a black hole at the table, and no one can see it but me.

Even Jules looks a bit bored as she helps clear the table once we're done eating and sits down with her dessert. She's been talking to Rocío more and more, and begging to go back up there. I love that she's made a new friend, but it's making me wonder if Boston is the right place for us long-term.

That's not the only thing making me reevaluate my life choices. We signed a big client at work, a local restaurant chain with six locations across eastern Massachusetts, and my boss has been pushing me to get the marketing deck completed by the first of the year. We're expected to unveil a six-month marketing strategy to rebrand the chain and launch several new marketing initiatives.

This project, along with the dozen other year-end reports I'm supposed to submit, has been the bane of my existence since Jules got suspended. I was hoping I'd get to take a day or two off to bring her Christmas shopping, watch movies together, make homemade gingerbread cookies—her favorite Christmas traditions, but I've been too busy working.

When I'm not working, I'm dazed and cranky with anyone who dares to approach, and that's mostly Jules. When she got suspended, I took it as a sign to look inward and determine what changes need to be made in the way I parent. What I figured out is that the most important change I need to make is to be more present for her. I vowed to put my phone and laptop away from six p.m. until she goes to bed every night. After that, I can work if needed or talk to Nic. But during that post-work/school period, she gets one hundred percent of my attention.

It didn't seem like an unreasonable plan. It wouldn't

require me to dip out of work early, and it wouldn't feel like I was pushing Nic away either. If she needed to do homework after dinner, I could practice witchcraft or catch up on emails. Everyone wins.

This has not been the case at all. Witchcraft has been shoved to the back burner, my calls with Nic are short and are mostly me yawning and trying to convince him I'm not tired, and work has been piling up. What's worse is that Jules's schoolwork has been winding down for the holiday break. She has another entire week off before her suspension resumes, and I have no idea how I'm going to balance that.

This is the part of my stress spirals where I wish the Lilith Fair would return. What I wouldn't give for the promise of a modern Lilith Fair 2.0 on my horizon. I was too young to go to the first one, and not getting to see Sarah McLachlan, Fiona Apple, Lauryn Hill, and Missy Elliot will haunt me forever.

Jules is going to be home with me, bored off her ass, and I'm going to be working twelve-hour days to get this deck finished.

And for what, really?

I make decent money, but my job doesn't come with high stakes. It's not like I'm saving lives. So why am I being pushed so hard? More importantly, why am I allowing myself to be pushed?

My boss refused to approve an assistant position to help lighten my load, and I know my counterpart, who manages marketing for restaurants on the western half of the state—one of the Jakes who loves to interrupt me in meetings—not only has an assistant of his own, but he took his family to Aruba for the holidays. Why in the festive fuck is he sitting on a beach sipping Mai-Tai's while I'm over here considering racing home on Christmas Eve to work on a presentation?

I shoot up from my chair, as caught off guard by the action

as everyone else at the table, and say, "I'm sorry, but Jules and I will be leaving early."

My daughter looks up at me with a confused pout. "How come?"

"We're heading up to Mapletown for a few days."

Jules throws up her hands, victorious, and takes one last bite of her cheesecake before we give hugs and wish everyone a Merry Christmas.

Quinn is thrilled to see us again when we check into the B&B, and gives us the same room as last time. She offers us hot chocolate and frosted cookies shaped like Christmas trees. We drop our bags in the room and take our treats to go before driving to Fast Glass. The parking lot is way more packed than I was expecting, but Dominic did tell me that his neutral, anti-Christmas tradition is quite popular among the locals.

I was skeptical at first, assuming more people would be annoyed by the lack of holiday spirit, but as Jules and I enter the bar, it's clear I was sorely mistaken. People are laughing, playing board games, and enjoying the bar's new food offerings without a strand of tinsel in sight.

"Hi, guys," I say as we grab two seats at the bar.

We're immediately surrounded by the staff, who shower us with hugs and cheers for our surprise pop in.

Nic spins Jules around, her feet flying in a wide circle as her delighted giggle fills the room. I'm rewarded with a kiss on my cheek, my neck, and just below my ear as he whispers, "Best Not Christmas ever."

Camilla stops by with Rocío after a busy day of Christmas shopping, and the girls jump around in a circle at the sight of each other. They grab an available two-top next to the bar, and Vyla brings them tall glasses of cranberry juice.

I end up in a conversation with Natalie, Camilla, and

Mayor Crane about my current work woes and Jules's suspension, and the mayor knocks me off my ass with two questions.

"Have you considered moving here? I know the schools don't normally accept transfers this late in the quarter, but I can speak to the school board if you're interested. Do you think Jules would be happier in Mapletown?"

My mouth hangs open as my mind races. Should I move here? I know that I'd be allowed to buy a place and settle here due to my ancestral witch blood. But *should* I? I can't deny that my trips to Mapletown have been the best part of my year. When I haven't had an upcoming trip on the calendar, the days have seemed endless, and I've wondered how I'll get through another in this bitter, dark time of year.

Then there's the whole job thing. They'd likely let me work remotely if I requested it, but since I make so many site visits to our clients' locations, there'd be a lot more driving, and not around here.

The second question is much easier to answer, because yes, Jules would be happier in Mapletown. There's no doubt in my mind. She loves living close to her cousin and grandparents in Boston, but her friend group at school is small and flaky. I've never seen her let loose like she seems to around Rocío, and knowing she could start a new school with a friend to guide her would make the transition much easier.

I look over at the girls huddled close together. Rocío is painting Jules's nails as Jules looks animated while telling a story.

"I think Jules would be happier here," I say to the mayor. "Could you get us a meeting with the principal?"

Camilla perks up. "I'm close with the principal. That'll be no problem. It's a small school, so I'm sure there's room for her."

Natalie gives me a thumbs up and an encouraging nod.

"And I'll make sure the school board knows about your quest to join the local coven. They'll eat that up."

"Oh, well, I'm not—" I begin, ready to explain that I'm nowhere near skilled enough to join the coven. I'd be the weak link of the bunch.

"I know," the mayor interrupts. "You're still dabbling. We've all been at that stage. You gotta start somewhere." She smiles brightly as she nods, flipping her tight curls off her shoulder. Even on Christmas Eve, she's rocking a pantsuit and white Adidas sneakers, which is her signature look, I'm told, and she's by far the best dressed person in the entire bar.

If I weren't completely obsessed with Nic, I'd ask the hot mayor if I could buy her next drink. I haven't dated a woman in years, but *damn.*

"I guess I'd have to find a realtor and all that jazz. I know property values around here are relatively low, but if I were to leave my job"—*fuck,* it feels good to say that—"I'm not sure I could afford a place without a lead on employment. I have a solid nest egg I could live off of for a while, but I was saving it for any gender affirming medical expenses Jules might need when she gets older. Whatever insurance won't cover."

Mayor Crane and Camilla share a sly glance. Then Mayor Crane beams proudly. "Lindsay, healthcare is free here."

I almost choke on my ginger ale. "Are you serious?" They must be kidding, because how can that be? "What do you mean?"

"Any medical treatment you receive as a resident of Mapletown costs you nothing. There are no co-pays, no premiums, no deductibles."

I can't help the volume of my voice when I shout, "You're shitting me!"

The jukebox plays on while every head in the bar turns toward me.

"Sorry," I say, holding up a hand, my cheeks hot with embarrassment. I turn to the mayor. "But how?"

Her chin lifts. "Mostly taxes, which are higher for our wealthy residents, but we also have benefactors on the National Oversight Council. Those who believe no one should go bankrupt to pay for live-saving medical treatments."

"National Oversight Council?" I repeat.

"It's a group of witches who oversee the monster towns in the U.S. Any advanced legal matters or budgetary issues the mayors can't handle ourselves are brought to their attention. This is a cause I fought hard for, and I'm extremely proud Mapletownies have access to it."

My jaw nearly unhinges one again. I wouldn't be surprised if some drool dripped out and landed on the bar.

Natalie laughs. "Pretty great, right?" Then it dies as a sad smile tugs at her lips. "I wish Mom could've lived here."

Her mom died of cancer, and who knows the level of care she could've gotten, or how things would've turned out if she and Natalie didn't have the looming threat of financial ruin over their heads the whole time.

If this is true, and gender affirming medical treatments will cost nothing, no matter how old Jules gets, then the money I have socked away can be used for something else. Something like starting a new life in a new place, perhaps.

We spend Christmas Day with Nic at the bar. Jules and I bake non-holiday themed cookies to give today's customers for free. Just a little something to make this day feel less debilitating.

I get a text from Camilla that afternoon confirming an appointment for us to meet the principal of Mapletown High School the following Monday. When I tell her that Jules is only thirteen, she assures me that if Jules is as smart as I make her sound, she might place at the high school level in her entrance exam.

This is all starting to feel very real, and I realize I can't keep this possibility to myself anymore. I decide to talk to Nic first, to make sure he's cool with the idea of me moving here.

"I wouldn't be moving here for you," I explain. "It's really for Jules. But you would be an added bonus, of course."

He traces my cheekbone with his finger in a featherlight touch that has goosebumps erupting across my skin. "An added bonus, huh?" His tone is wary, but the smirk on his face is nothing short of playful. He crosses his arms over his wide chest and says, "Fine, I'm cool with you moving here. Under one condition."

"What's that?"

"Can I finally call you my girlfriend? We ain't gettin' any younger, you know."

I launch myself in his arms and kiss across his cheeks and stubbled chin. "Well, when you say it like that, how could I ever say no?"

CHAPTER 15

LINDSAY

The interview is a breeze, and just as Camilla suspected, Jules aces the entrance exam. She gets placed with the freshmen and won't stop talking about how cool the layout of the school is when we're back in Boston. It's the week between Christmas and New Year's, and while everyone else seems to be existing in the liminal space of time when nothing matters, I'm up to my tits in revisions for my deck. My boss didn't hold back on his criticisms, and going through his notes on seventy-five percent of the slides is taking forever.

"Did you see the terrarium in the science lab?" she asks for the twentieth time as she dances through the kitchen. "They have vampire crabs and regal jumping spiders!"

"And you are expressly forbidden from bringing either of them home, do you hear me?" I don't even want to know what they look like. Ick. "I don't care if it's for an assignment that's fifty percent of your grade. They are not welcome in my house."

"So we're moving, right? When do we get to start looking at houses?"

It's an excellent question, and one that I haven't taken the time to figure out. I still have to ask my boss if I can switch to remote work. My parents have no idea I'm even considering this, and I need to pull Jules out of her current school and have her transcripts sent to Mapletown high. I'm sure there was a more efficient order to do this in, but as expected, that's not the path I'm following.

"I'll figure that out tonight, okay?"

"Okie doke." She grabs a sparkling water from the fridge and skips back to her room.

The following forty-eight hours become an exercise in not losing my shit. I'm on my third round of revisions for this godforsaken presentation, and for some reason, my boss thinks there's more to be done.

I'm getting emails at all hours of the day from him. Just quick, one-line emails containing feedback at whatever moment it hits him.

Things like, "We should include more case studies here. This isn't enough." "We don't need your opinion on this, we need facts," and, my favorite, "Please fix," next to a screenshot of whichever slide he's looking at.

Oh, fix what, you ask? No idea, because he doesn't elaborate.

I have a separate email minimized on my computer requesting to work remotely. Even though quitting altogether would be way more fun, I can't bring myself to do it. The idea of waking up without knowing where my rent or mortgage payment is going to come from gives me hives. I've never lived on the edge like that, and I'm not sure it's something I want to try at my age.

That's why I'm hoping my boss reads my email, acknowledges that the benefits outweigh the drawbacks—for the company, that is—and it won't change how available I make myself to my clients.

I take a break between revisions to look through the property listings Mayor Crane sent over. There are only seven in Mapletown, but the ones available do look promising. Four of them are cookie-cutter condos in a bigger development behind the coffee place and the bookstore. There's a two-bedroom apartment above the bookstore, which Jules might love, but the kitchen looks outdated for the price, and I don't like how small the bedrooms are.

The other two are three-bedroom, single-family homes with vastly different styles, but look equally nice based on the asking price. One is an older three-story colonial with a wide screened-in porch, a backyard pool, and a detached garage. However, the inside looks like it needs a lot of work. The other is a newly renovated Tudor style with an attached garage, a large walk-in closet in the primary bedroom, and brand-new kitchen cabinets and appliances.

My top pick is the Tudor because I'm unable to see the charm in old homes. What I see when I look at a century-old house is lead paint, the likelihood of asbestos, and buckets filled with water from a soon-to-be leaky roof. I want none of that. Give me move-in ready and entirely up-to-code, please and thank you.

The condos all look the same, but have renovated interiors, so I make those my backup option, as I shoot off an email to the listing agent to see how soon we can come up and take a tour.

I wake up on New Year's Eve with a belly full of dread as I open my email on my phone. There are seven emails from my boss requesting more changes. Seven. On New Year's Eve. Though I won't be in Mapletown, Nic and I have made plans to FaceTime as the ball drops. The bar is throwing a party, and though I wanted to attend, I just have too much going on with work at the moment.

Yesterday, I summoned the courage to send the email requesting my shift to remote work. No word from the boss yet.

I drop Jules off at my dad's house for their New Year's party in the early afternoon and promise to come back as soon as I can. She and Kayla have glowstick necklaces they plan to wear and sparklers they're going to light at midnight in Dad's backyard.

I go through the slides one by one and make the requested changes, then I haul my ass into the shower to get myself pretty for the coming of the new year. It's when I'm applying my blush that my phone dings with three email notifications.

The first is from my boss about working remotely. It says, "I appreciate the thought that went into this request, and if we were still in Covid times, I'd be open to considering it. Unfortunately, I fear the long-distance drive to and from your clients will be more of a hindrance than you've realized. Long commutes can weigh on a person, and I need you giving your best to your clients. It's a no at this time, but feel free to follow up in six months to reevaluate."

The second email is also from my boss, regarding my deck changes. "I'm concerned you're missing the core interests of their customers. Somehow, this is still way off-base and shoddy, given the revenue they're about to bring in. Where is your head? They're still within their sixty-day window to cancel their account with us. If I show them this presentation, I can almost guarantee they'll take their business elsewhere. I've left my notes on the final four slides. When we return to the office, let's sit down and discuss your current role with the company and if you truly see a future here."

The third email is from the listing agent in Mapletown. It

says, "Thanks so much for your interest in these properties. I'm available as early as nine a.m. on January 2, if you'd like a tour. If that's too short notice, please note that my schedule is flexible, and if you have a date and time in mind, I can likely accommodate you."

I sit at my vanity, processing the emails I just read. Clarity settles my muscles, and the decision is made so easily, I wonder why it took me this long. When I fantasized about this moment, I thought I'd be angrier, ready to stomp on a printer, slap one of the Jakes across the face, maybe even toss hot coffee all over one of my boss's hideous ties. But no. I feel none of that right now.

I send my first response to the listing agent. "Let's make it ten on January 2. Looking forward to it."

The second email, I send to my boss in response to my deck changes. "Thank you for your feedback. This job means nothing to me. I quit. Happy New Year." After I press send, I turn my phone on silent and put on my bad bitch blood-red lipstick, because that's exactly what I am.

THE FIRST HALF of January speeds by as Jules and I race to pack up the apartment, and I go through my pending tasks to complete before the move. Principal Torres has faxed Jules's transcripts to Mapletown High. Her classes for the third quarter have been selected, and she's already received her schedule. The owners of the three-bedroom Tudor appreciated my all-cash offer, which sped up the process considerably. I've already had the entire interior painted and wall-papered exactly how I want it. Nic was there to oversee that, as well as the Wi-Fi installation and the inspection before the sale. I have no idea how I could've done this without him.

Moving day is tomorrow, and Jules starts school next week. Nic and Riz have been given their day passes from the mayor with accompanying spells to come down and help us move. Packing is almost done, thank Christ, because it's exhausting.

My family took the news better than I expected. I was bracing for my dad to guilt me into staying so he could keep his granddaughter close. That didn't happen. He immediately saw how excited Jules was and gave his blessing.

I knew Isla would be supportive, but when she pulled me aside and said, "You've been carrying the load with Mom and Dad your whole life. I'll take it from here," I couldn't hold back the tears.

"They've got each other, and Dad's got Ruth. They'll be fine," she assured me in a tight sisterly hug. "Besides, I hear there's a rugged mountain of a man waiting for you up there, and I'm here for it."

Mom was the most reluctant with her well wishes, as expected. "What about your career?" she asked. "You worked so hard for it. Why would you throw it away?"

It felt like a lot of projecting, to be honest. When she from graduated law school and started working at a nearby firm, she wasn't home much. Dad had to take time off work to be home with Isla, and drive me to and from school, while Mom worked eighty-hour weeks. She enjoyed the challenge, at first, but within a decade, she was burned out and miserable. After that, she bounced around at various small firms until the moment she had enough money saved to retire.

When I told her, "Because I'm starting to hate my job, and I think I can find something else I find more fulfilling," I knew she'd understand. Ultimately, she let out a heavy sigh and wished me luck. It wasn't the most supportive response, but people show up how they know how, not how you want them to.

I sent Billy a courtesy text that his daughter was moving to a different state, and he replied, "Cool. Good luck." Then another text five minutes after that saying he won't be able to take Jules in a couple of weeks like we had planned because he's going somewhere with his new girlfriend for the weekend, and that he's "so sorry."

As I plop down on the couch now, I survey the empty walls and dusty corners of our apartment. We've been here since Jules was four years old, and we've made a lot of memories here. But I'm not sure how much I'll miss it. It's always felt temporary, like I was just waiting to have enough money saved for a down payment. Luckily for me, Mapletown is a thousand times more affordable than Boston, despite the higher taxes everyone pays. What's amazing is that they aren't much higher than what I've been paying here, yet in Mapletown, we get free healthcare.

All I know is that I got the sweet end of the deal.

What's more is that not working is *really* working for me. I still wake up early and struggle to sit idle for more than twenty minutes, but how I choose to fill my time is entirely up to me. I have five upcoming catering gigs in Mapletown—for which I'll be paid and have created my own catering menus—and Nic has asked me to join the bar staff part-time to consult on the menu and help Anton in the kitchen. They've gotten busier with the few dishes they've added, and the locals want more.

I'm not sure that either is going to turn into full-time, long-term careers, but for the first time in my life, I don't care. This is good enough for now, and the "for now" part of life is what I plan to focus on. Because "for now" is all I have.

Things start to feel less chaotic in week three of being an official Mapletown resident. I'm now receiving mail at the new house, every box has been unpacked and the cardboard recycled, and I have my beauty products lined up perfectly in my medicine cabinet. For me, that's the sign that I'm truly home.

Jules has already signed up for science club and she and Rocío will be performing a choreographed dance to a Chappell Roan song at the town talent show in one month. She loves her classes, her teachers, and being able to safely walk home from school. She's never been outgoing, really. I assumed she was an introvert. She's really coming out of her shell here, though, and it confirms I made the right decision.

The only blemish on the face of this spectacular life change is a demon with perfect tits and the personality of wet mulch.

Gemma spends a lot of time at the bar. She refuses to acknowledge my presence when I'm there, and from what I've seen, only speaks to Nic in hushed conversations. I've asked him about it, and he brushes it off like their conversations aren't even worth repeating. I'm not jealous. For the first time ever, I'm actually not in the slightest, despite the obvious way she chooses to pursue him—tits out, nails sharp, and a mouthful of double entendres.

I think I'm so confident in my relationship with Nic because he doesn't play games. He isn't afraid of PDA, and definitely not in front of her. He also spends most nights—into the early mornings—with his suckler latched onto my clit, making me squirt harder than a fucking firehose. Hard to doubt his loyalty when he's that committed to making me come.

It's their friendship that I have a problem with. On more than one occasion, she's asked him to meet her to help with household tasks, or to console her after another guy has ghosted her. He keeps telling me they've been friends for years, and that's all they'll ever be, but I'm not comfortable with him being her first call when something goes wrong.

I also don't like how he's sometimes withdrawn and distant after seeing her. He's made comments lately about how dumb he is, and despite the way he laughs it off, I can tell there's a deeper layer to those thoughts. Gemma popped back into his life not long after we started hanging out, so maybe he's always been like this, but it seems more frequent now. I have a hunch that Gemma's to blame.

If they're going to be friends, fine, have at it. But that friendship better lift both of them up, because I'm not about to let anyone gaslight my boyfriend into thinking he's stupid.

This is how it starts, though—the me of it all that ruins every relationship I develop. I get attached, then I get protective. Next, I overstep in the name of that protection, and it pushes people away. They see that I'm too much, and decide they need significantly less.

Shit, it almost drove Natalie and I into a friend breakup.

I've tried to change this part of myself over the years, but with no success.

Will it be the thing that ultimately drives us apart? Am I too much just as I am?

CHAPTER 16

DOMINIC

"Motherfucker, goddamnit." I throw the dirty rag I used to wipe my hands against the digital clock in my truck. Eleven forty, it reads. Almost midnight. I pull my phone out of my coat pocket, furious as to why my alarm didn't go off three hours ago like it should've.

Dead. Perfect.

I forgot to charge it last night when I got home from the bar, and didn't think of it when I went into work this morning. When I stopped by Gemma's after work to help her figure out what's wrong with her dryer, I forgot to ask if I could borrow her charger.

Now, here we are.

I'm leaving my ex's house late at night after missing movie night with Lindsay and Jules. I certainly didn't intend for tonight to unfold like this. I texted Lindsay when I left the bar that I'd be at her house by seven. That I'd bring pizza. She said she'd provide the popcorn. Jules was in charge of finding the newest *Jurassic Park* movie on whatever streaming platform didn't make you pay extra to watch it, and we were set to have lovely, cozy evening. Just me and my girls.

When I got to Gemma's, I shoved my phone in my coat pocket, knowing I had an alarm set for six forty-five, so I'd have enough time to wash my hands and head to Lindsay's house. I started working on her dryer, first checking and clearing out the vent, then using an air duster to clean out the lint trap. When that didn't seem to fix anything, I started pulling the machine apart.

Gemma tried talking my ear off at first, asking questions about Lindsay and how our relationship was going. I have trouble focusing on two things at once, so I barely acknowledged her presence. Then she sat down next to me on the floor, and at one point, parted her legs so I had a clear view up her very short skirt, under which she was wearing nothing.

"What are you doing?" I asked with a shake of my head. "What is this?"

"What is what?" she replied innocently. When I let out an irritated sigh, she giggled. "Okay, fine. You want to know what this is? It's me being abundantly clear about what I want." She lifted the hem of her skirt, allowing the overhead light to shine directly onto her pussy. "I want to ride your face while you fuck my pussy with your tongue. Then I want you to lift me over your head, and slam me onto the kitchen counter so hard it leaves a crack in the marble. Then I want you to fuck me so hard that I can't walk for the next three days. I want things to go back to the way they used to be with us. That's what I want."

My response was immediate. "Not happening. I'm with Lindsay. We're happy. Discussion over."

When she put her hand on my forearm and started to protest, I could also feel the signature tingle of her influence as a succubus, trying to pull me in. I lost my patience entirely.

"Enough! Look, I've told you more than once that friendship is the only form of *us* in our future. Now, do you want me to fix your dryer or not? Because if you don't leave me the fuck alone, I'm outta here."

She held up her hands, looking surprisingly spooked, and backed out of the kitchen. By the time I had the motor on the floor next to the thermal fuse and determined neither had any damage to them, my phone was probably long dead. It must've taken at least another hour to get everything reassembled.

Nothing happened between us since I shut her down, but that won't matter when I try to explain this to Lindsay. There's something about Gemma that Lindsay doesn't trust. I see her bristle when Gemma walks into the bar. The way she watches us with a scowl on her face. She really doesn't want Gemma and I to remain friends. I get that she's jealous. I even find it cute. If our situations were reversed, I can't say I'd be comfortable with a random guy constantly hanging around Lindsay either.

When Gemma first started hanging around the bar again, I, too, assumed she was just trying to mess with my head. But when she put her hands on my chest and tried to kiss me one night after I locked up, I pushed her away and told her to cut the shit if she didn't want to destroy our friendship. I told her that Lindsay is the love of my life, and we're building something real. Something that'll last, and that I'd be damned if anyone tried to get in the way of that.

Gemma looked hurt, even cried for a spell. When I refused to comfort her, it seemed to click. She promised that she'd respect what I have with Lindsay, and the two of us would be friends and nothing more.

After tonight, I don't know. She broke her promise, and for that, she needs to be held accountable, but how? Does that warrant me cutting her out of my life? Do I ice her out as punishment for a month or two and see if she feels remorse? I still feel indebted to her for helping me create a life here, and I'd hate for our friendship to deteriorate over something this silly.

Admittedly, there's also part of me that enjoyed working with my hands on the tasks Gemma asked me to help her with. Being handy is a skill I developed as a kid, when Mamaw couldn't afford to hire people to fix things around her trailer. The only time I do mind is when I get so lost in the task itself that I lose track of time, especially when that means I stand up my girlfriend and her daughter.

My stomach twists when I pull into Lindsay's driveway. The lights in the living room are still on, so I know she's awake. I'm inclined to turn around and drive home, leaving this conversation for the morning, but the not stupid part of my brain knows it's better to get it over with.

I trudge up the driveway and knock gently on the front door. When she opens the door, she looks strange. Not like herself. Her hair is in a messy bun, and she's wearing loose pajama pants with one of my hoodies, but she's pulling up the collar of the hoodie to block my view of the bottom half of her face. She quickly turns her back and ushers me inside.

"Jules is asleep, so we need to be quiet." She turns off the lamp closest to her before sitting on the couch. The rest of the lights are on, except for the overhead light, of course. Again, strange. "So where were you? I was worried. I've been texting." She leans forward to adjust herself and put a pillow on her lap, and in the dim light, I can see angry red spots on her forehead and around her nostrils.

The pieces of the puzzle snap into place, but this is no time to tell her what I know. First, I need her forgiveness.

I take her free hand in mine and stroke the back of it with my thumb. "I'm so sorry, Lindsay. I should've been here. I wanted to be. It's just…I lost track of time. I set an alarm to make sure I'd be here for the movie, but my phone died because I forgot to charge it last night—"

"Where were you?"

I swallow. "I was trying to fix Gemma's dryer."

She tosses the pillow aside and starts pacing across the rug behind the couch. "Gemma," she mutters quietly. "Of course you were with Gemma."

I hold up my hands. "It's not what you think. I truly was working on her dryer. I had the thing in pieces. We didn't even talk that much."

She rolls her eyes. "And when you were talking, what were you talking about?"

I should probably tell her the truth about the way Gemma came onto me, but what good would that do? Ultimately, I handled the situation the way I know Lindsay would've wanted me to, so I don't see the need to upset her now for no reason. I might not be the brightest bulb in the bunch, but I'm not *that* dim. "Nothing. I don't know. She was talking, and I wasn't really listening."

Her mouth forms a straight, displeased line. She gives me a scathing look, then throws up her hands in defeat. Letting go of the collar, I can see several more red spots on her chin and along her jawline. She seems to realize a second later and yanks it back up to her nose once more. "Forget it. It's not worth it."

Now I'm getting pissed off. If we're going to argue, I at least want to take part in the argument, yet Lindsay seems to be determining my punishment, and I don't even get to state my case? Fuck that. "What's not worth it?" The words she uses are what really get under my skin. *Not worth it.* Like the truth doesn't matter, regardless of what it is. That's not how I see this relationship, and it kills me that she might. To me, she's worth everything. We're worth *everything*.

She scoffs. "I don't want to fight with you about Gemma."

"Well, I don't want to fight with you either, but clearly something's bothering you, and I don't give a hoot if it's about Gemma or not, I just want you to tell me."

I watch her pace, her slippered feet stomping across the abstract pattern of the rug as if she's trying to punish it for disappointing her. Her gait is naturally heavy, but it looks more like a model walk when she's having a good day. Confident and unafraid to take up space. This is not that.

I get tired of the silence stretching between us. "Lindsay, whatever it is, just say it."

She rounds on me, her different-colored eyes wild with fury. When her mouth opens, I brace for a yell, but she must remember that Jules is in the next room because I watch her recalibrate before whispering fiercely, "Gemma's a fucking asshole, and I don't want you to be friends with her."

I sigh. "I told you, you don't need to be jealous. She means nothing to me." I reach for her, but she jerks away.

"I'm not jealous. That's not what this is." She stares off into the distance, and her hand lifts to her face.

I watch as her fingers slowly glide along her jawline, back and forth over there two red spots remain. I know I shouldn't, it's not the right time, but I can't help it. Reaching up, I bat her hand away from her face. That snaps her back into focus, and she looks at me, bewildered, and maybe hurt too.

"What are you doing?" She looks at her hand as if I burned it. "What the hell was that?"

"Mapping," I tell her, gesturing to her face. "I was trying to stop you."

Her eyebrows pinch together as she jerks back. "How did you even—"

"I asked Natalie about it after the picnic. I wanted to know what it meant."

She lets out a frustrated groan and shakes her head. "Unbelievable."

"Natalie told me you did that sometimes in college." I shrug. "I thought if I noticed it in the moment, I could—"

She tries to hide her face again with the hoodie. "This isn't about my coping mechanisms, okay? This is about you and Gemma, who I am not jealous of, by the way."

"Fine. You're not jealous."

She nods. "Even if I were, like, a little jealous of her, which would be completely justifiable, given that she's a smoking hot demon, that's not what I'm upset about."

I feel like we're talking in circles. "Then what?"

"She's not worth your time, Nic. She's a shitty friend. Why even keep her in your life when she doesn't treat you with respect?"

I back up a few steps, aghast at the direction this is taking. "How would you even know what kind of friend she is?" To my knowledge, Lindsay has only been witness to maybe four conversations Gemma and I have had. How would she have any idea how Gemma treats me? And why does she assume I'd put up with that kind of person? Maybe she just doesn't understand how much we've been through. "Gemma has known me since I first recovered, okay? She knows things about my past that no one else does. You have no idea what kind of friend she's been." Gemma knows who I used to be. The real monster. She saw the evil that lives inside, and she accepted me anyway. That right there is friendship. "She got me a placement interview here. My bar, my life—I owe it all to her."

"Yeah, well, it was nice of her to get the placement interview for you, but you earned your spot here on your own. The mayor wouldn't have let you live here if she thought you were a danger to other residents, so Gemma didn't do that. That was all you, okay? She doesn't get credit for that. Just so we're clear." She resumes her pacing, and I start to think we're going to have another marathon of silence when she whirls around. "I don't know why you feel like you owe her so much. Is it because you're just that kind and forgiving, or has she been manipulating you into thinking you don't deserve everything you have?"

Her words hit me like bullets. "Wait, so you think I'm either too weak to establish boundaries in a friendship, or too dumb to recognize when someone is trying to manipulate me?"

Lindsay has never made me feel like I don't belong, or that my lack of education and vast vocabulary means I'm not worthy of her time, but others have. So many others, from childhood to now look at me like I have four heads when I say the wrong thing, or if I mix up a common phrase. They see a giant undead bag of bones who pours drinks for a living and assume I can't tell the difference between apples and oranges, and until I can impress them with a big word, that's all I'll ever be.

I thought Lindsay saw the real me. Maybe I was wrong.

"I don't think that at all," she says, softening her tone. "I'm saying that's how Gemma treats you, and that's why she doesn't deserve you." She's moving toward me now, arms open. Her eyes are filled with fear. "I'm just trying to protect you." Her bottom lip wobbles when I don't go to her. "Nic, please. I-I...This is how I get when I care about someone. I just want to protect you."

That's the nail in the coffin. "I don't need your protection, Lindsay. I'm perfectly capable of determining who should and shouldn't be in my life." I walk backward until I'm by the front door.

"You're leaving?" she asks, swiping a tear off her cheek.

My fingers twitch at my side, eager to serve as her tissue. My lips are desperate to kiss the red spots across her face until they fade. I want nothing more than to comfort her, but my heart wouldn't be in it, so I stay where I am. She made me feel foolish tonight. I know it probably wasn't her intention, but I can't pretend my feelings weren't hurt in the process. "Let's call it a night, okay? Sleep it off."

She sniffles and eventually nods. "Yeah. Sleep it off."

I leave without looking back.

CHAPTER 17

DOMINIC

I don't sleep a wink. Instead, I toss and turn, yanking the ends of my hair out of a desire to create as much pain as I saw reflected in Lindsay's eyes before I left. What a fucking cockwaffle I was. So what if she's protective of me? Is that really a dealbreaker? That the woman I love senses when I'm not being treated right by the people and around me and she...makes me aware of it? Is that truly why I left her house last night? It seems so silly now.

When we first started talking, and we'd go weeks without being able to talk in person, I remember thinking, *I was given a second chance at life, and I get to spend it with her. I'm not going to waste another moment,* and here I am, wasting precious moments that could be spent with her, making her laugh, running my tongue across her sweet skin, holding her in arms while she sleeps.

I turn over and grab my phone off the nightstand. It's almost eight. Pulling myself out of bed, I start formulating a plan. A gesture of some kind. Yeah, that'll do it. Nothing too over the top. It's only our first fight, but it was enough of a doozy that I need to make sure the present I give her is something she actually likes. No more flowers. No more picnics. She likes chocolates, especially when they're filled with peanut butter, but that's not big enough.

My mind continues to pore over the options as I brush my teeth. With a fresh shower and a renewed sense of determination, I leave my trailer with a pep in my step. I make it about two feet before the sight before me has me stopping dead in my tracks.

It's Lindsay, and she's running. There's no sense of dread or fear in her expression, though. In fact, she looks happy. She's got a bag in one arm. I can't tell what's inside. When we lock eyes, she picks up her pace, and my feet respond with urgency.

We're panting when we come face to face. There's so much I want to say to her, but where to begin?

She beats me to the punch. "Nic, I'm sorry." Her eyes are wet, and to know I caused her a moment of strife feels like someone's running a chainsaw down the middle of my chest. "I don't care who you're friends with, including Gemma. I-I overstepped, and I'm sorry. I'm so sorry."

I hold her face in my hands, bending down until our noses are almost touching. "I'm sorry too. The fight was stupid, and I regret the whole fucking thing. You're way more important to me than Gemma. I'll choose you every time."

She looks up at me and smiles. *Fuck*, that smile. I'll never stop being in awe of it. She pulls me into a hard kiss, filled with forgiveness and desperation. Hauling her into my arms, I carry her back to my trailer.

"What's in the bag?" I ask when I drop her onto my bed. I take it from her hand and open it onto the table next to the TV. "Banana and mayo sandwiches?"

She nods. "I made you three. I didn't like the idea of you being stressed without your comfort food."

There were still a couple hours before the bar opens. In that time, I make her come three times with just my fingers, her sweaty body writhing beneath my hands. She insists I give her a break, and I only agree to it when she crawls between my knees and takes me in her mouth. Those plump pink lips swallow me deep. She lets me fuck her mouth until I'm leaning over the edge, so dangerously close to shooting my seed down her throat.

"I'm coming," I say through heavy breaths, and goddess that she is, removes her mouth and presents her perfect breasts, lifting them just beneath my cock like the most stunning blank canvas on which to paint. I continue with rough strokes as my come drenches her chest and runs down the center of her belly. Once my balls are empty, I watch her rub it into her skin as she moans with pleasure.

I lose consciousness after that.

LINDSAY

Winter becomes a steady cycle of snow falling, then melting, then falling, then melting, as erratic temperatures dictate the thickness of our outerwear. Nic and I get into a good groove. After the fight about Gemma about two weeks ago, I vowed to make an effort and give her some slack. If he trusts her, so can I. I greet her with a friendly hello when she comes into the bar, and whenever Nic says he needs to help her with something, I smile like I'm in the running for the Most Supportive Girlfriend award, and don't say another word.

We spend almost all our nights together at my house. I even sacrificed six of the hangers in my closet so he can keep stuff here. Things between us feel steady, and I couldn't be happier about the way Jules has bonded with Nic.

They have inside jokes now, a secret handshake that I've attempted and failed because there are so many parts to it. She's even started painting his nails a new color each week. It's a new Sunday tradition. After dinner, they load the dishes into the dishwasher together, then sit at the kitchen counter for their manicure time. This is when Jules talks to him most about school and her blossoming social life. He's so attentive, too. He asks follow-up questions, offers comfort without prying too deep when she reveals something that has upset her, and while he's blowing on his nails, he helps her practice her choreography for the upcoming talent show.

I didn't realize men with painted nails was a kink of mine, but my god, seeing him go about his day not giving a solitary fuck about how brightly colored his nails are has my pussy in a constant state of flood. When he's behind the bar pouring drinks with those deft hands, or lifting a keg onto his shoulder, and I get a flash of pink from his thumb, well, let's just say, I'm carrying extra pairs of underwear in my purse now.

The current color is a deep teal, and as we lay in bed, our bodies sated and spent, I run the pad of my thumb over it, making a mental note to ask Jules the name of this particular shade in the morning.

Nic rolls me over until I'm on my back, and his lips travel down the column of my throat with smacking, ticklish kisses that have me squirming beneath him. He pulls back and lays on his side, his strong jawline pressed against his palm as he stares at me.

"What?" I ask when he doesn't say anything.

He worries his bottom lip, the tips of his ears turning dark green. Then he brushes the hair off my forehead and says, "I, um, I love you, Lindsay."

I kind of thought this was coming, but not even the sweetest daydream could've prepared me for the real thing. I trace the outline of the white scar beneath his eye. The boy who stole my heart as a kid. The man who filled the cracks and made it whole again as an adult. How did I get so lucky? "I love you too."

Because that's what this is, isn't it? The comfort and safety of walking through life next to a person who understands you, accepts you, and wants only the best for you. I didn't know it was real, or that it ever could be for me.

He drops his head against my wrist and lets out a relieved sigh. When he lifts his head again, his eyes are glistening. "I'm so in love with you. I think I have been since you walked into the bar."

Our gazes catch, the emotion so thick he's almost blurry. We reach for each other, tangling our legs and closing every speck of distance that comes between our bodies. He starts kissing along my collarbone, then down my arm. I feel the flat of his tongue swipe across my nipple, and I settle into the familiar way he traverses my body. His love language seems to be tonguing every inch of my skin. I'm not mad about it.

His tongue circles my belly button, and he looks up at me, a mischievous grin stretching those perfect, heart-shaped lips. "I have an idea."

"Oh yeah?" I'm expecting him to propose sex toys, anal, maybe even pegging—all of which I'm down for.

Instead, he says, "Let's move in together."

Move in together.

Move in together?

Move in...*together?*

You know when you say something enough times and it starts to sound wrong? That's what's happening inside my head with the question Nic just asked. The more I dig for an answer, the more uncomfortable I become.

I could chalk that up to not living with a romantic partner since Billy and I tried it. That was over a decade ago, and it didn't end well. Now, I'm in my forties. My daughter is a teenager. My belongings take up exactly as much space as I let them, and they're in the exact right places.

Nic's still looking at me with pleading eyes, and I realize I haven't spoken in a long time. "You want to move in together?" Repeat the question. Hope he misspoke. It's not a great plan, but it's all I've got.

"Yeah, don't you think we're ready?" He sounds so certain. *How* is he so certain?

"Um," I stammer, "I mean, there's still a lot we don't know about each other." Like, where does he cut his toenails? If the answer is not, "In the bathroom over a towel that I immediately empty into the tiny steel trash bin," could I live with that? Another is, where does he store his granola bars with the powdered brain tissue? And how much does Dr. Yates send him each time? Will I have to empty out an entire cabinet for them? What I finally say is, "I'm not sure," because I'm not, and I don't want to lie to him.

I just said I love you, for fuck's sake. That's a big deal, considering how much I hate men and how ready I was to die alone. Can't we put the brakes on and savor one big step at a time?

He moves off me and crawls up the bed until we're side by side. "You're not sure? Really?"

Words are escaping me at the moment, so I nod.

He scratches the hair on his chin. "What about the hangers?" he asks, gesturing toward the closet. "I stay here all the time. I basically already live here."

"Uh, hard disagree," I reply, surprised he'd make that leap.

"Sleeping here and living here are two very different things." A memory wiggles its way to the front of my mind. "Besides, you haven't even told me the stuff about your past. The stuff that only Gemma knows."

It could be seen as a low blow. I'm not trying to trigger his past trauma, but if we're going to have this discussion, really consider moving in together, I deserve to know him as well as Gemma does, don't I?

He pushes the sheets off his body and sits on the edge of the bed, reaching for his pants. "I don't want to get into that right now."

It feels like he's proving my point. "See? How are we supposed to take a huge step like this when you don't even trust me enough to share that with me?"

"I shouldn't have to talk about that part of my life. With you or anyone else."

I'd argue that any subject cloaked in this much visceral pain is the thing that needs to be talked about the most. Maybe not with me, but someone. Not Gemma. A professional of some kind.

Not that I can say any of that to him now. He wouldn't be receptive to it.

This isn't just about me, though. "Forgive me for wanting to know everything about the person who will live under the same roof as my daughter. I have a duty to protect her, Nic. I don't know why you think I'd love you any less if you told me the truth, but not telling me makes me imagine the worst."

He pulls his t-shirt over his head and wipes his cheek. "I understand," he says, his voice shaking. "I really do."

Then the panic sets in. The finality in his tone, the sight of him fully dressed. He's leaving, isn't he?

Men always leave.

My mother warned me, didn't she?

There's a reason that memory stands out among the rest, right? Why I can see it so clearly, decades later? Either I wanted to believe she was too smart to ever be wrong, or life repeatedly confirmed the accuracy of her assumption.

They all leave eventually.

They certainly always have. Every situationship, every boyfriend, every casual hookup—they all ended the same way. Not with me pursuing the breakup. Billy is the only exception, but that was after dozens of prior breakups and even more final straws. The time I ended things, it was already long over.

"I don't want you to leave," I beg Nic, wrapping the top sheet around me and coming to stand in front of him. "We were just saying I love you, fucking, what, five minutes ago? Come. Come back to bed." Can't we press pause on this whole discussion? Table it until we know more about each other? Why does this feel like it has irrevocably changed what we have?

He doesn't say anything, so I keep talking. Maybe if I keep telling him how much I love him, that heartbreak will fade from his eyes. "Just give me time. Please. I want us to be on the same page before moving forward. That's all."

"Okay." His voice breaks halfway through that word, and I wonder if there's any truth in it. He pulls me against his chest, but his arms are loose around me, and there's a stiffness in his posture that I don't recognize. "I'm going to head home," he says after he presses a quick kiss to my hair.

Tears start pouring out of me. "I don't want this to end. Why does it feel like it's ending?"

They all leave eventually.

"It's not ending. We should both take some time to think. To get on the same page."

Maybe it is ending, and he's saying whatever he needs to in

order to get me to calm down. I don't think Nic would do that, though.

"I'll still see you at the talent show on Friday, right?" I call out from the doorway.

He doesn't turn around. He lifts his arm and replies over his shoulder, "Yeah. See you there."

Since I have nothing else but his word, I take deep breaths as I watch his truck pull out of my driveway, hoping that even though he's leaving, there will come a day when he returns.

CHAPTER 18
DOMINIC

The pint glass in my hand has a smudge near the rim, and no matter how roughly I run the rag over it, the smudge remains. What a perfect metaphor for the current state of my life. Is that a metaphor? Who the fuck knows.

The last forty-eight hours have not been easy. They've made me long for the darkness from that first year as a zombie, in fact, because that's exactly what I've become. A mindless creature shrouded in darkness, unable to form coherent thoughts, staggering through my waking hours with a gaping chest wound where my heart should be.

She said she loved me, then that she didn't trust me enough to live with me. I don't know how to reconcile the two. It was my fault for asking her to move in so quickly after we said I love you, but I was just expressing how I felt, what I wanted to do. I was ready, and I thought she was too.

I should've known she'd bring up Gemma and the secrets I haven't been willing to share. She was right, and it's perfectly reasonable that she'd want me to tell her before allowing me to live with her and her daughter. I can't begrudge her prioritizing Jules's safety.

What I realized is that I wasn't ready to look at the horizon and accept what was coming. We were always going to end up here, in the place where we can't move forward without her knowing about my past, and me knowing the second I reveal it, she'll go running in the opposite direction. Maybe I foolishly hoped she'd forget. That we could proceed without addressing it ever again.

"Boss!" I hear Riz shout from beside me.

"Are you okay?" He looks gravely concerned as he glances down at my hand.

"Oh, shit." Without realizing, I squeezed the smudged glass so hard it shattered in my palm.

"The hell's wrong with you, man?" Vyla pops up on my other side, crouching down to collect the shards around my feet.

"Sorry," I reply in a flat tone. My hand is bleeding a bit, but I feel only numbness. "I'll go wash up."

I splash water on my face in the bathroom, pleased to see that the cuts on my hand have already stopped bleeding. My world feels like it's crumbling, and I'm racing around the pile with scotch tape trying to put it back together.

How am I going to face her at the talent show?

She can say it's not over all she wants, but whether it's now or several months from now, she's going to ask me about my past again, and I can either tell her and risk having to see her terrified reaction of me every time we cross paths for the rest of our lives, or not tell her, after which she'll definitely dump me, and risk having to see her terrified reaction of me—based on whatever horrors she's imagined—every time we cross paths for the rest of our lives. Either way, I lose the girl of my dreams.

What I won't do is bail on Jules. I already made a sign to

hold up in the crowd during her performance. Maybe I can go and hide somewhere in the back. She'll still spot me with the sign, but I won't have to see Lindsay.

To make matters worse, as if that's even possible, my rut is late. It's never late. If it doesn't show up by Saturday, I should probably call Dr. Yates and see if she needs to change my medication.

I was looking forward to being out of my mind for a couple of days in the hope that it would distract me from the heartache. At least the moving in discussion saved me from having to tell her about my monthly fuck frenzy. That's something.

When I emerge from the bathroom, Vlad is blocking my path back to the bar. "Need a refill?" I ask.

"You look like shit, you know that?" His voice is scratchy, and his New England accent is thicker than maple syrup. He looks around the bar. "Where's your lady? Haven't seen her around."

This ancient vampire has never, not once, asked me anything personal. Today, of all days, he wants to become buddies? "Yeah, she's been busy." It's the best I can do.

He shakes his head. "She ain't busy."

I wait for him to keep talking, but when he continues to stare at me, I step around him and head back behind the bar.

He plops down in front of me with the same assessing glare. "Don't be an idiot."

"Is that supposed to be helpful advice?"

"It is if you can look at yourself in the mirror and acknowledge that you're being an idiot."

I sigh, impatient. "Would you like a refill?"

"Hey, don't take that shit for granted, young man. Some of us"—he points to himself—"don't have that luxury."

It takes me a minute to realize he's talking about being able to see his reflection in the mirror. Maybe it was his attempt at a joke, but either way, I know I look like shit, and I don't appreciate him pointing it out. "So...refill?"

"Yeah, O negative," he growls, adding quietly, "idiot."

The rest of the day moves at the speed of molasses. I tell the others to take off early and that I'll lock up for the night. They continue to look at me funny, but none will pass up the chance to skip out on closing tasks.

After the tables are cleaned, the floor is mopped, and the doors are locked, I step out into the frigid night, and hope frostbite takes me out before I make it to my trailer. I'm pulling my keys out of my coat pocket when I hear the snapping of a branch behind me. Before I get the chance to turn around, darkness swallows me whole.

~

LINDSAY

What's the point of love, exactly? I'd like for someone to explain it to me. Because the whole, "it's better having loved and lost than to have never loved at all," quote makes absolutely no sense. This, what I'm experiencing right now, this deep yawning chasm of heartache that feels like it's never going to close...this is worse. I don't care how much fun the falling in love was. How I felt like I was floating above the ground whenever Nic touched me, or how protected I felt inside his big arms. This is so much worse.

He said it wasn't ending, but considering we haven't spoken in days, I'm taking it as a period at the end of the sentence that was our relationship.

Jules keeps asking where he is, and since I all I can say is, "I don't know, honey," I think she's starting to catch on.

When she asks if he's coming to the talent show tonight, I say yes, because despite whatever's going on with us, he promised her he'd be there, and I expect him to deliver on that promise.

I'm not sure what I'm hoping for when I take my seat in the audience an hour later. My eyes scan the crowd, but I don't spot him. When the lights go down in the stuffy high school gymnasium, I cross my fingers that he's about to sneak in and cheer from the back row.

Camilla sits down beside me, her husband and Hugo in tow, and gives my hand a comforting squeeze. She doesn't ask where Nic is, because she knows he's MIA. I told Natalie too. She said he's been acting weird at work but hasn't said anything about me.

Natalie's working tonight, but I'm relieved to have at least one person to enjoy the show with.

When Jules and Rocío are called to the stage, Camilla and I hoot and holler at the top of our lungs. "Good Luck, Babe" by Chappell Roan echoes through the speakers, and the lights come up on our two angels. I forget about Nic entirely.

I know every move Jules makes before she makes it, and my hands mimic hers throughout the entire song. Their moves are impressively fast and tight, but I remind myself that this is the TikTok generation, and they've been dancing for an audience since before I started growing hairs out of my chin. When Chappell belts out, "I told you so," the girls hold a cheeky pose that charms the crowd.

The performance ends with Rocío landing a backflip with her elbows on her knees, and Jules leaning her elbows on Rocío's shoulders, both cheesing as cheers erupt. Camilla and I are on our feet screaming for them.

They don't win the show, but they do get second place, which comes with two fifty-dollar gift cards to Tome Time bookstore. After the show ends, I hear them discussing the list of books they plan to buy, so clearly it was a victory.

When we get out to the parking lot, Camilla and Morty say their goodbyes, and the girls give each other one last death grip of a hug before reluctantly letting go. Once her dance partner is out of sight, I watch Jules scan the faces of the crowd still exiting the high school, and my stomach sinks.

"Where's Dominic?" She turns to face me, her eyes wide with disbelief. "He didn't come?"

I suck in a breath and promise myself to only do this once. That because of how good he's been with Jules, he's earned this one favor. "He wasn't feeling well, pumpkin, so he couldn't make it. He said to tell you he'd be cheering you on from bed, though."

She looks disappointed but she buys the lie.

Maybe she'd be more upset if she weren't so used to the men in her life letting her down. *Welcome to the club, baby girl.*

I plan on texting Nic tomorrow and letting him know I covered for him, but this was the first and last time. Him bailing on her helped me shake off some lingering sadness, too, because how dare he let my perfect girl down? The fucking audacity of that is ridiculous.

Any man I choose to move in with needs to show up for me and my daughter. That's a line in the sand that I'm drawing today.

We get home and celebrate with some leftover bibimbap with kimchi and extra gochujang sauce, and ice cream sandwiches. I let her stay up as late as she wants, but once the adrenaline wears off, her eyes get heavy and she's in bed by ten.

I settle into the couch with a glass of red wine and allow myself to accept what tonight really means. He didn't show up for Jules; therefore, he didn't show up for me. He didn't come because he didn't want to. Because this is over. It was ending while he was telling me it wasn't.

I can't stop the tears that fall, so I curl into a ball and let them. I cry for so long, a dull throb forms behind my eyelids, and I try to sleep. To let the sobs fade into snores. But as my cheeks start to dry, I hear my phone ringing beneath my pillow.

When I pull it out, I'm taken aback by the name on the screen.

"Mom?" I say when I accept the FaceTime.

Her face isn't in the frame. I don't know what I'm looking at.

"Mom? You there?"

"Lindsay?" I hear several rustling noises, and then her face appears. "What's wrong? Are you okay?"

"You called me."

"No, your face. Have you been crying?"

I don't know what it is about hearing your mother ask that question, but it turns me into a weeping child with a skinned knee, desperate for the comfort only a mom can provide. Between shallow breaths and sniffles, I tell her everything. Or rather, everything that doesn't outright reveal that Nic is a zombie. She never interrupts. Just listens to me cry and waits until I'm finished talking.

I'm eager for her to take my side. To agree that men are useless and terrible, and they always leave. I expect her to validate my feelings.

Instead, she says, "Sweetie, I think you should give him a chance to explain."

What the hell?

"Are you kidding me? What about *they all leave eventually?* Remember?"

"Men always…leave?" She repeats the phrase slowly, as if it's brand new to her. "What are you talking about?"

I scoff. "Remember when you and Dad got into that huge fight right before the divorce and you took me and Isla to that hotel room? You told me *men all leave eventually.* That's what you said. And you were right."

Her eyebrows knit together. "I said that?"

Is she serious? "How can you not remember?"

She rests her chin in her palm. "Probably because your father and I had thousands of fights back then, and I probably said a lot of silly things like that. There are too many to remember." She chews on the inside of her lip. "Doesn't mean any of it was true."

"What do you mean? Men do always leave. They have for me."

"No, they haven't." When I look at her blankly, she adds, "Your father never left. We got divorced, sure, but he never left."

I'm struggling to process what she's saying, likely because one of my core memories now has this weird blurry film over it, making me question whether it ever happened.

"We were never supposed to get married," she says with a wistful grin. "We were best friends in college. I helped him cheat on his tests. Then we started dating, and I got pregnant. At the time, we did what we thought was right. We got married, and I dropped out of school to be home with you."

None of this is new information, but I can tell she's going somewhere with it. Somewhere different.

"I had no close friends to lean on, and my parents hated the fact that they fought so hard, went through so much to make sure I had a good education, and I threw it all away by getting pregnant. They wouldn't have supported an abortion either, so there was no way to make them happy."

"We were so thrilled when you came along." She's smiling bigger now, and I can't help smiling too. "It felt like we were doing everything right. But then, I don't know what happened. I became a different person. It was a struggle to get out of bed, to shower, and with you...I hated myself for it, but part of me didn't want to hold you."

She's never shared much about her postpartum depression, but I knew it was there, because it never really left. From as far back as I can remember, I was the child who made her sad, and Isla fixed whatever I'd broken.

"I didn't know the name for it at the time, and going to a therapist was seen as a moral failure, so I didn't. I tried to manage it on my own, but it was ruthless. It destroyed me." Her voice cracks a little, and I give her the same space she just gave me. "I tried to heal myself however I could, short of medication and therapy. So I kept trying new things, hoping one would stick. I remember thinking, maybe a chia pet is the secret to my loneliness, and maybe if I grow enough of them, I'll be the mother I want to be."

"A chia pet?" I chuckle. "Really?"

"They were a big deal back then." She waves a dismissive hand. "Then I started looking into law school. My future looked bright, and even when I got pregnant with Isla, I knew I could still do this, just at a slower pace, you know? Graduate and take the bar exam on my own time. I felt much more prepared for Isla than I did for you, and I regret that every day."

"It's fine," I tell her, but she's quick to press me on it.

"No, it's not. I can see how not fine it all was because now I'm in therapy and taking the proper medication, and I know that I wasn't the mother you needed me to be. The mother you deserved."

Here come the tears again.

"Another huge regret I still carry is not teaching you girls about where you came from, but I want you to understand that I didn't know either. Not really. Not like I do now. Because my father was in the army, our only goal when he was stationed somewhere new was to assimilate. To become as American as possible. We didn't even speak Korean at home because they wanted me to be fluent in English. I had to blend in wherever we went, and that's hard when you're the only Asian kid in school. Not every school I transferred to, but a lot of them."

I knew my grandparents were strict, and because he was in the army, they moved around a lot, but I don't think I realized how tough that lifestyle would've been on my mom.

"I guess what I'm trying to say is that I have a lot of regrets, but I'm trying to do things differently. I'm trying to enjoy my retirement. I want to try new things and old things and give things a chance that maybe I wasn't ready for earlier in my life."

The revolving door of hobbies certainly makes more sense now. And maybe I should just accept that Mom and I are on different journeys to reclaim our roots. Hell, even Isla and I are on different journeys. I shouldn't keep expecting Mom to be the one to teach me when I can learn about it myself and make it a bigger part of Jules's life than it was in mine.

"Do you regret not remarrying after Dad?" The question spills out of me before I can stop it. I have always wondered, though. I don't even remember her going on dates after the divorce. From the outside, it looked like she gave up on the concept of love altogether.

"No, not at all," she replies confidently. "I dated a few men, but I enjoy my alone time far too much to share my house with another person. If I wanted to remarry, I promise you, I would've."

"Well, maybe we're the same in that way."

She shakes her head, her gaze almost sad. "No, we're not,

Lindsay. You feel things deeply, and you love with every bone in your body. You're three parts passion, one part empathy. All you do is love."

"What about fury?" I ask, surprised she didn't mention my temper in her measurement of my soul.

"Passion is a coin with two sides. It can become love or fury depending on how it falls."

"I guess that's true."

She lets out a sigh. "For a long time, I was worried your dad and I messed you up so badly, you weren't capable of the kind of love we always wanted for you."

I jerk back. "And what about *this* makes you think I'm not messed up?"

"Sweetie, go look in a mirror. You might be messed up now, but it's not because you're incapable of love. It's written all over your face. Just like it was the day we met Dominic."

"What are you saying?" I ask, my heart pounding.

"I'm saying maybe he hasn't left at all. Don't make assumptions. Go go talk to him."

CHAPTER 19
LINDSAY

Nic isn't answering his phone. It's going straight to voicemail. He's not answering his texts either. What I'd normally dismiss as rejection by an asshole, I'm freaking out that maybe something terrible has happened.

As soon as it hits eleven on Saturday morning, I drop Jules off with Camilla and head straight for the bar. Vyla and Natalie are pulling the stools off the tables when I walk in, and Riz is wiping the tables down.

"When was the last time any of you heard from Dominic?" My voice is loud and thick and shaky with nerves, but I don't care. If my mom is right, he could be in pain and in need of help.

Riz and Vyla both say they saw him here at the bar two days ago, and Natalie saw him the day before that.

"Two days? That doesn't seem odd to any of you? Two whole days without any communication?"

The three of them look at each other, trying to decide if I'm right.

"Well, there have been stretches where he has a few days off in a row," Vyla points out.

"Yeah, and we knew his rut was coming," Riz adds. "He usually texts me the day it arrives and lets me know he can't come in, but I assumed—"

"His rut? What's that?" I have no idea what they're talking about, but I know for sure this is something he's never mentioned to me.

"His rut," Riz repeats. When I continue to look at Riz like he's speaking another language, he asks, "Has he not told you about that yet?"

I shake my head, panic creeping up my spine. "Okay, can we skip past the part where you all hem and haw about whether he should be the one to explain it and just fucking tell me?"

Vyla is the one to explain it to me, and even when she does, I ask her to explain it again.

"So, it's like a period, except that it only lasts forty-eight hours, and instead of bleeding or cramping, he has the constant desire to ejaculate?"

Vyla nods. "Yeah, basically."

"And during that time, he typically holes up in his trailer and asks us not to call or visit," Riz adds.

"But he'll still answer texts about orders or billing," Natalie points out.

Natalie knew this about her boss before I knew it about my boyfriend. I'll need to unpack that later.

"So he's likely in his trailer?"

They nod.

"Can someone text or call him to confirm that he's fine and just in the middle of his rut? Say it's an emergency or do whatever you have to do to get him to respond. I just...have a really bad feeling."

The three of them spring into action. Natalie pulls out her phone and starts typing. Vyla pulls hers out and calls him. Riz shouts over his shoulder that he's going to check Nic's trailer before racing out into the cold.

Vyla purses her lips. "Not answering."

"Did it go straight to voicemail for you?" I ask.

She nods.

Natalie's staring at her screen, waiting for a response. I take this opportunity to get my steps in by pacing around the bar. Five minutes eke by, then ten. He still hasn't responded to Natalie's text by the time Riz returns, amazingly not sweating or out of breath after running to Nic's trailer and back.

"He's not there," he says grimly. "These were on the ground outside." In his hand are Nic's keys.

I feel myself stumble, but I recover almost as quickly. Crippling fear is replaced by something deep. Feral. I suppose you could call it passion, or maybe it's the other side of the coin. "Where does Gemma live?"

Vyla insists on taking me to Gemma's house, while Riz and Natalie agree to stay at the bar until they hear otherwise from us.

"She's a demon, you know," Vyla says as we walk up her driveway. "A succubus. Do you know what that means?"

My nails dig into my palm as I clench my fist. In my other hand is a wooden baseball bat I found in Nic's office. "I know it might take more than a few swings to pop her head off, but I've got time."

She grabs my arm. "Lindsay, she's got enhanced physical strength. She's stronger than Dominic when she wants to be. She also has powers of manipulation and seduction." Vyla sighs. "Knowing what you might be walking into, do you still want to do this?"

Sure, I could come face to face with the man I love having

animalistic sex with the only Mapletown resident I hate, but what if he's not? What if she's taking out her revenge on him because he rejected her? I couldn't live with myself if it's the latter. "Yeah," I tell her, choking up on the bat. "Let's do it."

Vyla goes in first, keeping her feet light the deeper we go into the house. It's relatively quiet, apart from the occasional sound coming from somewhere upstairs. I poke Vyla in the arm and gesture up the stairs with the bat. She nods and puts a finger to her lips, reminding me to keep quiet.

As we ascend the stairs, I hear a soft, "Yoo-hoo, Dommy Dom," from the bedroom on the left. The door is cracked. He's in there. With *her*. I run into Vyla's back as I charge the rest of the way, and she picks up her pace to give me the room.

"What in the actual fuck is this?" Vyla demands after pushing the door open. It slams against the wall and rattles on its hinges.

I push my way around her, and I understand the tone of Vyla's question. It's not sex I'm looking at. Nic doesn't appear to be hurt, either. There are no visible cuts or bruises.

But he is asleep. Out cold, in fact.

Gemma's standing next to Nic's lifeless form, and her expression is completely unbothered.

I decide in that moment to beat the face off her face.

"What the fuck have you done!" I shout, swinging the bat in the direction of her skull. I don't get very far. Vyla's big hands grip my biceps and yank me back.

Gemma, to her credit, doesn't try to retaliate. If anything, she seems shocked by my rage. Then she takes a breath and rubs her eyes. "Okay, I may have given him a little too much of this sleep aid I got from the apothecary. I wanted him relaxed, not passed out." I don't know what she sees on mine and Vyla's faces, but whatever it is makes her shoulders tremble. "This isn't my fault, okay? I gave him the proper dosage, and it didn't seem to work, so I gave him more."

The bat falls from my hand and makes a loud clatter on the floor. "What did you give him?" I ask through gritted teeth. "And how much?"

I dial Camilla on speaker phone, and when she answers after one ring, I hold the phone toward Gemma. "Tell her," I say.

She lifts her shoulders with a *Tell her what?* expression, and it takes everything I have not to lunge at her and use my long acrylic nails to claw her fucking eyes out. "Tell. Her."

"Hi, Camilla, it's Gemma. I, um, sort of gave Dominic too much of a sleep aid from the apothecary and was wondering if there's anything I can do to wake him up."

"Wow, really, Gemma?" Camilla replies, her tone a deadly slither. "You drugged Dominic." A statement, not a question. "Describe what you gave him."

The apothecary is run by the town coven. They all take turns managing the place. I'm lucky that one of Camilla's shifts is happening right now.

"It's a gray powder," she says, her feet shifting from side to side.

"She's fucked," Vyla whispers in my ear. "It's over for her."

I don't entirely know what that means, but from context, I assume Gemma's in a lot of trouble, and she knows it.

"Did you mix it with water before putting it in his drink?" Camilla asks.

"You roofied him?" I bellow, and Vyla has to restrain me again, but she struggles as my rage builds. "You...you knew his rut was about to start, didn't you? What, so you were going to drug him and then..." I don't need to finish that sentence. We all know how it ends.

She waves her hands in front of her frantically like she's

trying to cool herself down. "Relaxed! I just wanted him relaxed!" she shouts back. "I thought if I could get him to chill, I could remind him of how much fun we used to have together. Then his rut would make it hard for him to deny me."

"You vile piece of shit!"

I fight against the strong hands that keep me in place, but then Vyla says, "Don't, Linds. You touch her without consent, and you'll end up in jail too. You'll never be able to come back here."

My breaths are coming out in labored pants as I sag against Vyla, feeling powerless and hating it. Camilla's voice fills the room, and I realize my phone is on the floor. "You guys still there?"

"I'm texting Otto," Vyla whispers.

The sheriff with tentacles who arrested Finn on Halloween night. Good.

I look back at her and nod.

"Yeah, we're here," I say to Camilla.

"Gemma, did you hear my question?"

Gemma picks at her red nails, looking everywhere in the room but at me. "I didn't put it in his drink, no." She clears her throat. "I, um, mixed it with saline and sort of...injected it into his neck."

"Jesus Christ, are you serious?" Camilla asks.

Her tone alone sends me careening off the edge of fury and into something so deep and hot there's no English word to accurately capture it. Interestingly, though, I don't lash out this time. I remain still. Something thrums in my belly, barely noticeable at first, but present. The feeling starts to grow, and my eyes drift to the floor-to-ceiling bookcase behind Gemma, almost overflowing with books. If she were anyone else, I'd compliment her shelf game and ask for recommendations, but since she's a fart in the shape of a demon, I focus on the eerie pull I feel from the top of the bookcase.

The tingle rises from my belly and into my lungs, and as alien as it is, I let it chart its course. It creeps up my spine and circles my neck and warms my cheeks. Gemma and Camilla are still talking, but I'm no longer listening. All of my focus is on the bookcase, and I feel compelled to keep my eyes on it, waiting for...a signal, maybe? Not that the bookcase feels sentient, or anything, but there's something about it–

I hear the splintering of wood first, and then the books fall. Every book blasts off the shelves and straight toward Gemma with a force that doesn't fit the scene. The bookcase is collapsing, but it sounds and feels like it's exploding. The books pummel Gemma, one by one. She cries out at first, holding up her arms to block her face, but there are too many of them and they just keep coming. She staggers to her knees, whimpering. Then a particularly thick hardcover book hits her square in the temple, and she drops, out cold. The shelves fall on top of the pile in jagged pieces, and the room goes quiet.

Somewhere beneath that pile of rubble is my mortal enemy, and I can't help but smile.

"Oh. My. God," Vyla says beside me. She scrambles to pick up my phone. "Camilla, you need to get over here right now." Then disconnects the call.

Nic is still out cold, though I'm not sure how, with all the ruckus. That drug must be crazy strong.

Camilla shows up a few minutes later, and surveys the scene in the bedroom. She quickly checks Nic's pulse, lifting his eyelids to check his pupils. "He'll be fine, I checked with the coven. He'll probably sleep for another day or so while it wears off." Then she looks at the bookcase, and back at me. "You did this."

It's not a question, but I'm honored she thinks I'm capable of this.

"Uh, no. The bookcase fell over. I was just enjoying the show."

Vyla chuckles. "Nah, babe. You did it."

There's a commotion downstairs, and Vyla leaves to take care of it. Camilla puts a hand on my shoulder. "Tell me, Linds, were you really mad when the bookcase fell?"

"Yeah."

"And were you looking at it when it fell? Like, couldn't tear your eyes away from it?"

"Yeah."

"And while you were looking at it, did you feel anything, like, say, a growing heat in your chest that moved up your body the longer you looked at it?"

"Yeah. Wait, how did you know that?"

She cups my face and lets out a squeal. "We've found your power, little witch."

I cover her hands with mine. "Whoa, really? What do you mean?"

"Uh huh. Good old-fashioned telekinesis."

As in, I can move things around with my mind? "That's crazy," I reply, dumbstruck. "How can you be sure?"

"Most witches who have it don't notice until something happens to draw out an extreme reaction. You're not in control of it yet, so until you are, it's going to appear when your emotions are most heightened, like"—she gestures at the pile of books and wood—"when your soulmate is almost sexually assaulted by a hideous monster, for instance."

"You think he's my soulmate?" I know it's the last thing I should be focusing on right now, but I can't help it.

"Oh, big time. A temporary relationship wouldn't affect you like this. Part of you knows he's it, even if the rest of you isn't ready to admit it." She nudges me with her shoulder. "But in other good news, we know what kind of witch you are now."

"Yeah?"

She nods. "You, my dear, are a gray witch."

I vaguely remember reading that in the list of types of witches, but I can't remember what it means.

As if reading my thoughts, Camilla explains, "Gray witches practice magic that's both light and dark. You straddle the line, which means you're incredibly powerful. Most covens keep their magic light, in an effort to fight for the greater good, but also because too many baby witches dabbled in black magic before they were ready and placed curses that seasoned witches had to go in and reverse. Dark magic is highly advanced, but to gray witches it comes naturally. You were born with the power to right wrongs using your magic. Do you understand? You can redirect bad energy to where it needs to go. You can correct injustice. *You can avenge.*"

I sit with what Camilla said and let it settle as a million things happen around me.

Gemma is unearthed from the pile of books, still unconscious, handcuffed, and dropped into the back seat of Otto's cruiser. Vyla and I provide our statements, and Otto, without being able to say for certain, thinks Gemma will be sent to the rehab facility in Iceland for an extended period of time based on the severity of the crime committed. If she passes the test at the end of her stay, she can leave but she will never return to Mapletown. She'll also have to wear a neon yellow bracelet at all times that identifies her as a convicted sexual predator.

Her house and her belongings will be auctioned off by the town. She'll lose everything.

Camilla calls Morty, and he and Riz maneuver Nic onto a hospital bed, which they carry out of Gemma's house and transport into my living room. When Camilla is back home with the kids, she texts me and says that Jules will stay at her house for the next two days, so that Nic can recover in private.

I'm tempted to press her on it but I decide not to. I have no idea what's going to happen when Nic wakes up. Will he be deep in his rut and start ripping off my clothes, or will he come out of the drug induced haze slowly and want to talk about our future?

Over the next twelve hours, I continue to check Nic's pulse and keep a fresh cold cloth on his forehead. I remember Riz said he left Nic's phone in his truck when he drove it over here, and I hurry out to grab it so I can charge it for him. On the floor of the passenger side, there's a bright yellow poster rolled up and secured with a rubber band.

In big black letters, it says, "Go Jules! Dancing Queen! You've got this. -Zad"

Zad? Could that be short for... I suck in a breath. "Zombie dad," I mutter aloud. Has she been calling him that? Without me noticing? How?

My gaze drifts to the center console, and I find a folded piece of lined paper in the left cupholder. I shouldn't be snooping like this, but when the top of the paper reads, "Lindsay Abbadelli: Likes and Dislikes," I refuse to stop. On this list, he's written everything I've mentioned liking or hating.

"Likes: Alanis Morrissette, Green Day, Drew Barrymore, Lilith Fair, cooking, sleeping with her foot out of the blanket, coupons, getting her nails done, everything Jules, fancy clothes, and peanut butter cups."

"Dislikes: Picnics, men, Jules's father, too much Carolina Reaper sauce, banana and mayo sandwiches, seafood, spiders, Gemma, and when she doesn't know where I am."

He's even got, "Flowers" in the dislikes column, with an arrow next to it and, "Allergic to baby's breath."

There's also a circled note at the bottom of the page that

says, "Mapping. She doesn't always realize she's picking at her skin. She doesn't want to do it, but there's something about it that soothes her. Keep an eye out for her touching her face. Try to help."

I press the page to my chest and try to steady my breathing. How could I ever doubt the love this man feels for me? It no longer matters what Gemma knows about him that I don't. He can keep his secrets if that makes him feel better. The man who wrote this is the man I want beside me, under my roof with Jules. I have no doubt about that now.

We all die alone, and I was prepared to do just that. Men have done nothing but disappoint me. I was sure I'd be better off without them. Then a teddy bear in a zombie-skin suit flipped my world upside down.

Now I just need to wait for my teddy bear to wake up.

CHAPTER 20
DOMINIC

My throat is burning. I'm not sure of much at the moment, but I do know that. I smack my lips together, which hurts since they're so dry.

"Hey," a silky voice says from beside me. "Thirsty?"

I grunt in response, my lips parting farther. I feel the straw when it hits my tongue and desperately start sucking the cool liquid down my throat.

"Slow down," the voice says. "If you drink too much, you'll get sick."

My eyes flutter open and hovering above me is the face of an angel. An angel with long dark hair and different-colored eyes. "Where am I?" I ask in a very scratchy grating voice.

She tells me I'm at her house, that I've been drugged by a woman named Gemma.

Gemma! As soon as I hear the name, my memories come flooding back.

I felt a pinch on the back of my neck while standing outside my trailer. The next thing I knew, Gemma was flying? No, that can't be right. Maybe she was dancing. Yeah, dancing around me in a tight navy-blue dress, telling me to relax so we could have fun. And then...there's not much beyond that.

Lindsay starts crying as she holds my hand. "I was so worried about you when you didn't come to the talent show."

I pinch my eyes shut. "I fucking missed it?" I ask, devastated. "Unbelievable. How'd Jules do?"

"They won second place."

"That's great." Then realization hits. "Did she wonder where I was?"

She nods. "I told her you weren't feeling well, which isn't untrue."

Shame sits like a boulder in my gut. "I'm so sorry, Lindsay. I wanted to be there. I made—"

"I know," she says, cutting me off. "I found the sign in your truck."

I lift my hand to cup her cheek. "Why are you crying? I'm okay, lioness."

The nickname makes her cry harder. "I'm sorry, Nic. I'm the one who's sorry."

"What do you mean?"

She swallows, as if summoning the courage to say what she's about to. "You don't have to tell me anything about your past, okay? If it's hard for you to talk about, then don't talk about it. I'll still love you. I don't care. I love you now, and nothing will change that. Just don't leave me again. Never leave."

Her forehead drops to my chest, and I can feel my heart breaking beneath my bones. She's giving me so much of herself, all because she was worried about me. If I truly love her as much as I say I do, as much as I think I do, then I owe it to her to reveal the truth. I can only hope that she still has enough love left in her to forgive me.

I spot my phone on the table beside the bed. "Can you give me my phone, please? I need to show you something."

She looks up at me, eyes bloodshot and snot running down her nose. I want to tattoo this image on the inside of my eyelids so I never forget how radiant she is. Then she hands me my phone.

It doesn't take long to dig up the well-hidden file. I never go near it, but I could never forget what's inside. I click on the video in the folder and hand the phone back to her, willing my thumping heart to slow down.

"Press play whenever you're ready."

She does, and I hear the unmistakable sound of me screaming. There's a clanging of chains against thick steel bars, and the bizarre, inhuman groan that falls out of me and everyone else newly infected with the virus.

I don't look at her while she's watching it. I can't.

I hear her gasp when Dr. Yates uses a cattle prod to shock me through the cage, and a strangled whimper when the footage changes to me in a medical chair, my arms and legs strapped down. This was months after the cage clip, when I regained my ability to speak.

"What did you do?" Dr. Yates asks.

"I don't know," I say through ragged sobs.

"Yes, you do. Tell me."

She pokes me with the cattle prod and I shout, "I killed people!"

"How many people?"

Another shock.

"Ah!" I howl in pain, bucking against my restraints. "Three! My br-brother."

Another shock.

"Who else?"

"The two cops who found us."

"How did you kill them?"

Another shock.

"Ah, please! Not again. I'll tell you whatever you want."

"How?"

"I-I ripped their heads off!"

"Then what?" Dr. Yates's tone is cold and firm.

"I ate them," I mutter, voice lowering a few octaves without the additional shock. "I ate their brains. Th-then I left their bodies to rot."

The video stops.

I still can't open my eyes. I don't want to see the look of disgust and horror twisting Lindsay's beautiful features. It'll crush me.

"You can go if you want," I say, barely louder than a whisper. "I'll understand if you want to go."

I hear my phone being put down on the table, then I feel her forehead pressed against mine, her breath hot and sweet as it fans my lips. "Hey. Look at me."

I open my eyes to find hers filled with longing. It's not at all what I expected.

"I'm not afraid of you, Dominic. Do you hear me?" She pulls back to hold my gaze. "Is that what you were worried about? Me seeing that and, what, running away?"

Does she really have to ask? "Well, yeah."

She shakes her head. "That video isn't scary. It's fucking devastating. What you went through..." she trails off, trying to hold the tears back. "I'm just so sorry you had to survive that. That you have to carry this guilt around for something you don't remember doing. For something you did when you weren't even you."

"That's an excuse," I explain. "You can't excuse this, Lindsay. I killed people. Didn't you hear me? Two cops. My brother. I killed my brother."

"No," she insists. "You chased a violent need to stay alive while a virus ravaged your body and robbed you of coherent thought. Don't compare what you did to a drunk driver or whatever. It's not the same."

"But the result is the same." I pull out of her grasp, frustrated that she's ignoring the most important part of it. "Those three are still dead, and they wouldn't be if it weren't for me."

At that, she nods, and I feel like I'm getting through to her.

"That may be true, but that person in the cage, that…thing, it wasn't you, and I don't care if you agree with me or not. You're not without flaws, okay? I'll admit that, but you were clearly someone else when you did that, and you're in no way that same person today. I know your secret now. I watched the video with my own eyes, and I don't love you any less."

"How?" I demand. "How?"

"If anything, I love you even more."

"This is lunacy."

"Nope," she says, pressing a kiss to my palm. "It's love."

"Ugh." I roll my eyes. "I won't let you do this. You can't forgive me."

She laughs. "Oops, too late. I already did."

Then she runs her fingers through my hair, and selfish monster that I am, I lean into her touch when I know the right thing to do is pull away.

"Listen, I'm not trying to make light of their deaths. It's incredibly tragic, and it shouldn't have happened. Nothing could ever make up for that loss."

"Finally, you see sense."

"But would you like to know why it was so easy to forgive you?"

I let out an exasperated sigh. "Why?"

"Because no amount of jail time, torture, or even an eternity in hell will punish you as much as you continue to punish yourself, and likely will until your time on this mortal plane is over. And even then, it won't bring those three back to life. That's your burden to carry, but from where I'm sitting, I see a man trying to learn and grow and do better every single day. You take every opportunity to help your community. You're a loyal friend, and a wonderful, generous partner." She pauses, holding me in her gaze. "Whoever that guy in the cage was, he's gone. You need to let him go."

My voice cracks as I ask, "How?"

"For starters, you can start leaning on me for help. You're not alone in the world anymore, Nic. I can help you make sure you never lose yourself. I should probably get on a Zoom call with Dr. Yates so I can fully understand your medication, the side effects, and what to do if you run out, things like that. Also, the brain powder. I want to make sure we always have a lot of it in the house."

I don't know what to say, so I say nothing. Eventually, I pull Lindsay into the bed next to me and let myself fall apart in her arms. She holds me the entire time, rubbing my back and whispering *I love yous* into my ear.

When the tears subside, she asks, "So, any other secrets you'd like to share?"

I almost shake my head no, but then I remember. "Yes, actually." I turn to face her. "You should know that I'm bisexual."

She cackles. "No shit. Me too."

"Really?"

"Yeah."

"I thought I heard Natalie tell Vyla you were straight."

"Oh," she replies, confused. "Natalie might not know, come to think of it. It's not something I talk about or share on social media. But yeah, I'm as bi as a bottlenose dolphin."

My eyebrows lift. "Bottlenose dolphin?"

"Yeah, they're famously bisexual."

Huh. Who'da thunk?

"Have you dated men in the past?"

I nod. "One before the change, and one during my recovery, before Dr. Yates released us. Though, both were more casual hookups than serious relationships." It feels good to get that off my chest. I didn't expect Lindsay to judge me for it, but you never know. Bisexual men aren't as widely accepted as bisexual women. "What about you?" I ask. "Any secrets?"

"Ooh," she says, rubbing her palms together. "Let's see... I've gotten Botox on my forehead, and I might want to do it again someday. Once, I pretended my cat died to get out of a really bad date. Um..." She continues, listing them on her fingers now. "I pierced my sister's ears with a thumbtack, they got infected, and I told my parents her friend did it. Sometimes I forget to wash my legs in the shower, and, oh! I've been known to flirt with the employees at Wendy's so they'll give me free fries."

I sit there, awestruck, trying to absorb her list of offenses.

"What do you think? Can you still love a monster like me?"

I gently nip at the tip of her nose. "Nothing could ever make me stop."

EPILOGUE

LINDSAY

A MONTH LATER...

"Wait, can you show me again?" I ask Anton. We're prepping ingredients in the kitchen, and he's trying to teach me a cutting technique that I will never be able to replicate. It's impressive as hell to watch, though.

"You put your cucumbers here, your tomatoes here, your onions here, and your potatoes here," he says, pointing at the different vegetables on four separate cutting boards. "Then you get your knives," he lifts four sharp blades in the air using his tentacles, "and you dice!" His limbs move at lightning speed as the veggies are diced into small, neat shapes. His eyes stay on me, while his tentacles move independently with expert precision.

"Wow," I say with an appraising clap. "Incredible."

He's become one of my favorite people in town. We work well together in the kitchen, prepping ingredients, managing different stations, and splitting the tasks evenly for the current dishes on the menu. We've been brainstorming a new spring selection—just a few new dishes that we can easily fold into the rush—and he's just as eager to try new recipes as I am.

I still only work part time, but since my shift ends at four each day, Anton has everything measured out and organized before the dinner crowd rolls in. That also leaves me enough time to meet Jules when she gets home from science club.

"Lioness?" Nic calls out from the bar.

I find him standing in the middle of the floor with a hand behind his back and a smirk tugging at his lips.

"What are you up to?"

"I've got a surprise for you." Then he nods for me to follow, and like a puppy, I do.

When we get outside, he stands behind me and covers my eyes as we continue to walk deeper into the field behind the bar. We must walk for ten minutes like this before he pulls us to a stop.

"Okay, open your eyes."

It's his trailer, but the door is hanging open.

"Step inside."

I follow his command and find a completely empty space, apart from a stack of old desktop computer monitors and what looks like an old copy machine. On a chair in the corner sits a pair of safety goggles and a sledgehammer. "What exactly—"

"It's a smash room," he says with a grin.

"A smash room?"

He grabs the goggles and gently pulls them over my eyes. "Camilla said you need to manage your rage before you can start practicing your telekinesis with the coven, so I figured this could be a way to do that."

He places the sledgehammer in my hands and backs out of the trailer.

"You want me to obliterate this shit with a hammer?" It's not my birthday, but it certainly feels like it.

He pops his head through the open window. "Yes, darling. Bash it up good, okay? Remember, it's for your craft, so don't hold back."

I swing the hammer up over my head and try to summon my most rage-filled memories. They come in waves, and I let my body take over. Hard plastics and sheet metal bend and crumple beneath my weapon, and I picture the faces of Billy, Gemma, and my former boss as I continue to swing and smash.

It doesn't take long for my arms to tire out, and I can already feel the soreness setting in. Clearly, I need to work on my upper body strength if I plan to spend more time in the smash room, which I absolutely do.

I toss my goggles off, drop the hammer, and race into Nic's arms as he stands outside, pride evident in his expression. Then I launch myself into his arms. He catches me easily and twirls me around.

"You made me a smash room," I sing-song as calm settles over my body. It's the same way I felt after bringing the bookcase down onto Gemma—bone-deep serenity.

"You know I did," he replies, slowing down and setting me on my feet. "Your rage is who you are, lioness. We're not trying to tame it; we just need to figure out how to help you channel it into something greater."

I gaze up at Nic's face and let myself get lost in those light blue eyes for a moment. "Are you sure I'm not too much for you?"

"I'm sure. You'll never be too much for me, Lindsay, and you're not going to scare me away. I see every layer of you— even the ones you try to cover up—and I want them all." He kisses me, his tongue swiping into my mouth, playful, but also a promise. "We should get home," he says, the sound of his voice rougher and lower than usual. I know what that means.

"Your rut?"

He nods, groaning as he palms my ass. "My rut."

He told me he shouldn't drive when he's in his rut. It's just not safe. But clearly having me behind the wheel during his rut isn't safe either, because he's pressed up against my side, tracing the shell of my ear with his tongue, and it feels so good I can barely focus on the road.

Miraculously, I get us home in one piece. Jules is sleeping over at Rocío's tonight, so we don't need to worry about peeping teens as we race into the house ripping our clothes off.

I worried at first about combining his stuff with my stuff when we moved in together, where it would all go and if there'd be enough room, but it turns out, I never had to worry, because Nic doesn't really have stuff. His wardrobe is painfully limited, all of his skin, hair, and body needs are met with only three products—lucky bastard—and beyond that, it was a handful of trinkets and books that we pulled from his trailer. My things remain delightfully spread out and right where I need them.

"Fuck, you're soaked," he moans against my neck as he inserts a finger. I wiggle out of my leggings and kick them off with my socks and underwear. His t-shirt follows, then his heart-shaped lips latch onto my nipple, and I feel his teeth graze the tip as he starts fucking me with his hand.

It's nice. Fucking extraordinary is a better word for it, but it's not enough.

I reach down and cup his hard cock through his boxer briefs. "Need you to fuck me," I beg as I suck the skin at the base of his throat.

His boxers go flying behind him, and he lifts me up, slamming my back against the wall as he gives the same attention to my other aching nipple. When I wrap my legs around his hips, it takes one swift motion for him to push inside me and seat himself to the hilt.

"Oh, yes," I cry out as he drives into my wet heat, my back banging so hard against the wall that all the framed photos around us are rattling. "Harder." It's hilarious that he ever worried about being too rough for me to handle. This body of mine is made for his rough side.

The suckler finds my clit, and I forget my own name.

"You feel so fucking good," he groans against my lips as he thrusts, my hips meeting his with matching intensity. "I'm not gonna last."

It's the only warning I get before he pulls out and bends me over our dining room table, my ass in the air as come drips down my inner thighs. He slaps my ass once, twice, and I yelp in pain and pleasure both. He responds by gently kissing and rubbing my tender flesh. I feel him swipe a finger along my folds, then a surprising drop of warm liquid at my back entrance. "Nic," I pant, desperate for him to proceed with whatever he as planned. "Please."

He spreads my come around the tight ring of muscle, and just when I prepare my body to take him there, he thrusts back into my pussy.

"Holy fucking shit!" I cry out as the suckler dips into the wetness Nic pooled there and starts flicking and sucking and teasing my asshole with its tiny inner tongue. Every nerve comes alive as my body starts to tremble and my legs feel like jelly.

Nic reaches around, swiping across my clit with his thumb, and I'm so lost to the sensations of everywhere he's touching that I feel like I'm floating. To be outside and so very inside one's body at the same time is a new kind of euphoria, and something I could only experience with him.

"I'm close, baby," he growls against my back.

His tongue traces the length of my spine, and when his thrusts become erratic, I follow him into the abyss. Sounds leave us that don't sound like us at all, my nails sink into the tablecloth, and I'm fairly certain I've ripped it. I revel in the hot spray of his come as it covers my back.

We end up on the floor in a heap next to each other, our chests heaving as we come back to ourselves. He takes my hand and kisses my palm and along my wrist as I snuggle into his side.

"I think you killed me," he says with a laugh.

I playfully smack his reaper tattoo. "Psh, you're already dead."

"Excuse you, I *was* dead. Now I'm back."

He smooths my hair as I drape my thigh over his. "Anything you'd change about our love story?" I ask him.

Lifting his head, his gaze searches mine. "Yeah, after that first kiss, I never should've let you go. You?"

I shake my head. "No. Since I didn't believe a love like this existed, every moment has been a breathtaking surprise."

"I'm glad I proved you wrong, gorgeous."

THE END.

Also from Ivy

<u>ALIENS OF OLUURA</u>

Saving His Mate

Charming His Mate

Stealing His Mate

Keeping His Mate

Healing His Mate

Enchanting Her Mate

(This series isn't finished. There's plenty more to come!)

<u>STRANDED ON EARTH</u>

Her Alien Bodyguard

Her Alien Neighbor

Her Alien Librarian

Her Alien Student

Her Alien Boss

<u>THE CURSED COMPOUND</u>

Alliance with the Alien Pirate

(This series isn't finished. There's plenty more to come!)

<u>MAPLETOWN MONSTER MATES</u>

<u>Adored by the Grumpy Ghost</u>

<u>(This series is just getting started. Each can be read as a standalone.)</u>

<u>SINGLE DADS IN SPACE</u>

Rescued by the Alien Dad

(Multi-author series releasing in time for Father's Day 2026. Preorder now!)

A Note from Ivy

Can you tell how angry I've been lately about the state of the world? I channeled all of it through Lindsay. She's my hero. I think she's probably the person I wish I could be in real life. I'm nowhere near as confrontational or bold, but a girl can dream.

What she and I do share, though, is dermatillomania. I've picked my skin for as long as I can remember, and it's something I still carry a lot of shame about. It's also a huge reason why I don't often show my face on camera. This is a severely underreported condition, primarily due to that shame, but studies suggest it affects about 1 in 20 people, which a much higher prevalence in women (go figure).

It's become a coping mechanism for me, and during moments of severe stress or anxiety, you might find me in front of the bathroom mirror, attempting to "fix" my perceived flaws while scarring my skin. There are also moments throughout the day when I don't even know I'm doing it. Like Lindsay, I'll be watching TV and my hand will find my face and I'll just start mindlessly mapping.

It doesn't make sense, I know, and believe me, I've spent years trying to process it with my therapist.

Luckily, I nabbed a Good One, and my husband has been nothing but supportive. We've tried several tactics to minimize this behavior in me, and the most effective by far is having him in the bathroom with me while I do my nightly skincare routine. This is the part of the day when I'm mostly likely to pick, and having him next to me removes the temptation because it's not something I'd ever do in front of an audience.

If you're also a picker and have found ways to overcome this habit, I'm all ears. Please teach me your ways.

Now, back to the anger. Lindsay feels every emotion deeply, and the way she expresses herself can seem like "too much" to some people who've crossed paths with her. Lately, I've noticed that this is a fairly common experience among women—the fear of being seen as "too much" and I wanted to tell a story wherein a "too much" woman didn't have to change a single fucking thing to find her person. Because guess what? Women who are "too loud," "too sensitive," "too big," "too confident," "too opinionated," are EXACTLY who we need to be championing right now. These are the ones who bring down empires.

Dominic knows he's no less of a humongous, protective beefcake when he's standing in awe of Lindsay embracing her rage. He feels her power and he isn't afraid of it. In fact, he nurtures it, because that's how Good Ones behave.

I suppose you could say this book helped me process *gestures at everything* the many atrocities we're facing right now. It didn't erase any of them, but if I couldn't use Lindsay to scream into the void, I'm not sure I would've been able to get any writing done at all.

Now, onto the next Mapletown couple, yes?

I didn't drop any breadcrumbs in this story because the next is separate from the first two and centers around a shocking event that occurs a few months in the future.

Our couple for book 3 will be...the brilliant Mayor Emma Crane and the ridiculously attractive robot bodyguard her family assigns to protect her! HEALED BY THE REBELLIOUS ROBOT is coming soon.

Thank you so much for reading!

Xoxo

Ivy

P.S. To my wonderful husband, thank you for being a Good One in a world full of men so easy to hate. To my beautiful four-legged babies, Clover and Ruby. Fucking hell, I love you both. To my fabulous PA, Nikki, thank you for being from Tennessee and teaching me what banana and mayo sandwiches really taste like. I adore you.

To my editors, Chrisandra, Jenny, and Kenzie, thank you for not firing me when I asked for yet another extension. To Rouge for my adorable cover. To Dani, my sensitivity reader, for providing such insightful and brilliant notes on Korean culture. This book would be a jumble of words without you.

ABOUT IVY

Ivy Knox has always been a voracious reader of romance novels, but quickly found her home in monster/alien romance because let's be real, most human men are disappointing. When she's not lost on faraway worlds created by her favorite authors, she's creating her own.

Ivy lives with her husband and her two dog daughters in Chicago. Everything she does is to give them a bigger backyard and a better life. When she's not reading or writing, she's probably watching *What We Do in the Shadows*, *The Fall of the House of Usher*, *Bridgerton*, or *The Good Place* for the millionth time.

www.ingramcontent.com/pod-product-compliance
Lightning Source LLC
Chambersburg PA
CBHW071500140726

47997CB00005B/1801